THE WHITE SNAKE AND HER SON

THE WHITE SNAKE AND HER SON

A Translation of
The Precious Scroll of Thunder Peak
with Related Texts

Edited and Translated,
with an Introduction,
by

Wilt L. Idema

Hackett Publishing Company, Inc.
Indianapolis/Cambridge

Copyright © 2009 by Hackett Publishing Company

All rights reserved
Printed in the United States of America

14 13 12 11 10 09   1 2 3 4 5 6 7

For further information, please address:

Hackett Publishing Company, Inc.
P.O. Box 44937
Indianapolis, Indiana 46244-0937

www.hackettpublishing.com

Cover design by Abigail Coyle
Text design and composition by Carrie Wagner
Printed at Malloy, Inc.

Library of Congress Cataloging-in-Publication Data

Bai she zhuan. English. 2009
  The White Snake and her Son : a translation of The Precious Scroll
  of Thunder Peak, with related texts / edited and translated, with an
  introduction, by Wilt Idema.
    p. cm.
  Includes bibliographical references.
  ISBN 978-0-87220-995-4 (pbk.) -- ISBN 978-0-87220-996-1 (cloth)
  1. Tales--China. I. Idema, W. L. (Wilt L.) II. Title. III. Title: Translation of
The Precious Scroll of Thunder Peak, with related texts.
  GR335.B3513 2009
  398.20951--dc22
                                                                2009010478

The paper used in this publication meets the minimum requirements
of American National Standard for Information Sciences—
Permanence of Paper for Printed Library Materials,
ANSI Z39.48–1984.

CONTENTS

Preface	vii
Acknowledgments	ix
Introduction	xi

MA RUFEI
The Story of the White Snake — 1

ANONYMOUS
The Precious Scroll of Thunder Peak I — 9
The Precious Scroll of Thunder Peak II — 51

FOUR ANONYMOUS YOUTH BOOKS (*ZIDISHU*) — 87
The United Bowls — 87
Sacrifice at the Pagoda — 93
Weeping at the Pagoda — 97
Leaving the Pagoda — 103

APPENDIXES — 111
  I. *Li Huang* and Other Classical Tales of Bewitching Snakes — 113
  II. West Lake Monsters — 119
  III. The White Snake on Stage — 135
  IV. The Virtuous Seductress — 151
  V. The Elder Brother of Zheng Defeats Duan in Yan — 157

Bibliography — 161
Glossary — 169

PREFACE

The exploits of Mulan, the legend of the White Snake, the romance of Liang Shanbo and Zhu Yingtai, and the thwarted love of Weaving Maiden and Buffalo Boy continue to fascinate Chinese audiences all over the world. As the embodiment of Chinese people's wisdom, virtue, and pursuit of love, these tales have been told and retold throughout the twentieth century; they have also been performed on the stage, adapted for the screen, and rewritten as dramas for television. They have inspired theme parks and postage stamps, violin concertos, and Western-style operas. In their modern transformations these traditional tales have been hailed as the quintessence of Chinese culture, as instruments for cultural renewal, and as tools of criticism.

The earliest extant premodern versions of these Chinese tales and legends are no less varied and multiform than their modern adaptations. By the time they were recorded, each of these stories had already undergone a centuries-long period of development and change. Depending on the time, region, and genre in which it was created, each version is unique and brings its own perspective and meaning to the story. Moreover, each of these texts reflects the idiosyncrasies and personality of its author (whose name has usually been lost). We could make no greater mistake than to assume that these stories embodied a single, unchanging, essential meaning, even though many modern and contemporary scholars write about these stories as if they did.

Despite the popularity of these tales and legends among modern and contemporary authors and intellectuals, in late-imperial times such tales and legends (with the exception of Mulan) were mostly ignored by the scholars and literati of the Ming (1368–1644) and the Qing (1644–1911) dynasties. Nonetheless, these texts flourished in the realm of oral literature and in the many genres of traditional popular literature (*suwenxue*). This series aims to introduce the contemporary English reader to the richness and variety of traditional Chinese popular literature of late-imperial China, and to the wide discrepancies between the different adaptations of each story by translating at least two different premodern adaptations in full. Each of these sets of translations will be preceded by an introduction tracing the historical development of each story up to the beginning of the twentieth century. The translations will be followed by a selection of related materials that will provide the readers with a fuller understanding of the historical development of each story, and help them place the translated text in the development of Chinese popular literature and culture.

ACKNOWLEDGMENTS

First of all it is my pleasure to thank the staff of the Harvard-Yenching Library for their assistance in locating materials on the legend of the White Snake. This little volume utilizes only a fraction of the rich holdings of the Harvard-Yenching Library in the field of traditional Chinese popular literature acquired in the course of the last few years.

I also would like to express my gratitude to the students and teaching fellows who pointed out typos and malapropisms in drafts of the translations included in this volume, and to which they were exposed in class. Professor Sarah Allen of Wellesley University kindly went through all of the translations and saved me from many mistakes against good English usage. Gustavo Espada assisted in making scans of the artwork.

Last but not least I would like to express my thanks to the copyeditor and production staff at Hackett Publishing Company. Their meticulous attention to detail has greatly enhanced the quality of the final product.

All remaining shortcomings are of course irrevocably and completely my own.

Wilt L. Idema

INTRODUCTION

The Chinese legend of the White Snake, the admirable demon who loves her victim, has enjoyed an ever-growing popularity during the last five hundred years. The legend originated in Hangzhou and was from its very beginning associated with Thunder Peak Pagoda (Leifengta)—one of the scenic sites on the banks of Hangzhou's famous West Lake—as it was believed that the demon had been imprisoned under this building. From Hangzhou the legend spread all over China, and it was continuously rewritten as a vernacular story, a novel, a string ballad, a precious scroll, and many other genres of balladry. It was also adapted for the stage from early on, in both elite and popular theater. Combining romance with martial arts, these plays showcased elaborate pageantry, and plays about the White Snake became a staple of the repertoire of many genres of local opera.

In the twentieth century, the White Snake first appealed to modern Chinese intellectuals as a femme fatale, but later she was reinterpreted as a symbol of the new woman who bravely confronts patriarchal authority in her struggle for free love. This development can for instance be traced in the lifelong fascination with the White Snake of the modern playwright Tian Han (1898–1968), whose version of the White Snake legend as a Peking opera not only was popular in the 1950s but also was one of the first Peking operas to be revived following the Cultural Revolution (1966–1978). The ongoing reinterpretations of the legend in the twentieth century and beyond have inspired new operas and novels to this very day, inspiring writers as diverse as Li Pik-wah (Li Bihua, Lilian Lee), Yan Geling, and Li Rui (b. 1950). The legend also time and again provided inspiration for the new media of China's twentieth century, such as movies and television dramas, musicals, and ballet. The first screen adaptation was a two-part silent movie of 1926, starring the famous actress Hu Die as the White Snake. Of the many later movie versions, Tsui Hark's *Green Snake* of 1993 is probably the most popular. In some of the more recent works, the demonic aspect of the White Snake has been highlighted once again, and the relationship between the White Snake and her maid Little Blue has at times been given a homoerotic coloring.[1]

Outside China the legend was adapted into Japanese as early as the eighteenth century. The earliest Western-language version appeared in French as early as 1834,

---

[1] A comprehensive survey of premodern and modern adaptations of the legend of the White Snake is provided in Fan, 2003.

and English-language versions followed later. An English-language opera on the theme of the White Snake for production in the 2009–2010 season has been commissioned by Opera Boston in cooperation with the Beijing Music Festival.

The Legend of the White Snake in 1624

The legend of the White Snake has only a relatively short history. Despite the often-seen assertion that the legend may originate in the Southern Song dynasty (1127–1278), there exists no positive evidence of such a story before the Ming dynasty. From the sixteenth century onward, however, we encounter stray remarks stating that a snake demon had been captured under Thunder Peak Pagoda on the southern side of Hangzhou's West Lake. The earliest full-length version of the legend is a vernacular story included by Feng Menglong (1574–1646) in his *Stories to Caution the World (Jingshi tongyan)* of 1624. It is number twenty-eight in this collection of forty stories, and carries the title "Madame Bai Is Imprisoned Forever under Thunder Peak Pagoda" (*Bai niangzi yongzhen Leifengta*).[2] Feng Menglong's *Stories to Caution the World* had dropped from circulation by the end of the seventeenth century, only to be rediscovered in the early twentieth century, but this elaborate story of the demon White Snake has been reprinted with only modest changes in later compilations of vernacular stories dedicated to West Lake such as *Fine Tales about West Lake* (1683; *Xihu jiahua*) and *West Lake Anecdotes* (1792; *Xihu shiyi*), and so remained in general circulation.[3] It made its way to Japan in the eighteenth century,[4] and in the last few decades

---

[2] The young lady dressed in white claims to have the surname Bai, which is written with the same character that is used for the color white (*bai*), so some translators choose to translate the surname as White. In some later texts, the young lady claims to be Bai Suzhen, which might be rendered as Blanche White. She is accompanied by a servant-girl named Qing'er, or Xiaoqing. *Qing* is a naturally dark color, and depending on the context, the word may be translated as "black," "blue," or "green." In some traditional color woodblock prints, Qing'er/Xiaoqing is dressed in blue; in others, in green. In these translations I have chosen Little Blue, but Little Green would also have been a possibility. For instance, Tsui Hark's 1993 movie of the legend of the White Snake, based on the modern retelling of the tale by Li Pik-wah (Lilian Lee) in English, is called *The Green Snake*.

[3] English translations of the *Jingshi tongyan* tale have been provided by H. C. Chang, 1973, 205–61; Yang Hsien-yi and Gladys Yang, as Anonymous, 1959; Shuhui Yang and Yunqun Yang, in Feng Menglong, 2005, 474–505; and Diana Yu, 1978. The translation by H. C. Chang comes with a substantial introduction and detailed annotations. A translation of the *Xihu jiahua* version has been provided by Waley, 1952, 183–213. The limited changes introduced in the *Xihu jiahua* version tend to stress the purity of lady Bai's love and put Fahai in a more negative light.

[4] In Japan this vernacular story inspired Ueda Akinari (1734–1809) in *Ugetsu monogatari* to a short story, set in medieval Japan, entitled *The Serpent's Lust* (*Jasei no in*). The story provided the inspiration for a silent movie as early as 1921, also entitled *Jasei no in*, which was directed by Kurihara Kusaburo (Thomas Kurihara) and based on a screenplay by Tanizaki Junichiro. It is also one of the two stories

it also has been repeatedly translated into English.[5]

The action in this vernacular story takes place around the middle of the twelfth century, and starts on the banks of West Lake in Hangzhou, where the young pharmacy assistant Xu Xian[6] during a drenching rain meets with lady Bai (lady White), a beautiful young widow, and her servant Little Blue. At their request, he takes the two of them on board the boat he has hired to take him back to the city, and he also lends them a fine umbrella. When he later visits the women to reclaim his umbrella, lady Bai proposes marriage to him, and when he replies that he is too poor, she gives him a fifty-ounce ingot of silver to pay for the expenses. Xu, who is an orphan, lives with his elder sister and her husband—the latter a lowly government officer, Mr. Li, who immediately recognizes the silver as part of a sum stolen from the vault of Commander Shao and informs the authorities. Xu is arrested, but when police officers try to arrest lady Bai at her house, she disappears in a flash. Nonetheless, the officers recover the silver, whereupon Xu is only lightly punished by banishment to Suzhou.

Thanks to a letter of introduction from his brother-in-law, Xu is permitted to live with the innkeeper Wang. There he is visited by lady Bai and Little Blue, and after some initial misgivings, Xu is soon convinced once again to marry lady Bai. But when he visits one of the local temples, a Daoist master tells him that he is bewitched by a demon, and gives him amulets[7] to burn. The amulets turn out to be ineffective, and the next day lady Bai goes to the temple to confront the master. Utterly humiliated, the latter flees town. When some time later Xu, now married to the lady, once again wants to visit the temple on a holiday, lady Bai dresses her husband in a set of fine clothes. These turn out to have been stolen from a local pawnshop, together with many other goods. Xu is once again arrested, but when police officers want to arrest lady Bai and Little Blue too, the two women have disappeared. Even though the stolen goods are miraculously returned to the pawnshop, Xu is banished once again, this time to Zhenjiang.

Upon his arrival in Zhenjiang, Xu Xian begins working in the pharmacy of a certain Li Keyong. One day he encounters once again lady Bai, who claims she has just arrived from Nanjing. She allays his wariness, and the couple starts living

---

that provided the plot for Mizoguchi Kenji's movie *Ugetsu monogatari* of 1953. The original Chinese story provided the inspiration for Japan's first full-length color animation movie *White Snake Enchantress* (*Hakuja den*, also known as *Panda and the Magic Serpent*) of 1958, directed by Okabe Kazuhiko and Yabushita Taiji.

[5] The story also was twice adapted for the screen in Korea, viz. in 1960 and 1978.

[6] In many earlier versions of the story, Xu Xian is written as Xu Xuan, and in some texts the names are used interchangeably.

[7] The word "amulet" here refers to magical formulas written on paper and intended to be burned. It is one of the most important skills of a Daoist priest to be able to write powerful amulets.

together again. Li invites the couple over for his birthday party, and, deciding he wants to rape lady Bai, he follows her to the toilet. To his revulsion, when he peeks inside through a crack in the door, he sees no beautiful woman but instead a huge white snake, and he faints at the sight of it. Lady Bai informs Xu of Li's attempt to rape her, tells him not to return to his job, and provides him with money to start his own pharmacy, which is very successful. Later, after making a donation to a monk, Fahai, of the Golden Mountain Monastery (*Jinshansi*)[8], he is invited to attend the celebration there of the birthday of the Dragon King on Double Seventh. He goes despite the misgivings of his wife. At the monastery he meets the monk Fahai, who warns him of the danger she presents to him. When lady Bai and Little Blue approach Golden Mountain Monastery in a frightening rainstorm by boat, they hide themselves in the River at the sight of Fahai.

When a general amnesty is declared on the ascension of Emperor Xiaozong after Emperor Gaozong abdicates, Xu is allowed to return to Hangzhou. When he arrives at the house of his brother-in-law, it turns out that lady Bai and Little Blue have arrived there just a few days earlier. Lady Bai tells Xu that she will drown the whole city of Hangzhou if he does not love her as before, so he is very fearful. When Xu's brother-in-law, at his wife's instigation, tries to observe lady Bai that night in her room, he sees instead a huge snake. Together with Xu, he invites a professional snake-catcher to exorcise her, but the snake-catcher ends up scared out of his wits on seeing the huge serpent. When a desperate Xu is about to commit suicide by drowning himself, he once again runs into Fahai. The latter gives Xu a begging bowl (Fahai's own), and when Xu returns back home, he places it over the head of an unsuspecting lady Bai and pushes it down; thereupon, she shrinks from her monstrous size into nothing more than a harmless little snake whom Xu easily traps beneath his bowl. Fahai then enters and captures Little Blue, who turns into a blue carp. Fahai locks the two creatures in a jug, which he buries at Thunder Peak Monastery. Xu later collects donations and has a pagoda erected on top of the buried monsters, and then becomes a Buddhist monk himself.

Thunder Peak Pagoda was a well-known sight at West Lake. Originally erected in the tenth century on the southern banks of the lake, it had never been built up to its intended height, and this gave it a squat, yet massive appearance. In the middle of the sixteenth century it lost its wooden exterior in a fire, leaving only its delapidated brick core.[9]

---

[8] This famous monastery was built on a small island in the Yangzi (the Long River), not far from Zhenjiang. In the nineteenth century, however, the island was linked to the river bank.

[9] For more on Thunder Peak Pagoda as one of the famous sights of Hangzhou, see Wang, 2003 (a and b). What remained of the structure finally crumbled in 1924, inspiring the modern writer Lu Xun (1881–1936) to write some of his best-known essays, viz. "The Collapse of Leifeng Pagoda" and

Earlier Amorous Encounters of Man and Snake

Feng Menglong was not the author of "Madame Bai is imprisoned for ever under Thunder Peak Pagoda." While the story shows signs of later editing, it most likely was written at some time during the first century of the Ming dynasty. Over the last century scholars have made considerable effort to track down the sources of Feng's vernacular story.[10] A legend claiming that Thunder Peak Pagoda was guarded by a huge serpent that lived at its base may have been in existence as early as the twelfth century, but that snake is not credited with a prior record of amorous crime. Stories about men who meet with a woman dressed in white, share her couch, and (almost) lose their lives—upon which it is discovered that the woman is a snake—are many. One of these tales is a vernacular story, entitled *West Lake's Three Stupas* (*Xihu santa ji*), which may date from the thirteen or fourteenth century, and is included in the mid-sixteenth century collection *Vernacular Stories from the Qingping Mountain Studio* (*Qingping shantang huaben*) compiled by Hong Bian.[11] In this Hangzhou story the woman in white is accompanied by an old hag in black (who turns out to be an otter), and a young girl (who turns out to be a black chicken). The woman in white eats the heart and liver of her lovers as soon as she has exhausted their vital energy, and the male protagonist is eventually saved from the same fate by the intervention of his uncle, a Daoist priest, who imprisons the three demons under three stupas in West Lake.[12] These three stupas were said to have been built first by the famous poet Su Shi (1036–1101), when he served as prefect of the city, but had been destroyed by the end of the fifteenth century (and would only be reerected more than a century later). A translation of this curious text, which may well have been intended for performance, is included as Appendix 2.[13] The earliest known account of a fatal amorous encounter between a man

---

"More Thoughts on the Collapse of Leifeng Pagoda," in Lu Hsun, 1964, 82–84 and 94–100. The current structure at the site dates from the beginning of the twenty-first century. Construction was preceded by extensive archaeological research of the terrain, which revealed the existence of a hidden crypt below the pagoda foundations. *Leifengta mibao* 2005; *Leifengta yizhi* 2005; *Leifeng yizhen* 2002.

[10] In Chinese, see Zhao Jingshen, 1936, 1–44, and Pan Jiangdong, 1981; in English, see Hsu Wen-hung, 1973, and Wu Pei-yi, 1969.

[11] This collection would appear to have dropped from circulation by the end of the sixteenth century. Parts of the collection came to light in the 1930s.

[12] That this story might reflect an earlier version of the legend of the White Snake was first suggested upon the rediscovery of *Vernacular Stories from the Qingping Mountain Studio* by the Japanese sinologist Aoki Masaru.

[13] French translations have been provided by Pimpaneau, 1965, and Dars, 1987, 248–65. For another English translation, see Wu Pei-yi, 1969, 170–97.

and a snake is the classical tale of Li Huang, which may date from the ninth century and is found in the *Extensive Record of the Taiping Era* (*Taiping guangji*)—a huge, thematically arranged compendium of classical tales from previous centuries compiled in the final years of the tenth century. The tale of Li Huang is set in the Tang dynasty capital Chang'an, and the amorous young man is eventually reduced to a puddle of water. A translation of this tale is provided in Appendix I.[14] Beyond that, scholars have pointed to the rich tradition of tales of amorous meetings of men and goddesses and men and demons in earlier Chinese literature.[15] Inspired by the close parallel to Keats's poem *Lamia*, other scholars have widely searched for a common Eurasian source for tales of passionate affairs between men—and snakes disguised as women.[16]

Traditional and modern readers continue to be intrigued by the contradictory characterization of the White Snake who is on the one hand devoted to her lover, yet creates no end of trouble for him. A fusing of rain maiden and dragon lady, lady Bai embodies both the fertilizing capacity of rivers and lakes, and their destructive power in floods. As a reflection of men's sexual anxieties she embodies both their insatiable desire and their fear of being dominated, drained of strength, and destroyed. Lady Bai may shower Xu Xian with affection, but she is ultimately a dangerous outsider who must be exorcised. In the earlier demon stories, and in the vernacular story published by Feng Menglong, the young man is the central character. And while modern readers often chide Xu for being bereft of love for the White Snake and turning against her, traditional adaptors of the legend may well have considered him admirable for that very reason: though initially seduced by her many charms, he eventually realizes the danger she poses, and seeks refuge in religion.

The White Snake on Stage and the Birth of Her Son

In an act that is symbolic of Xu Xian's final insight, it is he, not the monk Fahai, who places the begging bowl on the head of the White Snake and pushes it down; the role of Fahai is still very limited in this vernacular story by Feng Menglong. With earlier versions focusing mainly on Xu, it is only later that we see the White Snake become the central character in her own legend, and the role of Fahai becomes more prominent too, as now both are portrayed as battling for the body and soul of a rather weak-spined Xu. From at least as early

---

[14] Scholars have focused on stories of encounters of mortal men and white snake demons. It should be pointed out that among Tang dynasty classical tales one also finds a tale of a demon who loves her partner. However, in Shen Jiji's (c. 800) *Renshi zhuan*, the animal partner is not a female snake, but a vixen.

[15] See Whalen Lai, 1992, and Yen, 1975 (a and b).

[16] See, for instance, Nai-tung Ting, 1966.

as the eighteenth century, this battle, as played out on stage, culminates in the flooding of Golden Mountain Monastery—as the White Snake mobilizes all creatures of rivers and seas, and Fahai responds by calling on all the protective deities of Buddhism for help.

When Feng Menglong published his *Stories to Caution the World*, the legend of the White Snake was also already quite popular on stage. It had been adapted as a long *chuanqi* play by Chen Liulong, about whom we know nothing. His play has been lost, and all we know about it is its title *Thunder Peak (Leifeng ji)*, and the very low opinion expressed about it by Qi Biaojia (1602–1645) in his *Classification of Plays from the Far Mountain Hall (Yuanshantang jupin)*. By the middle of the eighteenth century, the official and playwright Huang Tubi (1700–1771) wrote a new version, entitled *Thunder Peak Pagoda (Leifeng ta)*. His adaptation followed the vernacular story printed by Feng Menglong very closely, but when it was performed, the actors soon expanded it with scenes that narrated the tale of a son that was born from the union of Xu Xian and the snake—this son eventually passes the examinations as top-of-the-list and sees his mother liberated. Huang Tubi suggests—in his disgusted comments on watching such a performance—that these scenes had been newly created by the actors, catering to the conventional desire for a happy ending, but it is quite possible that they were simply borrowed from the earlier play by Chen Liulong. A manuscript of the play as it was usually staged, and said to be based on the performances of the famous mid-eighteenth-century Yangzhou actor Chen Jianyan and his daughter, has been preserved. An extensively rewritten version of that version, still entitled *Thunder Peak Pagoda*, was produced in 1772 by Fang Chengpei (second part of the eighteenth century).[17] Extensive summaries of these three plays (and information on their authors), as provided by the contemporary scholar Guo Yingde, have been translated in Appendix 3.

In giving Xu Xian and lady Bai a son, Mengjiao, the actors followed the lead of the legend of Dong Yong. The earliest versions of that legend only narrate how the filial son Dong Yong was assisted by Weaving Maiden in paying off the debt he had incurred in providing his father with a fitting burial. Weaving Maiden came down to earth, posed as his wife, and quickly produced the required amount of silk, whereupon she returned to heaven. Later versions of the legend portray the couple as having a son who, when bullied by classmates for not having a mother, sets out to find her.[18] An even closer parallel to this

---

[17] Fang Chengpei's play is often highly praised by modern critics because it almost completely does away with the "demonic air" that still clings to the character of lady Bai in many other versions. A scene-by-scene summary of this play is presented in Wu Pei-yi, 1969, 198–215.

[18] The earliest version of the legend of Dong Yong in which he and Weaving Maiden have a son is a long ballad of the ninth or tenth century found at Dunhuang. For a translation, see Waley, 1960, 155–62.

two-generation version of the legend of the White Snake is provided by the legend of Chenxiang, the son of a student who had been pursued by the amorous goddess, Third Daughter of Mt. Hua. When the elder brother of the goddess learns of her affair, he has her imprisoned under a mountain, leaving her student lover to raise their son alone. When Chenxiang grows up, he too is taunted by his classmates. He then leaves home to learn magic arts with the Eight Immortals, defeats his uncle in battle, and frees his mother from her prison.[19] Perhaps the most famous and popular story of a son who frees his sinful mother from her prison deep below the earth is the legend of Mulian, who freed his mother from the Avici Hell thanks to the magic of the Buddha.[20] One of the anonymous youth books translated in this volume, *Sacrifice at the Pagoda*, clearly describes the pagoda as a grave, and explicitly compares Xu's son Mengjiao to Mulian. Xu Mengjiao, however, does not rely on Daoist magic or Buddhist meditation, but on his own filial piety and writing skills, and he is able to bring about his mother's liberation once he has passed the metropolitan examinations as top-of-the-list and has sacrificed imperial offerings to his mother.

The addition of a son, fundamentally changed the nature of the legend. It began as a demon story, but as retold and elaborated over time, the demon defeats, in sequence, the secular authorities who attempt to arrest and subdue her, a Daoist priest, a Buddhist monk, and a hereditary snake-catcher. As the number of specialists who see through her disguise and try to exorcise her increases, we need an explanation of why lady Bai can maintain her hold over Xu Xian. It is not enough anymore to state that she is very beautiful, as happens in simple demon stories. Lady Bai is now described as not only seductive, but also as loving and caring. Most importantly perhaps, she is never at a loss for words when explaining the strange events that cause Xu his troubles with the law. In Feng Menglong's vernacular story, however, lady Bai remains a demon,

---

[19] On the legend of Chenxiang, see Dudbridge, 1990. A translation of the *Precious Scroll on Chenxiang* by Idema will appear in Bender and Mair, forthcoming.

[20] On the legend of Mulian, see Teiser, 1988; also see Cole, 1998. The similarity between Xu Mengjiao and Mulian was already pointed out by Wu Pei-yi, 1969, 112, who also highlights the similarity to Huaguang's delivery of his mother from hell in the sixteenth-century novel *Journey to the South (Nanyou ji)*. In the various versions of the legend of Mulian, his mother is punished in hell for her indulgence in eating meat. In *Nanyou ji*, Huaguang's mother has been locked up in the Fengdu hell because of her insatiable craving for human meat—even when freed from Fengdu, she still suffers from this craving until Huaguang can provide her with peaches of immortality. For Mengjiao's visit to Thunder Peak Pagoda, Wu Pei-yi finds a source in "Saving One's Mother by Venerating a Pagoda," an item in the *Zimen chongxing lu* by the late-Ming Hangzhou monk Zhuhong. In that story, too, a son saves his mother from the torments of hell after three years, but it is never stated that his mother is buried/imprisoned under the stupa/pagoda he venerates, and he never has any desire to destroy the stupa/pagoda.

and when all her sweet words fail to allay her husband's fears, she is not above threatening him with death and destruction to make him come back to her. Demon stories can traditionally only end with the death of the demon's victim, or with the demon itself being captured and subdued, the latter of which happens in the vernacular story version of the legend through the concerted effort of the monk Fahai and Xu Xian, whose eventual suppression of his desires is symbolized by him becoming a monk himself.[21] There may be no more fitting symbol to celebrate man's victory over the lure of the female than the rising shape of a pagoda. The tales of the imprisoned mother and her liberation by her son, however, would appear to be very much the Chinese counterpart of the Freudian family complex.

In his *Mothers and Sons in Chinese Buddhism*, which focuses on the legend of Mulian, Alan Cole concludes that tales of loving and saving one's mother must have possessed powerful attractions for sons. Such tales provided a medium through which mother-son feelings could be expressed and celebrated, while putting sons in the roles of hero and saint. Moreover, the son was also provided with a way to pay back all he owed to his mother. But at the same time the son got to imagine his mother begging him for help. "He is now in power while she is in need and remains at his mercy." The implied sadism in this discourse became more noticeable as time went by: "Besides granting the son an image of power, these myths also gave him images for fantasizing about his mother's degradation and punishment. They required him to visualize her in bestial conditions in hell."[22] The sin for which the mother is punished may be described as indulgence in her own lust, but it is basically her female sexuality. In late-imperial times the sin of sexuality was reified as the blood women shed in menstruation and childbirth, blood that was seen as polluting. But as the same sexuality is also the source of life, a son has to save his mother from hell, and so he did in the ritual "Destroying Hell," which used to be part of a woman's funeral in many parts of China.[23] Kristofer Schipper has suggested that such rituals may go back to Zhou dynasty times, if not earlier, and are reflected in the story of "The Elder Brother of Zheng Defeats Duan in Yan" (*"Zhengbo ke*

---

[21] As in other stories of true and tragic love, the lovers would often be described as immortals who are punished for one moment of carnal desire by being sent down to the world of men, where they will suffer through all the miseries of love in order to expiate their sin, after which they may return to heaven, having repaid their karmic debt. In one of the youth book texts, *Weeping at the Pagoda*, lady Bai and Xu Xian are described as the reincarnations of an immortal maiden and a heavenly incense boy. If the two are seen as true and tragic lovers, Fahai can be interpreted as a lecherous monk. In the same *Weeping at the Pagoda*, he is said to be the reincarnation of a scabby turtle ("turtle" being a common curse word, meaning a pimp or a cuckold).

[22] Cole, 1998, 234–235.

[23] See Seaman, 1989.

Duan yu Yan").²⁴ That story is found in the *Zuo Commentary* (*Zuozhuan*) and was included in many anthologies of prose that were studied in late imperial China by young literati all over China in preparation for their examinations, even though it can hardly qualify as a good model of essay writing. A translation is provided in Appendix 5. The story tells of the troubled relationship between Duke Zhuang of Zheng and his mother, who hates him because he was a breech birth. She showers her affection on his younger brother Duan. When Duan plans to rebel, his mother agrees to open the city gates for him. The rebellion fails, and the duke imprisons his mother, swearing he will only meet her "below the Yellow Sources" (that is, after he is dead and buried). He later regrets this rash vow, is stimulated to remorse by the filial piety of one of his retainers, and frees his mother. In order to keep his word, he digs a deep tunnel, and mother and son are reunited, singing songs. Understood as myth and not as history, the story tells the tale of a jealous son who punishes his insatiable mother because she showers her affection on some other man. Once he has done so by burying her in a prison (the Chinese word for hell is "earth-prison"), he can only undo his act by descending into the earth himself.

If the actors wanted to devote numerous scenes to the adventures of lady Bai's son, they had to drastically simplify the action of the vernacular story, and they did so by fusing Xu Xian's adventures in Suzhou and Zhenjiang. They also enhanced the stage action by having Xu collapse upon seeing his wife in her original snake form—whereupon she sets out to the Southern Pole Star Palace to steal the herb of immortality in order to bring him back to life (if an earlier theft almost cost Xu his life, a second one restores him to life). These plays were very rich in spectacular stage action as they featured gods and demons, and even brought all the creatures of rivers and lakes on stage, especially in the scene in which the White Snake tries to flood the Golden Mountain Monastery. The spectacular nature of its stage action may well have contributed to the popularity of this play with the Qianlong emperor, who was an aficionado of elaborate pageantry. *Thunder Peak Pagoda* was performed for the emperor's amusement on the occasion of his visit to Yangzhou during his Southern Tour of 1765, and the Yangzhou salt merchants were told to arrange for a performance of the play in Beijing in 1771, on the occasion of the celebration of the eightieth birthday of the empress-dowager. Whatever the artistic qualities of the scripts by accomplished literati such as Huang Tubi and Feng Chengpei may have been, it is clear that the actors' version remained the favorite of audiences. Adaptations of *Thunder Peak Pagoda* in the many varieties of local theater are always based on the actors' version,²⁵ and this was also the

---

²⁴ See Schipper, 1989, 127.

²⁵ Chinese migrants to southeast Asia took their theater with them, and to this day the White Snake

version that authors of prosimetric narratives, such as string ballads *(tanci)* and precious scrolls *(baojuan)* of the eighteenth century and later, followed. The fifty-three-chapter *tanci* adaptation entitled *The Virtuous Seductress* (*Yiyao zhuan*), as performed by Chen Yuqian and revised by his students, was one of the most popular items in the repertoire of Suzhou storytellers. Its length prohibits a complete translation. The summary of its contents provided by Tan Zhengbi and Tan Xun appears in English in Appendix 4. A much shorter version of the legend based on the popular stage versions (and the *tanci*) appeared as a thirteen-chapter novel, which was first published in 1806 as *The Strange Tale of Thunder Peak Pagoda (Leifengta qizhuan)*.[26] Ma Rufei, the most famous Suzhou *tanci* performer of the nineteenth century, provided a potted rendition of this version, all in verse, as "an opening piece" *(kaipian)* in six sections, performed as a prologue to the main entertainment of the day. A translation of this text has been included in this volume.[27] Most modern critics concur with Huang Tubi in condemning the addition of Mengjiao, as they believe that it detracts from the tragic nature of the story. In their view, lady Bai's struggle in traditional society against patriarchal authority, and her pursuit of true love was doomed from the start. But even Tian Han's much acclaimed modern play culminates in the destruction of Thunder Peak Pagoda by Little Blue, and with lady Bai's liberation.

Precious Scroll and Youth Books

The anonymous *The Precious Scroll of Thunder Peak* (*Leifeng baojuan*), which is translated in this volume, provides a full account of the later, traditional version of the story.[28] Divided into two scrolls *(juan)*, its first section focuses on lady Bai's seduction of Xu Xian, her search for the immortal herb to bring her husband back to life, and her fight with Fahai at the Golden Mountain Monastery, this last resulting in a destructive flood. The second section focuses on her imprisonment under Thunder Peak Pagoda, her son's discovery of his

---

is popular on the Thai stage. See Diamond, 2006.

[26] The novel was translated into French as early as 1834 by Stanislas Julien and published as *Blanche et Bleue*. A Malay translation of this novel was published in 1893. Julien's French version was retranslated into German in 1967 as *Die wundersame Geschichte der weissen Schlange*.

[27] The translation is based on Fu Xihua, 1959, 147–50, which reproduced the text in the woodblock edition of *A First Collection of Southern Ballad Short Introductions by Mr. Ma Rufei* (*Ma Rufei xiansheng nanci xiaoyin chuji*) of the Guangxu reign (1875–1908) of the Qing.

[28] The translation is based on the text as provided in Fu Xihua, 1959, 191–269, which is based on the woodblock edition by the Jingwenzhai of Hangzhou of the thirteenth year of the Guangxu reign (1887). For a list of available editions, see Che Xilun, 2000, 147–48.

true identity, and his attempts to save his mother, leading to her liberation and return to heaven. In this way, the text pays equal attention to lady Bai's pursuit of Xu, and her deliverance by her son.[29] The text is preserved in a number of late-nineteenth-century woodblock prints, the earliest of which, hailing from Hangzhou, dates from 1887. Each of these editions has been preserved in multiple copies, which would seem evidence of their considerable popularity. In the early decades of the Republic, the text was also reprinted by three different Shanghai lithographic publishers, which must have greatly increased the readership of this *baojuan*, which now was called *The Precious Scroll of Lady Bai* (*Baishi baojuan*).

The text alternates between prose and verse. In performance, the prose passages would be narrated, while the verse sections would be recited or sung to a simple recurrent melody. This "prosimetric" format is quite common in Chinese narrative ballads, and is already encountered in the "transformation texts" (*bianwen*) of the eighth to the tenth centuries discovered at Dunhuang.[30] In performance, the prosimetric format allowed the singer the opportunity to rest his voice somewhat after a long verse passage, and for the audience it provided greater variety.

The genre of precious scrolls is often considered a continuation of "transformation texts," not only because of formal similarities, but also because of its strong preference for Buddhist subjects. While from the fifteenth century on religious leaders used precious scrolls to disseminate their teachings, pious narratives without any sectarian connotations continued to be a major staple of the genre.[31] From the nineteenth century on, many old and new tales were written up as precious scrolls, and the subject matter of these texts was not necessarily limited to Buddhist topics.[32] Even in these late precious scrolls, the opening poem and final comments continue to have a Buddhist coloring, and the performance of precious scrolls maintains a strong liturgical character even today.

The Precious Scroll of Thunder Peak is in many ways a typical representative of nineteenth-century narrative precious scrolls. The verse sections are uniformly

---

[29] This is in contrast to earlier versions such as the *tanci* and the novel, in which the final section of the liberation of lady Bai by her son is relatively short. As a result the character of Xu Xian's elder sister as the adoptive mother of Mengjiao is much more developed. Also see Yu, 1999.

[30] On *bianwen*, see Mair, 1983, 1989.

[31] The standard English-language introduction to the genre is Overmyer, 1999, but this work focuses on the sectarian *baojuan*.

[32] English translations of such precious scrolls are rare. For two different precious scroll adaptations of the legend of Meng Jiangnü (who by her weeping brings down the Great Wall), see Idema and Lee, 2008, 112–59, 181–213.

written in lines of seven-syllable verse (a very small number of lines is preceded by an additional three-syllable phrase).[33] Each line of verse consists of a complete sentence, or at least a complete clause, but a single line of verse also may consist of two or even three short sentences. Each section of verse maintains the same rhyme throughout, but it would appear that occasionally, especially in longer verse sections, the first couplet stands somewhat apart as a formulation of a more general truth. On three occasions characters, upon first entrance, introduce themselves in the first person after first reciting a couplet or a four-line poem. This may indicate that our anonymous author based the work on a play or a *tanci* in writing this text. As in other narrative *baojuan* from this period, the religious pantheon freely mixes immortals and gods, Buddhas and demons. The action begins at the banquet hosted by the Queen Mother of the West, and it is attended by the Eight Immortals and the bodhisattva Guanyin, who plays an important role throughout the tale as *dea ex machina*, intervening whenever events threaten to take an ugly turn for our main characters.

The four youth books (*zidishu*) translated in this volume date from the nineteenth century.[34] The genre of youth books had become popular in Beijing by the middle of the eighteenth century, when texts in this genre were widely performed by the younger members (*zidi*; literally, "sons and younger brothers") of the capital Manchu elite.[35] The texts, however, also circulated in written form as reading materials.[36] While some texts only circulated as manuscripts, others also were printed. One could either buy or rent the texts from specialized bookshops such

---

[33] As one syllable or character can be a full word, two seven-syllable lines are close in content to one four-line stanza in traditional English ballads.

[34] The texts are translated from their editions in Fu Xihua, 1959. *The United Bowls (Hebo)* is found in Fu Xihua, 1959, 101–3, where it is presented as an independent work. It is based on a woodblock edition of the Jiaqing period (1796–1820) by the Wensuitang of Beijing. The same text is also encountered as the final chapter of an eight-chapter adaptation of the legend. *Sacrifice at the Pagoda (Jita)* is reprinted in Fu Xihua, 1959, 110–11. That edition is based on a Guangxu era (1875–1908) manuscript. *Weeping at the Pagoda (Kuta)* is found in Fu Xihua, 1959, 107–9. That edition is based on a Tongzhi era (1862–1874) manuscript from the Bieshutang in Beijing. The eight-line opening poems for each chapter have been translated from *Tanta* in Liu Liemao and Guo Jingrui, 1993, 1037–40. *Leaving the Pagoda (Chuta)* is found in Fu Xihua, 1959, 113–15. That edition is said to be based on a Xianfeng era (1851–1861) manuscript from Hundred Copies Zhang. The opening poem has been added on the basis of the edition of this text in Liu Liemao and Guo Jingrui, 1993, 1049–53.

[35] Youth books are also known as "bannermen tales" in English-language scholarship. The most comprehensive study of the genre in English is Chiu, 2007. A few youth books featuring country folks with a poor command of the Chinese language contain passages in Manchu, but texts completely written in Manchu are unknown. See Wadley, 1991, and Elliot, 2001.

[36] When by the end of the nineteenth century youth books were not performed anymore, the performers of drum ballads (*guci*) adopted many of the texts. Drum ballads were popular all over northern China and were performed in many local styles.

as One Hundred Copies Zhang. Youth books consist of one or more chapters, and as titles often contain only single episodes from longer narratives, this allows the authors to elaborate at greater length on the emotions of the characters. The texts are all in verse, and the basic line consists of seven syllables, but because the music to which youth books were performed apparently was very slow, many additional syllables could be added to each line, so even lines of fourteen syllables are not uncommon.[37] This irregular line length is to some extent reflected in the translations. But whereas the verse passages in the precious scroll are workmanlike and efficient in moving the story forward, the youth books indulge in lyrical and descriptive elaboration. The four texts in this collection clearly go back to different versions of the complete story, which all must have departed considerably in matters of detail from the precious scroll version. I have selected for translation those youth books that focus on the second part of the story, beginning with the imprisonment of the White Snake under Thunder Peak Pagoda.

---

[37] The Chinese texts of youth books are available in a number of fine editions, and have started to attract the attention of English-language translators. For other renditions of youth books, see Scott, 1995; and Idema and Lee, 2008, 45–60. Also see Goldman, 2001.

THE WHITE SNAKE
AND HER SON

MA RUFEI

The Tale of the White Snake
An Opening Section

I

Xu Xian went for a walk in spring to sweep the graves,
And he feasted his eyes on the ten miles of West Lake.
Who could have known that suddenly a shower would fall?
From the bank he hailed a little boat to take him back home.
 Unexpectedly he met with a couple of mistress and maid,
Two glamorous charmers like a flower, resembling a jade![1]
These demons Blue and White were extraordinary beauties,
So he fell a hundred percent in love, a hundred percent joy!
 Because he had been a virginal male for seven generations,
She wished to repay old karma, deeply moved by his kindness.[2]
They joined the boat and idly talked, chatting and laughing,
And they didn't hide from each other their name and village.
 All three together, they went to the shrine of Lord Tin—
They served him tea, borrowed his umbrella, hung around.
The servant Little Blue acted as the Old Man of the Moon:[3]
They were united in wedlock that night in the bedroom!
 She urged him to open his own drugstore selling herbs,
But he told her that he didn't have the money he needed.
She claimed to be the daughter of a regional commander,
With a private fortune of millions of cash at her disposal!
 The young man believed her and took her story to be true—
How could he know she had dispatched five demons to get
The silver from the county strongroom, so creating disaster?

---

[1] In Chinese poetry, jade refers to white jade.

[2] Some versions of the legend include the detail that, as a snake, lady Bai had once long ago been saved from death by an earlier incarnation of Xu Xian.

[3] According to a well-known classical tale of the Tang dynasty, the Old Man of the Moon ties prospective marriage partners together with a red thread. In later literature the Old Man of the Moon is a common designation for a matchmaker.

II

Xu Hanwen[4] was a dashing and sophisticated young man,
And his only remaining close relative was his elder sister.
Once he returned home, she asked him where he had been:
"You went for a walk to sweep the graves until this time?"
    He said: "I met this precious daughter of a regional commander,
Willing one hundred percent, in love one hundred percent!
Her servant girl Little Blue served as the Man of the Moon,
So we became husband and wife in the bedroom last night.
    My ladylove also gave me silver of the highest quality,
She has a private fortune of millions—I'll never be poor!"
Since time immemorial women show no understanding—
Who'd think it was silver from the Qiantang County vault!
    His sister's husband, a courtroom usher, had his suspicions:
"He must have met some moonlight fairy or some demon!"
And when Xu Xian produced a silver ingot from his gown,
He saw at first sight it was stolen goods—what a fright!
    He immediately made a full confession to the authorities,
And yamen runners took Xu Xian to the county office:
The stolen goods were evidence he was the true thief,
And mistress and maid could only be a pair of robbers!
    Immediately police officers were sent off to the shrine
To arrest in one swoop that couple of mistress and maid!
Who'd know they'd hide their true shape by some magic?

III

He had the goods but was not the thief: banished to Suzhou!
The yamen runners who were his escorts did not tarry.
In a terrible mess, in rags and tatters, he arrived at the inn,
So the first thing he did was deliver the letter he carried.[5]
    In a new gown and shirt, shoes and socks, and silk scarf,
He was cleansed of the misery and shame of a moment ago.
Then he met the women a second time in Strung Pearls Alley.
The neighbors invited them in; they were beaming with joy!

---

[4] Hanwen is the style or adult name of Xu Xian.

[5] When Xu Xian was banished to Suzhou by the Hangzhou authorities for his complicity in the theft of government funds, his Hangzhou employer provided him with a letter to a friend in Suzhou, asking him to look after Xu's well-being.

Husband and wife had been parted after only a short time,
So as soon they were reunited, their tears streamed down.
She immediately wanted to give him some silver again,
But he was afraid it was stolen goods, so didn't touch it!
   They opened a drugstore under the name of Baohetang,
And he didn't have to worry about his food and clothing.
   On the fourteenth of the Fourth Month, in the middle week,
He went to the temple of Patriarch Lü of Undiluted Yang,[6]
And made a request to a Daoist priest trained at Mt. Mao.[7]
The amulet on a strip of paper startled mistress and maid,
Who only let go once they had strung him up in the sky!
   On Double Fifth lady Bai made the mistake to drink realgar wine,[8]
And against her own will she had to show her original shape.
As soon as Xu Xian saw her like this, his souls all flew away,
So he collapsed on the floor, off to the Lands of Darkness!
   Alas, in her own house she lacked the immortal medicine,
So she decided to go and steal it on the top of the mountain.
As soon as she had run into the immortal lad White Crane,
The Southern Pole Immortal Greybeard did her a great favor:
In his compassion he secretly gave her the numinous herb,
And greatly satisfied with herself, she rode off on a cloud.[9]
   Once he had taken the concoction, he returned to the living,
And from this moment on, he secretly harbored suspicions,
But for the time being he played his part of a happy husband.

---

[6] Patriarch Lü of Undiluted Yang (Lü Chunyang) is Lü Dongbin, one of the Eight Immortals. Lü Dongbin was widely believed to roam the world, killing demons with the sword he carried, and was venerated as a god.

[7] Mt. Mao, to the south of Nanjing, is one of the holy mountains of Daoism. The mountain was said to have been the home of the three Mao brothers, who were venerated as founding fathers in the fourth-century Shangqing tradition of Daoism. During the Song dynasty (960–1278), Mt. Mao was home to a new set of revelations which emphasized exorcism. The Daoist priest deduces from Xu Xian's appearance that he is the victim of a demon and promises to provide him with an amulet that will subdue her. His magical skills are no match, however, for those of lady Bai.

[8] Double Fifth was a summer festival celebrated on the fifth day of the Fifth Month. On this day, everyone was expected to drink wine laced with realgar, which was believed to have the power to expulse all evil powers.

[9] As cranes eat snakes, the immortal lad White Crane, an acolyte of the Southern Pole Immortal Greybeard, is an implacable foe of lady Bai. The God of the Southern Pole Star determines longevity.

IV

When the Gu family of Kunshan recognized the stolen goods,
He was arrested, and, by the magistrate, banished to Zhenjiang.[10]
For a third time he ran into this couple of mistress and maid,
And for a second time they made arrangements to open a shop.
    By the power of his compassion and wisdom the monk Fahai
Knocked on his gate and on purpose asked for his sandalwood.[11]
Because of the breath of the demonic blue and white snakes,
He was concerned that Xu Xian eventually might lose his life.
    He accepted him into Buddhism and made him his disciple;
Now taking refuge with the Three Jewels, he would be safe.[12]
Mistress and maid ascended the mountain, asking him to come back,
But all of a sudden, the Chan master displayed a heart of stone.[13]
    Crab generals and shrimp soldiers all strengthened her forces,
And Golden Mountain was all of a sudden inundated by floods.
    But the power of Buddha and Dharma is indeed without limit:
Meditation staff and cattail hassock undid mistress and maid!
Fortunately she was pregnant with a future top-of-the-list![14]
    The number of her evil karma, it appeared, still was not filled;
By chance he was computing yin and yang inside his sleeves.[15]
"I have no idea where these two demons may have gone off to;
Most probably they have already arrived at Broken Bridge!"[16]

---

[10] On one occasion when Xu Xian wants to go out in Suzhou, White Snake provides him with beautiful gadgets to wear. It turns out these had been stolen from the Gu family, and when servants of that family recognize these articles, Xu is once again arrested for theft.

[11] The precious sandalwood had belonged to a merchant, whose boat was wrecked on purpose by lady Bai, so Xu Xian would be enabled to retrieve this treasure.

[12] The Three Jewels refer to the Buddha, the Dharma (the law, or the Buddha's teachings), and the Sangha (the monastic community of monks and nuns), constituting the totality of Buddhism.

[13] Chan (*Dhyana, Zen*) means meditation. It also became the name of one of the most influential Buddhist sects, which in the West is better known by the Japanese pronounciation of the term, "Zen."

[14] A top-of-the-list (*zhuangyuan*) is the designation of the person who passes the triennial metropolitan examination for selection of candidates for official service with highest honors.

[15] Broken and unbroken lines (yin and yang) make up the six lines of the hexagrams in the *Book of Changes*. Here Fahai is secretly, with his hands tucked into his sleeves, counting out the lines of the appropriate hexagram in order to understand the true nature of his opponents and their fate.

[16] Broken Bridge (*Duanqiao*) is one of the bridges in the Su Dike in West Lake. Its original name was Duan Family Bridge (*Duanjia qiao*), and the actual bridge is not broken at all. The meeting of Xu Xian, lady Bai, and Little Blue at Broken Bridge, at which an enraged Little Blue tries to kill Xu and has to be

The old monk sent him off to be united with them once again,
And set a date for a later meeting that was still some time off.
   Little Blue gnashed her teeth as she was seething with hatred;
She looked at Xu with rage in her eyes, like a highway robber:
"Such an act of treacherous perfidy is truly impossible to forget!"

V

"Congratulations! Your unicorn son already is one month old!"
Before her dressing mirror, lady Bai applies makeup, combs her hair.
The most dangerous thing in this human world is a man's heart:
A cruel husband without any feeling of duty, any feeling of love!
   But in final analysis he didn't have any intention to harm her—
So what was the cause of the united bowls appearing in the mirror?[17]
   They made their appearance at the order of Chan master Fahai;
The cause of this disaster was all due to this one old ascetic.
In one moment he wiped away all the love of those few years,
   And now her remorse and regret were too late—in her panic
She could only jump up and down, grasp with both her hands:
Husband and wife, mother and son were cruelly torn apart!
She exclaimed: "My dear son!" she exclaimed: "My husband!
   I realize I've committed a crime that is so big it covers heaven.
I raised the wind and waves that flooded the Golden Mountain!
By drowning these millions of lives I created a deep evil karma,
So when I will die on this day, where will I eventually end up?
   From this moment on, we'll be unable to see each other again!"
Awash in tears, she lowered her head and exclaimed: "My son,
   Your clothes for the next few years I made with my own hands,
Your own mother has spent quite some effort in making them.
Your aunt will nurse you and spoon-feed you like a mother,[18]
Her work and labor in raising you will far surpass that of me.
   When you grow up into an adult you must filially serve her;
Do not become one of those who forget all love and all duty.
Make sure people won't call you as mean as an owl or a stag!"

---

dissuaded from doing so by the pregnant lady Bai, was very popular on stage; it was also often depicted in New Year's prints (*nianhua*).

[17] The begging bowl of the Buddha is often seen as an object of great magic power, which is shared by the begging bowls of holy monks. Fahai apparently uses two begging bowls to capture the demon.

[18] The aunt here refers to Xu Xian's elder sister.

VI

From his earliest youth Xu Mengjiao was extremely intelligent;
He devoted himself to the study of books, and never grew tired.
Other people made fun of him as the offspring of a snake-spirit,
But he didn't distinguish between snake and demon as for family.
   "Now the Black Dragon may well be the offspring of some snake,
But it raises clouds and rides on them, drifting on seas and lakes."[19]
But he never had seen the kind face of the mother who bore him,
And when he came home, he cried and cried all through the night.
   When he was free he at once went to Thunder Peak Pagoda,
And, facing north, he burned incense and candles most sincerely.
He devoted all his effort and strength to the study of the books,
And all of sudden his name appeared at the top of the tiger-list![20]
   As top-of-the-list he passed the exams, and came back home,
Bringing with him a patent of nobility for his original mother.
But when he personally tore down Thunder Peak Pagoda,
   He did not find a single snake coiled up below its foundation.
How could he know that the Golden Mother already had ferried her across?[21]
She ascended the nine heavens, riding a cloud of compassion.
Xu Xian had shaved his hair and become a monk, day and night
Beating the bell and the drum, as part of his ascetic practice.
   The filial son Mengjiao so found his father and his mother:
They disclosed the immortal design, then ascended the hills.
With the Three Teachings accomplished, all hatred was gone.[22]

---

[19] The divine Black Dragon is the rain god.

[20] If the emperor is a dragon, his ministers are tigers.

[21] Golden Mother is one of the common designations of the Queen Mother of the West, as gold or metal is the element of the West in the scheme of the Five Elements. The Queen Mother of the West is one of China's most ancient female divinities. She is believed to hold court atop Mt. Kunlun, and to be the ruler of all female immortals. "To ferry across" originally is a Buddhist term, referring to the achievement of enlightenment, as nirvana is often desinated as "the other shore." Here it refers to achieving immortality and ascending to heaven.

[22] The Three Teachings refer to Confucianim, Daoism, and Buddhism. Xu Xian becomes a monk, and so achieves the teachings of Buddhism; lady Bai becomes immortal, which is a Daoist practice; and Xu Mengjiao passes the Confucian examinations and becomes an official.

THE PRECIOUS SCROLL OF THUNDER PEAK

From left to right: Xu Xuan, Mrs. Li, and Li Junfu

ANONYMOUS

The Precious Scroll of Thunder Peak in Qiantang County of Hangzhou Prefecture in Zhejiang

Part One

Now *The Precious Scroll of Thunder Peak* is first opened:
Repaying a virtue, repaying a favor she comes to Wulin.[1]
You good men and faithful women listen with reverence:
When you see your nature with a clear mind it turns true.

The story of *The Precious Scroll of Thunder Peak* took place during the years of Emperor Zhenzong of the Great Song.[2] Let me explain that Mt. Emei in Jiading Prefecture of Sichuan is densely populated by demons born from the womb, from an egg, from moisture, and from magic, and that its grottoes are fully occupied by human beings of the nine classes and the divine immortals.[3] Miraculous animals appear here again and again. In one of these grottoes lived a white snake. Because she had practiced self-cultivation for over one thousand seven hundred years, she did not desire anything immoral, and did not harm any living being. As she continuously absorbed the essence of the sun and moon, she could take on a human shape, ascend and travel on clouds and mists, and call and command the wind and rain. With a firm mind and sincere intention she consistently revered the bodhisattva Guanyin of the Southern Sea.[4] Her heart and mind always recited her name, and

---

[1] Wulin is one of the alternative names for Hangzhou.

[2] The Northern Song reigned from its capital at Kaifeng from 960 to 1126. The reign of Emperor Zhenzong lasted from 998 to 1022.

[3] Mt. Emei in western Sichuan is one of the holiest mountains of Chinese Buddhism. See Hargett, 2006.

[4] Guanyin ("Observing the Sounds") or Guanshiyin ("Observing the Sounds of the World") is the Chinese translation of the name of the bodhisattva Avalokitesvara, who became a widely venerated deity in China from the fourth century onward. According to a chapter in the popular *Lotus Sutra*, Avalokitesvara will come to the aid of anyone who sincerely invokes his name, and can take on thirty-three different shapes in doing so. From the tenth century onward, Avalokitesvara was increasingly revered in the shape of a beautiful young woman. It is in this shape that Guanyin became one of the most beloved divinities throughout East Asia. See Yü, 2001. The story of her incarnation as the princess

her mind and nature achieved supernatural intelligence. Now it happened to be the day of the great congregation of the peaches of longevity at Emerald Pond.⁵ Traveling on an auspicious cloud Guanyin followed the sounds, intent on saving creatures from suffering and greatly displayed her tender compassion. When she saw this white snake, she called her and took her along.

> If only a single drop falls down from her willow wand,
> One is seated on a lotus flower here in this world of man.
> The bodhisattva Guanyin displayed her tender compassion,
> And took along Bai Suzhen who had cultivated her mind.⁶
>   Even though this demonic creature was no human being,
> She had created merit by a thousand years of self-cultivation.
> That's why Guanyin took her along with her to Emerald Pond—
> Her tender compassion ferries us across the ford of delusion.

Just look how all the many assembled immortals together came out to welcome the bodhisattva. Each and every one kowtowed and, arranged according to rank, they went to the site of the banquet to offer their congratulations on this happy occasion of the birthday. In truth:

> Tender compassion surpasses reciting the Buddha's name a thousand times;
> Committing evil destroys all merit acquired by ten thousand sticks of incense.

> At the edge of the world the many immortals congregate,
> As her phoenix-carriage descends from the ninth heaven.
> One only has to spend seven days here on this mountain,
> And thousands of years have passed in the world of man.

Miaoshan provided the materials for one of the earliest preserved precious scrolls, viz. *The Precious Scroll of Incense Mountain* (*Xiangshan baojuan*). For a translation, see Idema, 2008. Putuoshan, a small island in the Zhoushan archipelago off the Ningbo coast in Zhejiang, became a major piligrimage site for Guanyin devotees. Guanyin, as she manifests herself on this island to her worshippers (seated on a rock next to a bamboo grove, and holding a vase of pure water and a willow wand), is known as Guanyin of the Southern Sea.

⁵ Emerald Pond atop the mythical Kunlun Mountain at the western edge of the world is the dwelling place of the Queen Mother of the West, the ruler of all female immortals. In her paradisiacal garden the peaches of immortality ripen once every three thousand years. The anonymous author of this text seems to associate the banquet of the peaches of immortality hosted by the Queen Mother of the West with the birthday of Guanyin. In some texts of this period, however, Guanyin and the Queen Mother of the West are identified, or one is considered to be a manifestation of the other.

⁶ Bai Suzhen ("Blanche White") is the name given to lady Bai in many eighteenth- and nineteenth-century versions of the legend.

"Dear immortals, please sit down, sit down!" Now on the occasion of the birthday of the bodhisattva, they all came to the banquet to congratulate her.

> The loftiest virtue by far is the merit of extending life:
> A white crane carrying a flower reaches the ninth sphere.
> The Old Man of Eternal Longevity offers her his blessings;
> The Queen Mother of the West presents her with magic peaches.
>   Han Xiangzi// plays his jade flute—[7]
> Determined to practice cultivation he abandoned his wife.
> When snow locked Indigo Pass and no horse could proceed,
> He converted Han Yu, who so ascended to the ninth sphere.
>   The emperor's brother-in-law Cao// loves to roam freely—
> Not caring for riches or glory he rejected his brocade gown.
> Of all things in this world practicing self-cultivation is the best—
> He beats the execution-ground, immortal clappers in his hands.
>   Zhongli of the Han// is short by nature—
> Understanding the depraved character of the ways of the world,
> He practiced the miraculous Way in the Zhongnan Mountains,
> And his achievements are the loftiest of all Eight Immortals.
>   Lü Dongbin// is a dashing fellow—
> On his back he carries his dragon-sword to behead all monsters.
> Compassionate, he saves from suffering, transmitting the Way—
> For all eternity, to this very day, he is the most famous of all.
>   The Immortal Maiden He// looks most charming—
> Wearied of accompanying the red dust, she preferred solitude.
> She firmly practiced true self-cultivation for thousands of years,
> And returned to the realm of immortals to enjoy its freedom.
>   Lan Caihe// is by far the youngest of them all—
> He rejected all riches as he loved to practice self-cultivation.
> Practicing on famous mountains he achieved the true fruit;
> Holding a coir basket in his hands he rides the ocean's flood.
>   Iron Crutch Li// bellows and roars—
> A dark face and thick eyebrows; he limps because of his leg.
> With full devotion he cultivated the methods of life eternal;
> Leaning on his crutch he ascended the clouds to float about.
>   Old Gardener Zhang// is most advanced in years—
> His hair and his beard are all gray, and his locks are thinning.

---

[7] The first line of this four-line stanza has been broken into two short lines of three characters each, and the division between these two short lines is indicated by "//." This is also the case in the following seven stanzas.

As he is riding backward on his donkey he laughs out loud,
Having abandoned this world with all its riches and splendor![8]
    The immortals all came to the peaches of longevity meeting,
And they all had a drink at this immortal birthday gathering.
Mushrooms at the grotto entrance displayed their lucky colors,
Cranes and deer before the steps presented auspicious jades.
    The Greybeard of the Southern Pole enjoyed a game of go,[9]
And Patriarch Dongfang's desire was still to steal the peaches.[10]
Chen Tuan suddenly woke up after sleeping a thousand years;[11]
Patriarch Peng reached the advanced age of eight hundred.
    These all at one time had been no more than some dry bones,
But once they achieved the elixir, they ascended to heaven.[12]
The immortals offered their congratulations to Her Majesty,
Wishing her continuous happiness and limitless longevity.
    Her Majesty the Queen Mother thereupon gave the order
To bestow on them eight of the big peaches of longevity.
The immortals thanked her for the gift of the immortal peaches,
And riding their auspicious clouds they followed the winds.

    I will not expound on the circumstances of these immortals,
But let me disclose the White Snake's karmic background.

---

[8] The preceding thirty-two lines provided snapshots of each of the Eight Immortals, who enjoyed great popularity from the thirteenth century onward; see Kwok and O'Brien, 1990. The legends of each of these immortals were first collected in the sixteenth century as a vernacular novel entitled *Journey to the East (Dongyou ji)*, which is available in a French translation by Nadine Perront; see Wu Yuantai, 1993. The tale of Han Xiangzi—the grand-nephew of the famous Tang dynasty confucianist Han Yu (768–824)—who refused to consummate his marriage and is said to have converted his great-uncle to Daoism after the latter was banished to Chaozhou in 819, was developed in the early seventeenth century by Yang Erzeng into another vernacular novel, *The Complete Tale of Han Xiangzi (Han Xiangzi quanzhuan)*. Philip Clart translated this novel; see Yang Erzeng, 2007.

[9] The Greybeard of the Southern Pole Star determines the length of one's life.

[10] The historical Dongfang Shuo lived in the second half of the second century B.C.E. He served at the court of Emperor Wu of the Han, and enjoyed a reputation as a poet and wit. Legend made him an immortal; it is said that he once stole some of the peaches of immortality.

[11] Chen Tuan lived during the tenth century. He lives on in legend as an immortal who could sleep for one hundred days on end.

[12] The process of self-cultivation resulting in immortality is often described in alchemical terms. Through a strict regimen of physical and meditational exercises the practitioner develops, through the fusion of contradictory but complementary elements in his or her body, the elixir or medicine of immortality.

The story goes that Her Majesty the Golden Mother of the Western Pond noticed the girl by the side of the mahasattva Guanyin, and promptly asked where she came from. The Golden Mother[13] then disclosed her karmic background: "All who want to become an immortal have to pay back the virtues and favors shown to them in the past before they can join the ranks of the immortals. Seventeen hundred years ago you were a tiny little snake, and a beggar was about to cut you in half with one stroke of his knife in order to take out your gall. Fortunately there was a timber merchant by the name of Lü Tai who was filled with tender compassion. He bought you for a hundred copper coins and set you free, and that's why you could practice self-cultivation to this day. But this man has been reborn in Hangzhou, and his name is now Xu Hanwen. You should go there and repay his favors, and then you can come back to join the congregation." When lady Bai had heard these words of the Golden Mother, she immediately took her leave, and after she also had kowtowed to the mahasattva Guanyin, she returned to her mountain.

Our story also tells that in her grotto there also lived a black carp fish demon, who was called the Seven Stars Daoist.[14] He had practiced self-cultivation for many years, and the two demons had become sworn siblings. The white snake greeted her sworn brother, and said: "I once made a religious vow, which I have not yet fulfilled, so I have to take my leave of you to go to the Tianzhu Monastery in Hangzhou in order to venerate Guanyin."[15] The Daoist replied: "In Hangzhou, I remember, you have West Lake with its superior scenery. If you go there, my sister, I am afraid you will be ensnared by the red dust.[16] The merit of your seventeen hundred years of self-cultivation has not been easily obtained, and one misstep will be enough to lose it all!"

> The bond of marriage is determined by one's former life—
> She had attended the feast of the peaches of immortality.
> The Seven Stars Daoist told her original karma, and said:
> "Dear sister, please listen to what I will clearly explain.
> Now West Lake is a place of great splendor and beauty,
> All people there are dashing romantics, without a care!
> When you go there, I fear your mortal heart will return,
> So you will fall into transmigration and lose your merit."

---

[13] Golden Mother is an alternative designation for the Queen Mother of the West, as the West is associated with metal in the Five Elements correlation theory.

[14] The "black carp" is the northern snakehead. The Seven Stars are the stars of the Dipper (Ursa Major), a powerful divinity.

[15] Hangzhou's Tianzhu Monastery is to this day a major center of Guanyin veneration.

[16] "Red dust" is a common metaphor for the mortal world and all its sensual attractions.

When lady Bai had heard him, she replied as follows:
"My dear brother, please listen to what I will have to say.
   In going there I, your sister, have no other intention but
To venerate Guanyin in Tianzhu with greatest sincerity.
I am determined to go and visit the Spirit Vulture Peak[17]
To pay homage to the Buddha and beg him for a miracle.
   Your little sister definitely will not tarry on the road;
I will come back and practice self-cultivation with you.
I definitely will not pay attention to splendor and beauty,
So, dear brother, please be not worried on my behalf."

The Seven Stars Daoist said: "Dear sister, if you have made up your mind to go, I certainly will not stop you. But please make sure to return quickly, so I will not have to be anxious all the time." Lady Bai said: "Well, let me then say good-bye!"

When painting a dragon or tiger, it's hard to paint their heart;
When you know a person, you know his face, not his karma.

When Suzhen had said her good-bye to her dear sworn brother,
Who was more to her than a real brother, she wanted to leave.
Now as soon as she pointed her fly whisk to the sky above,
A magical cloud had formed within a moment, within a blink!
   Riding on that cloud she ascended the sky—indeed, the fame
She enjoyed for her magical arts was not unfounded at all!
"A hundred mountains and thousands rivers I cross at will;
The Long River and also the wide ocean I pass at liberty."[18]
   In one single journey she traveled to the city of Hangzhou,
But our scroll now first expounds on the Dharma King!

Sakyamuni Buddha, seated on his precious throne of nine kinds of lotus flowers, was explaining the sutras and preaching the Dharma to the arhats and Buddhas and heavenly kings, when suddenly he observed this demonic cloud, and said: "Just look at that white snake! She has practiced self-cultivation for seventeen hundred years and now she goes to Hangzhou to repay a favor from a former life, but she will harm millions of living beings! I will immediately dispatch a Divine Guardian[19]

---

[17] The Spirit Vulture Peak is frequently mentioned in sutras as the place where the Buddha preached that particular sutra.

[18] Long River is a literal translation of the common Chinese name for the Yangzi River.

[19] In traditional Chinese vernacular fiction Divine Guardians (*jiedishen*) constitute a special class of fierce supernatural warriors protecting the Buddha, the Dharma and the Sangha. More literally, *jiedishen* might be translated as "divine upholders of the truth."

to block her way. I want her to swear an oath, so there can be no mistake." Once the Divine Guardian had received this order, he went forward and shouted: "Evil demon, where do you plan to go? Your punishment will not be light if you bother or harm any living being! Quickly return to your mountain, and then I will forgive you. But if you disobey this order of the Buddha, your life cannot be spared!"

> Hearing these words the white snake trembled with fright,
> She had her cloud set her down and knelt down in the dust.
> She begged and implored the tender god to do her a favor,
> She piteously prayed him to be kind and show compassion.
> "My only intention is to travel to Hangzhou, so I may
> Pay homage to the bodhisattva Guanyin and then return."
> The Guardian blocked her way: "You cannot be forgiven!
> Everything you say is an empty lie, not one word is true!"
> Lady Bai could do little else but swear, awash in tears,
> A binding oath that was as weighty as a thousand pounds:
> "If there is anything that goes amiss during my pilgrimage,
> You may pin down my body and make me bitterly suffer."
> Hearing these words, the Guardian allowed her to go on,
> And returned on his cloud and reported to the Buddha.

Only when lady Bai saw that the Divine Guardian had left after she had sworn this oath did she feel relieved: "I wanted to go to Hangzhou and find that Xu Xian to repay his favors,[20] and to finish up this bit of karma." She thereupon ascended her cloud and went straightway to Wulin.

> Flying through the air lady Bai at last arrived in Wulin,
> And near the West Lake she had her cloud set her down.
> "I've no idea whatsoever where that Xu Xian may live,
> By the looks of it, this Hangzhou is quite a large place!"
> In her heart she also was secretly pondering to herself:
> "Where am I going to hide my body tonight? Far away
> I see a mansion with its storied buildings and rooms,
> So let me go there and see what the situation may be."

When lady Bai drew closer to the mansion to observe what was going on, not a soul was stirring. But suddenly she saw in an empty spot some demonic ether: "That is quite terrifying! I wonder which evil demon this may be. Let me go forward to have a look, so I will know what is going on."

---

[20] The original text uses both Xu Xian and Xu Xuan as the name of Bai Suzhen's predestined lover, but this translation uses Xu Xian consistently.

As soon as she saw the blue demon she was frightened:
Her two eyes bulged as big as two giant bronze bells.
   Her merit great after a thousand years of self-cultivation;
Often changing into human shape, she mixed with men.
In ancient times living in the foundations of Wu's palace,[21]
She transformed herself either into a human or a demon.
   As soon as she saw lady Bai, she opened her mouth,
Saying: "What kind of demon dares enter my gate?"
The two demons battled fiercely for quite a while,
But eventually the blue demon's merit was too shallow.
   With sweet and friendly words she now hastened to say:
"Please accept my apologies, please forgive my crime!"
Lady Bai opened her mouth and spoke as follows:
"Having been born and raised on Mt. Emei, I have
Practiced self-cultivations for seventeen hundred years;
My transformations are many, my magical powers great."

The blue snake said: "I have heard about you for a long time, but now I have the good fortune to meet you. Hearing Milady's words, it is my greatest desire to serve you, so please allow me, mistress, to become your maid!" When the white snake heard the blue snake say these words, she was very pleased, and said: "If that is the case, I will change your name and call you Little Blue."

   Throughout the night, from evening time till early dawn,
The two of them kept on talking, becoming close friends.
That morning they made their toilette, and then they went
Together to Tianzhu Monastery so as to pray to Guanyin.

When lady Bai arrived in front of the Jingci Monastery, she asked Little Blue: "What is the name of this pagoda?" Little Blue replied: "This is Thunder Peak Pagoda." Lady Bai exclaimed: "Damn it! When I swore that oath in front of the Divine Guardian,[22] I had no idea there was a pagoda with this name at West Lake. Could it be that my fate is predestined?" Little Blue said: "Milady, don't be frightened! We have already arrived at Golden Sand Harbor. Let's rest here for a while, and then go on."

---

[21] The palace of Wu refers to the palace of the kings of Wu-Yue who ruled Hangzhou and the surrounding area as an independent kingdom for most of the tenth century.

[22] While our text does not say so, apparently the oath of the White Snake included a line stating that if she sinned she might be imprisoned under Thunder Peak Pagoda.

> As soon as she saw Thunder Peak, she was frightened:
> "Only now do I know the weight of the oath I swore!"
> Filled with regret, her brow was now locked in a frown:
> "How I fear that that Thunder Peak will pin me down!"

"Never for one moment I forget the virtue of Heaven and Earth;/ With every thought I wish to repay the favors of father and mother. I am Xu Xian, and my style is Hanwen. I've just turned twenty-three. My family originally hails from Cixi County in Ningbo Prefecture, but at a very young age I was brought by my father to Hangzhou. Because later my father and mother died, my elder sister and I were left as orphans. My sister is married to Li Junfu as his wife, and her husband serves as a police agent of Qiantang County. He was so kind as to recommend me to Millionaire Wang of Great Peace Bridge, so I could become a clerk in his pharmacy for a living. The millionaire treats me as kindly as one of his own kin. Today is the Clear and Bright Festival,[23] so I have prepared some sacrificial foods to take to my parents' grave to offer to them. I have called the boy Little Two to come along and carry them for me."[24]

> The two of them set out and left through the city gate,
> At Clear and Bright, to sweep the graves and sacrifice.
> Having set out the sacrificial foods, he lit the incense;
> He deeply bowed down in front of his mother's grave.
>   The paper money having been burned, they cleaned up,
> And then he told Little Two to go back ahead of him.
> I will not show how Xu Xian went and enjoyed a walk;
> I will tell again about that couple of mistress and maid.

As soon as lady Bai saw Xu Xian, she secretly thought to herself: "That fellow is quite out of the ordinary!" And she whispered: "If I could tie the marriage knot with such a man, I would not in vain have been roused to passion." Little Blue said: "Milady, what is so difficult? Let me play a little scheme to ensure that Xu Xian will come to our gate tomorrow so he and Milady can consummate their marriage."

> She arranged a clever scheme to catch the golden carp:
> Lady Bai's miraculous trick was not something simple!
> The merit achieved by Little Blue was still too shallow,
> So how could she understand the hidden secret plan?

---

[23] The Clear and Bright Festival takes place on the 105th day following the winter solstice. On this spring day, relatives visit the graves of the deceased relatives and clean them, offering sacrifices to their ancestors.

[24] This first-person self-introduction, which starts with two lines of verse, resembles the self-introductions in traditional Chinese plays.

> That same moment black clouds arose in all directions,
> And a fierce wind and heavy rain drenched his clothes.
> In this fierce storm of lightning and hail where to flee?
> So Xu Xian came up with the idea of hailing a boat.

Even though Xu Xian had an umbrella with him, it was still impossible to walk. When he suddenly saw a little boat by the bank of the river, he promptly hailed it to take him back. On the bank Little Blue called to them: "Captain, where are you going? Can you take us aboard?" The boatman said: "This boat has been hired by this young gentleman, who wants to go to the Qiantang Gate." Little Blue said: "The Lord of Heaven sends down such a heavy rain! Sir, please do us women a favor!" Xu Xian replied: "Where do you two girls want to go?" Little Blue said: "We want to get off at Double Tea Lane." Xu Xianthen said: "Please come on board, you ladies, and we will go there together." Little Blue said: "Many thanks for your kindness. We are causing you so much trouble. But, sir, please tell me where you live? And what is your name? Please tell me in detail." Xu Xian then told her: "I live in this city and my name is Xu Xian—my style is Hanwen. At present I work as a clerk in the pharmacy of Millionaire Wang of Great Peace Bridge. But where do the two of you live? And what are your names? Please tell me in detail." The two of them replied: "Sir, please allow us to inform you."

> The two of them worked their plan with clever words:
> As soon as she had met her man, her passion ran deep.
>   Little Blue opened her mouth and told the situation:
> "As for her ancestors, her family hails from Jiaxing.
> The late master her father was as a military officer,
> And he served as a regional commander at Tong Pass.
>   But alas, he got into a conflict with a crafty official,
> Who accused him at court of most heinous crimes,
> Even stating that her father was planning a rebellion,
> That he was in secret communication with foreigners.
>   Our lord and king believed this scoundrel's accusation,
> And his imperial edict ordered the whole family killed.
> His wife just wept and died and went to the shades;
> The only one to escape this disaster was their daughter.
>   The young lady had studied magic arts since her youth—
> The transmitted teachings of the immortals are no lie!
> She collected some gold and silver and some clothes,
> And since she escaped she has been living in Hangzhou,
>   Here on Double Tea Lane, now already for three years—
> Alone and lonely, orphaned, wretched: lacking a man."

Xu Xian said: "So she is an upper-class young lady! Please forgive my rudeness!"

The boatman shouted: "We've arrived at Great Peace Bridge!" Little Blue then said: "Sir Xu, I have a request. You see that it is still raining like before, and from here to Double Tea Lane is still quite a distance, so could we perhaps be allowed to borrow your umbrella?" Xu Xian said: "Of course, no problem! Please take it!" Little Blue said: "Many thanks! But the issue is that there is no male person in our household, it's just the two of us, mistress and maid, so there is no one to bring it back. So tomorrow you must come to our place." Xu replied: "That is no problem either." Thereupon they each went their way.

When Little Blue had come home, she said to her mistress: "Tomorrow Xu Xian definitely will come early to fetch his umbrella, and then you can entrust your future to him. But what to do about the fact that Xu is so poor that he does not have the money for engagement gifts?" Lady Bai said: "That is no problem.

> With magic arts I'll steal the silver from the vault,
> Demons will carry it across, so I can tie the knot."
> Her oh-so-tender fingers grasped her phoenix sword;
> She spit out magic water and recited incantations.
> She summoned her five demons who arrived en masse,
> And told them: "Steal the silver in the Qiantang vault!"
> They stole the twenty pristine ingots from the vault,
> And moved them to her house—nothing remained.
> The next day she prepared for the arrival of her guest,
> But in our scroll we now will turn again to Xu Hanwen.
> Back home throughout the night he could not sleep,
> As secretly he pondered—he was overcome with joy:
> "If I could get this woman to become my wedded wife,
> She'd make a nice and proper, fine and perfect partner!"

When Xu Xian arrived at the gate of lady Bai's, Little Blue invited him inside with a smile as soon as she saw him. When lady Bai saw him, she was very pleased, and said: "Sir, please come inside to have a cup of tea." Xu Xian replied: "You are too kind!" But when lady Bai insisted, Xu accepted her invitation. When the three of them arrived inside, they greeted each other formally and sat down, whereupon lady Bai said: "Yesterday we made bold to borrow your boat, and you also were so kind as to lend us your umbrella. Even though it truly was a chance encounter, you really were very nice to us." Xu Xian replied: "Why would you have to be concerned about these trifling matters? But I am afraid I have to take my leave." Little Blue at his side then said: "Sir Xu Xian, please take your time. Our young lady would like to offer you a cup of wine, so please don't refuse!" Xu Xian said: "We have never had any interaction before, so how can I cause you so much trouble?"

> One cup of fine wine repaid the favor of the umbrella;
> The three of them were filled with love in their heart.
>   That smart and clever, oh-so-intelligent Little Blue
> Set out the wine and the food in the blink of an eye.
> The young lady sat down at the other side of the table,
> While Little Blue very ardently poured him his wine.
>   When Xu Xian had finished off three cups of wine,
> Little Blue immediately started to ask him questions:
>   "Dear sir,
> Have you by any chance already taken a main wife?
> When were you born, in what year and what month?"[25]
>   Xu Xian promptly replied in the following manner:
> "Your servant now has reached the age of twenty-three;[26]
> The month of my birth was a *jiyou*, the day a *xinwei*;
> I was born at the end of the day, at the hour of *you*.[27]
>   To my misfortune my parents passed away early,
> And because I am poor, I could not yet find a bride.
> I only have one elder sister, who is a full sibling,
> And she is married to Junfu, who lives in this city."
>   When Little Blue heard this, she spoke as follows:
> "So you were born in the same year as my mistress!"
> Hearing these words lady Bai could not but blush:

---

[25] As part of regular marriage ceremonies, the dates of birth of the prospective partners are compared in order to assess their compatibility.

[26] Twenty-three is also the age at which Student Zhang falls in love with Yingying in *The Story of the Western Chamber* (*Xixiang ji*). This play probably was traditional China's most popular love comedy. Until the age of twenty three, Student Zhang has refrained from all sexual intercourse because he has never met a woman of his liking, but then, when both of them happen to be staying at the same monastery, falls head over heels in love with Yingying. When he first sees her, she is dressed in white, because she is in mourning for her father.

[27] The characters *jia, yi, bing, ding, wu, ji, geng, xin, ren,* and *gui* constitute the ten "Heavenly Stems." The characters *zi, chou, yin, mao, chen, si, wu, wei, shen, you, xu,* and *hai* constitute the twelve "Earthly Branches." By combination of one of the characters of the first cycle and one of the characters of the second cycle, a new cycle of sixty combinations is produced, which from ancient times was used for the consecutive counting of years, months, days, and hours. Soothsayers used the combination of the "eight characters" specifying the year, month, day, and hour of birth to assess the compatibility of prospective marriage partners. In traditional China, a day was divided into twelve hours, each double the length of a Western hour. The hour of *you* corresponds to 5:00–7:00 P.M.

"I cannot disobey the Buddha and repay his favors!"
"The young lady here is an orphaned, single maiden,
Her parents have both died and she has no relatives.
If a man has no helpmate, he cannot be said to be noble;
If a woman has not husband, her lotus heart is pained.[28]
   A pair of mandarin ducks[29]—you should be a couple:
My mistress is young of years, you're greening spring.
     Dear sir,
There's no reason why you should refuse my proposal:
Both parties will benefit, so let's have this wedding!"

When Xu Xian had heard this, he said: "Dear sister, what kind of nonsense are you talking now? Your mistress is the pampered daughter of a noble family, so how could she become my bride?" Little Blue replied: "A marriage is determined in a prior life;/ five hundred yeas ago you were tied together. Discuss it with your elder sister, but don't miss this opportunity." Xu Xian said: "I am very grateful for your kindness, but how can I not be flabbergasted? And I don't have the money for the engagement gifts and the wedding preparations, so what can I do?" Little Blue replied: "That's no problem. Just wait here for a while and I will take care of that matter for you." Little Blue went inside and explained the matter to lady Bai. She then took out two silver ingots which she wrapped in a handkerchief, and which she offered in both her hands to Xu Xian, saying: "I've discussed this with my mistress. Here you have two silver ingots. Take them home with you and discuss the matter with your sister. Select a lucky day for the engagement, and then we will finalize the marriage."

   To take a widow as one's wife is not the proper way;
Money that one hasn't earned is followed by misfortune.

"To give the guy these silver ingots wasn't a good idea;
When the authorities find out, he will suffer disaster!
Xu Xian will be punished, suffering torture and shame,
Police officers everywhere are investigating this case.
   The magistrate is sorely upset about the stolen silver,
So this fine marriage karma will be cruelly ripped apart."
When Suzhen heard the people outside talking about it,
She made careful computations, counting on her fingers:
   "Fortunately the magistrate is very pure and honest, so
He will only be punished oh so lightly and not be killed.

---

[28] Lotus (*lian*) has the same pronunciation as one of the Chinese words for love (*lian*).

[29] The monogamous mandarin ducks are a widely used symbol for mutual love and devotion.

> Husband and wife will meet again at some later date—
> He'll suffer some empty fright, not some dire disaster."

Lady Bai said: "I made a mistake! I should not have given him those ingots. But fortunately the official is pure and honest, so he will only suffer a fright. And according to fate he and I will meet again some other day."

Now tell that when one day this Li Junfu saw that his brother-in-law had silver from the vault, he went and reported him to the magistrate: "I've found the criminal and the booty." The county magistrate asked: "So where are they now?" Junfu replied: "The criminal is called Xu Xian, and he is my brother-in-law." The magistrate then said: "You scoundrel! You must have been unable to get to the bottom of this case, and now try to get out of it by offering up your brother-in-law! Get out the ankle-presses!" Junfu reported: "My lordship, this is indeed the truth! I have seen two ingots of his that carry the stamp of Renhe County."[30]

When the magistrate had summoned Xu Xian for questioning, he said: "When I see your fine features, you don't seem a criminal to me. So where did you get these ingots? You must tell me the truth!" Xu Xian told him the full story in all detail, and the magistrate then asked the yamen runners: "Whose mansion is this in Double Tea Lane?"[31] The yamen runners reported: "Your lordship, that place was originally the location of the palace of the Prince of Wu. Now, we hear, it is a haunted place frequented by demons, and at present no one is living there." When the magistrate had heard this tale, he promptly took out a red slip, and dispatched ten yamen runners: "Quickly arrest those demons and bring them to this office for interrogation." "Yes!"

> The yamen runners then went to Double Tea Lane,
> But the main gate was closed with no one around.
> When they knocked on the gate, nobody answered;
> Together they broke it open, and entered the hall.
>   There they observed charming girls, two in number,
> Who looked like immortals descended to this world.
> When these runners had stared at them for a while,
> Little Blue explained the situation to them as follows.

Little Blue said: "You guys act quite brazenly without any reason! This is the house of a family of officials, and yet you break down the gate to enter! Do you know what punishment you deserve?" The runners replied: "We have come here today at the order of His Lordship the magistrate, for the very purpose of arresting two demons for interrogation. Friends, let's take action!"

---

[30] The two counties of Renhe and Qiantang shared the administration of the city of Hangzhou.

[31] The yamen is the office of a Chinese official.

In a flash the two demons suddenly had disappeared;
There was a huge flare of light—then they were gone.
The runners stood there and watched for quite a while:
These two indeed turned out to be demonic creatures!
   But in one of the rooms they found a wooden chest,
Which they carried off to the yamen hall for inspection.
They reported this to the magistrate who took his seat,
In order to see what the contents of the chest might be.

When the magistrate immediately took his seat, he found in that chest nothing else but the eighteen pristine ingots, so all the silver from the vault had been fully recovered. He had the silver stored in the vault as before, and then instructed Xu Xian: "You still are not awakened from your delusion! If you stay here, I should have you executed. And these demons too are bound to harm your life. I therefore will banish you to Suzhou to avoid such a disaster." Xu Xian could only express his gratitude to His Lordship.

   A pure judge's sentence—his fame was well-founded!
   He dearly loved the common people—great was his grace!

   A document was dispatched to the city of Suzhou:
Xu Hanwen was to serve as a soldier for three years.
The document did not state he had committed a crime;
But he had to avoid his own house to ensure his safety.
   Now when Junfu came back home to his own house,
And explained the whole situation to Xu's elder sister,
The latter flew into a rage when she heard this story,
And she cursed her husband as a man without morals:
   "You have no shred of decency, you are so vicious!
A human face but the heart of a beast—you are no man!
Our father and mother only had the two of us as children;
If hand and foot must separate, it will break my heart!"[32]
   The more she thought and imagined, the more she cried,
The sound of her wailing and grief—quite heart-rending!
Junfu thereupon addressed her in the following manner:
"My dear wife, please don't cry, please wipe your tears!
   At present he may be banished to the city of Suzhou,
But after the three years of his sentence he'll be back."
But the wife did not listen to what her husband said,
But cried and wept throughout the day, awash in tears.

---

[32] "Hand and foot" is a common metaphor for siblings.

[Old male:][33] "Amassing virtue I do not damage the grass before the steps,/ Perfecting blessings I cultivate the flowers in my heart. As soon as I learned that Xu Xian had encountered this disaster, I hurried to the county yamen." After he had greeted Xu Xian, he asked: "Now you have encountered this great misfortune, I am very distressed. But fortunately the magistrate is pure and honest, so you were not subjected to shame. When you get to Suzhou, I have there a good friend, by the name of Wu Zhaofang. His residence is the pharmacy in Zhan Zhu Lane, and he is a very generous man. I will give you a letter for him, in which I have provided a detailed description of the injustice you have suffered. When he sees my handwriting, he is bound to give you a job. I also have here some taels of silver for you to use on the road. When you get there, send me a letter at the earliest opportunity so I won't have to worry. And then I have here yet another tael for this officer to buy some wine." Xu Xian replied: "Many thanks, Mr. Wang! When will I ever be able to pay you back for this large gift? Now I have to say good-bye."

> When Xu Xian eventually arrived in the city of Suzhou,
> He presented himself at the pharmacy to deliver the letter.
> Upon reading the letter the millionaire told him to stay;
> He took care of him very well, providing wine and food.
>   He entertained Xu Xian with great respect and kindness;
> A banquet to welcome the traveler was set out in the hall.
> While the two of them were drinking and talking merrily,
> A servant came forward to report on some urgent matter.

He informed the millionaire: "There are two ladies outside who say they are the womenfolk of this young gentleman and have come to see him." The millionaire said: "Let me come outside and have a good look. According to his story they must be some demons." But he only saw two girls whose features had a hundred beauties and a thousand charms, and whose faces obscured the moon and shamed the flowers; their bearing was gracious and their behavior most proper. When Little Blue saw the millionaire come out, she stepped forward, made a curtsy, and said: "You must be Mr. Wu." The millionaire replied: "Indeed, I am. May I ask you two ladies what brings you here?" Little Blue said: "We have learned that our master is presently here in your mansion. First of all we would like to pay our respects to you, sir, and your noble wife. Secondly we came here to find our master." The millionaire then said: "Young ladies, please come inside." Lady Bai and Little Blue followed the millionaire inside. On seeing them Xu Xian shouted: "Mr. Wu, why did you allow these demons to come

---

[33] "Old male" is the designation of a role type in drama, so one can surmise that our anonymous author worked on the basis of a play text, but the term is also used to specify a type of delivery in *tanci*. The following short speech is by Mr. Wang, Xu Xian's employer in Hangzhou.

inside?" The millionaire said: "Dear Mr. Xu, you shouldn't be so frightened. How can there be any demons in the bright light of day? There must be some explanation. Young ladies, please be seated." The two young ladies then said: "Dear Mr. Wu and Mr. Xu, please listen as I give you a report.

> "Dear sir,
> In winter one knows the quality of pine and cypress—[34]
> How difficult it has been to see you, my dear husband!
> I implore you, my dear husband, do not harbor doubt,
> This all must have been due to some earlier evil karma.
>   The one hundred tael of fine silver which I gave you,
> Were only meant to defray the costs of the wedding.
> I had no idea that the county vault had been robbed,
> And that Junfu would become so vicious at first sight.
>   When my late father was still alive and holding office,
> The money at his disposal all came from official vaults.
> Each ingot of silver would carry its own local stamp,
> And I have come to see every prefecture and county!
>   When the magistrate saw the ingots, his greed arose,
> And he sentenced you, irrespective of the situation.
> When he banished you to the distant city of Suzhou,
> Day and night I was filled with worry, had no peace!
>   Little Blue and I then knew no better plan of action
> Than to collect my gold and silver and make this trip.
> It is not that I have no sense of decorum and shame,[35]
> It's all because of the great affair that settles my future.
> But how could I know that you would be so perverse
> As to declare, against all reason, that I am a demon!
>   Under these conditions I don't want to be your wife,
> I'll be happy to shave my head and to become a nun.
> From this very moment you and I will separate—
> Please take good care of yourself, don't feel sad.
>   There's no other reason why I want to become a nun
> Than that you, darling husband, will enjoy a long life.
> If we cannot be a couple in this present existence,
> I hope in a coming existence to become your wife."

---

[34] Pine and cypress are symbols of fidelity and loyalty in adversity, as they stay green in winter.

[35] A young lady of the upper class was not supposed to show her face in public, let alone travel without a proper escort.

> When lady Bai had come to this point in her speech,
> She was awash in tears, enough to soak her clothes.
> When the millionaire had listened to this sad tale,
> He also immediately joined in to convince him.

The millionaire shouted: "Mr. Xu, where in the world do you find virtuous women like these? Her story has cleared everything up. I will tell a boy to go to her boat and carry the luggage of Mrs. Xu to your room." He also called for his wife to join the banquet. Her Ladyship said: "I have been standing behind the screen for quite some time already!" Lady Bai curtsied to Mrs. Wu, and they took their seats as host and guest. Mrs. Wu said: "Behind the screen I could only hear how virtuous you are. But you are so talented and beautiful too!" And she said to Mr. Xu: "You cannot wrongly believe those slanderous words, be filled with doubt and blame her without reason! Young lady, you shouldn't blame him either. He is a young man who has just suffered a grievous wrong. But now the case has been cleared up, and the two of you should celebrate the ritual of happy reunion!" The millionaire also said to his wife: "Today is a lucky day of huge dragon virtue and happy phoenix heaven, so let the two of us act as the hosts, so they can consummate their marriage here in our house." Xu Xian said: "The favors you bestow on me are like a mountain, and surpass even those of parents who give us a second life!"

After they have lived at the mansion for a while, Xu Xian proposed to his wife: "I want to open my own drugstore, so I will ask the millionaire to pay attention and find me a suitable building. What's your opinion?"

The millionaire said: "Leave it all to me if you want to open a drugstore. I will take care of this for you."

> Out of the kindness of their hearts the millionaire couple
> Then hurried to make all preparations without any delay.
> Red and green lanterns were hung, and candles were lit;
> The Three Stars of Longevity were displayed in the hall.
> Bands of musicians played mouth organs, fifes, and pipes:
> Instruments mixing in harmony as drums were sounded.
> The love of husband and wife was like fish and water;
> The whole family enjoyed priceless joy and harmony.
> In all tasks she fulfilled, Suzhen wanted to be perfect—
> Carefully considering all aspects she managed affairs.

When lady Bai had been his wife for over two months, she brought out three thousand tael of silver, and said to her husband: "Two thousand five hundred should be invested in drugs, and three hundred should be kept for small expenses. With these two hundred we should thank millionaire Wu for arranging our wedding."

> When Xu Xian had heard her speak in this manner,
> He promptly hired two laborers to carry the silver.
> They delivered the silver to the mansion's high hall,
> To thank the millionaire for all his help and favors.
> "We, husband and wife, enjoyed your kind care;
> A lasting gratitude for this is engraved on our hearts."
> When the millionaire saw the silver, he first refused;
> Refusing to accept it lightly, he said many phrases.

The millionaire said: "When you stayed at my humble dwelling, we often treated you shabbily, so why should you bother to waste such effort? How could I in good conscience accept such a large gift? Dear Mr. Xu, please make sure to express my thanks to your wife. May I ask you, Mr. Xu, which day have you chosen to open your store? It will be my pleasure to take care of all minor matters."

> Xu Xian immediately replied in the following way:
> "The grand opening is set for tomorrow at noontime."
> Husband and wife had spent three days getting ready;
> In the kitchen wine and food had all been prepared.
> They then invited the millionaire and also his wife,
> And Xu Xian and his wife expressed their gratitude:
> "We enjoyed your hospitality while staying with you;
> You helped the two of us out in matters large and small.
> We have no way to repay this virtue and these favors,
> So we can only wish you two a long and happy life."

The millionaire answered them both, saying: "We thank you very much indeed!" When they took their leave from Xu Xian and his wife, lady Bai said: "Mr. and Mrs. Wu, please take your time."

After Xu Xian had expressed his thanks to the millionaire, the business of his drugstore became quite flourishing. When the Double Fifth festival had arrived, our story tells that Xu Xian himself had fetched a charcoal burner, and when he came upstairs, he saw that his wife was not feeling too well, so he said: "Milady, please get up, and I will go down to the kitchen to get us some wine, so you and I can celebrate Double Fifth." But lady Bai said: "I should keep you company, but because I am feeling so tired, you must go to the shop without me to have some drinks [with the assistants]. It is your duty as their boss to treat them well, you cannot slight them." Without answering her, Xu Xian promptly went downstairs, but came back with the wine. As he put it on the table, [he said:] "Milady, please get up, so you and I can drink a few cups. Don't disappoint your husband." At this time it was exactly noon. Lady Bai finally had to give in to Xu Xian's entreaties, and even though she had no desire to do so, she could not but force herself to get up. Xu Xian poured her a cup of realgar wine,[36] which he handed her with both hands. When lady Bai had drunk only half a cup, she was overcome by the force of the alcohol, but as he kept on entreating her to drink, she could only finish her cup. Xu Xian then went downstairs to drink merrily with his assistants.

When lady Bai had drunk this one cup of realgar wine, it seemed to her as if her belly was carved by a knife. This had hurt her womb energy, whereupon she lost womb blood.[37] Struck by the blood glare, she had, before she could suppress that impulse, manifested her original shape and turned into a white snake, lying all coiled up on the bed. When soon thereafter Xu Xian's drinking party with the assistants in the shop had come to an end, he thought to himself: "Little Blue has some illness, so there is no one who looks after Milady. Let me go upstairs to see how she is doing."

> Xu Xian walked over and came to the second floor,
> Arriving in front of the bed he called his wife's name.
> He called her a number of times but got no response,
> So he pulled the gauze curtains aside to have a look.
> He did not see his own wife, that very lovely woman,
> But he saw a white snake—what a frightening sight!
> The body was long and huge and coiled up on the bed;
> The head was as big as a bucket, the eyes bronze bells.
> Her beautiful face and fine features had disappeared:
> It scattered his spirits and souls, set his gall a-tremble.[38]
> Giving a cry he collapsed then and there on the floor;
> His limbs were as cold as ice: gone off to the shades!
> When Little Blue heard the bumping sound upstairs,
> She promptly ran upstairs to see what had happened.
> She saw there her master flat on the floor, passed out;
> His limbs were as cold as ice, his face was all blue.
> When she lifted the bed-curtains and so had a look,
> She saw her mistress showing her serpentine shape.
> Her man was scared to death, gone to the shades,
> And she had not noticed it at all, not in the least.

---

[36] Realgar is a suphur–arsenicum compound.

[37] Blood shed in menstruation and childbirth (or a miscarriage, as in this instance) was believed to be extremely polluting. It was therefore believed to have the power to defeat magic, as magic requires purity.

[38] The gall was considered to be the site of courage.

Our story goes that Little Blue struck her a few times in the face and called a number of times: "Milady!" When lady Bai had resumed her original human shape, Little Blue said: "Milady, you practiced self-cultivation for seventeen hundred years and your merit is huge, so why did you manifest your true shape? What has happened to all your merit?" Lady Bai told Little Blue: "My husband pestered me to drink a cup of realgar spirits. That hurt my womb energy, so I showed my original shape. Luckily my merit is huge, because otherwise I would have lost my life." Little Blue said: "Milady, if you had wanted to show your shape, you should have called for me, so I could have locked the door to the room, and then you could have shown your shape. Now your husband has been scared to death by you. So what to do now?" When lady Bai heard this, she got up and had a look. "Oh my dear husband! My husband! What do I have to do now?" Little Blue said: "Milady, there's no time for grieving and wailing, we first have to come up with a plan to bring him back to life."

>Once she had seen in what shape her husband was,
>Suzhen cried and wept, and her tears coursed down:
>"A moment ago you urged me to have wine with you,
>So how come you passed out and do not come to?
>　In an earlier life you were so kind as to rescue me,
>That's why I wanted in this life to repay your favor.
>Because of you I have suffered many tribulations;
>Two or three times I have suffered bitter hardship.
>　This disaster today is because of that realgar wine,
>You yourself are to blame for this fatal misfortune.
>How do you want me now to bring you back to life?
>Alas, when I see you there it really hurts my heart!"
>　Little Blue addressed her with the following advice:
>"We'll have to find a plan to bring him back to life.
>The merit of your self-cultivation must be sufficient
>To go and fetch the immortal herb to save his life."
>　When Suzhen heard this, she answered as follows:
>"Little Blue, what you said makes no sense at all!
>Where in this mortal world do I find a miracle herb?
>It's nowhere to be found on this whole wide earth!
>　It is only to be found in the Southern Pole Palace:
>You revive from nine deaths and come back to life!"
>When Little Blue heard her tell this story, she thought:
>"There is no way you can go to the Southern Pole!"

Little Blue said: "When you go to the Southern Pole Palace, you'll find there the two boys Crane and Deer, who guard that grotto-mansion. They are quite terrifying, so how could you go there?" Lady Bai replied: "If I want to save my husband's life, I will have to risk my own. I hope I will be able to return safely so we can meet again. If I am captured by Crane and Deer, not only can my husband not be saved, but I also will lose my life! Oh my dear husband, how I've harmed you!" She also said: "Little Blue, move my husband onto the bed. And quickly fetch me some water, so I can bathe myself and put on another set of clothes. Quickly hang up an image of the bodhisattva Guanyin. I will go to the Southern Pole Palace, and you will light candles and burn incense and on my behalf most devoutly pray that the bodhisattva Guanyin may protect me and my husband!"

> All she could think about was how to save her husband,
> She didn't fear a hundred mountains or thousand rivers.
>   She wrapped her body in a full set of new clothes,
> And on her head she wore a scarf like Miaochang.
> On her back she carried a pair of miraculous swords;
> In her oh-so-tender hands she grasped a fly whisk.
>   She thereupon knelt down on the cattail hassock,
> And prayed to the bodhisattva with sincere devotion.
> She also turned around and instructed Little Blue
> To spare no effort in taking care of her husband.
>   "And if someone outside asks you what's going on,
> Just say he has some disease and is staying in bed."

When Suzhen, riding on her magic cloud, had arrived at the Southern Pole Palace, she saw Deer asleep and blocking the gate, so she could only jump across him to get inside, and when she looked all around, she only saw in the courtyard just one immortal herb. It was as big as an official bushel and more than thirty feet high. All around it was thickly covered with green leaves, and at the very top one red flower had opened. The flower displayed all colors, and its brilliance was extraordinary. It sparkled and glowed with an auspicious brightness, and richly exuded a lucky fragrance. In the First Month[39] it opened one flower, and for each month it produced one petal. If there was an intercalary month, it produced one additional little petal. On the first day of the month the flower bloomed, and at the end of the month the flower fell. That is why Old Greybeard collected these flowers and distributed them to the immortals. Once you had swallowed this flower, you would live forever and never age. You

---

[39] The First Month is the first month of the traditional Chinese calendar. As Chinese New Year falls on a date between January 20 and February 20, the First Month on average starts more than one month later than January 1.

would even revive from nine deaths. At this moment lady Bai thought: "There is only this immortal herb in this palace, so this must be it!" She immediately flew up to the very top, and plucked two petals. When she put them in the bosom of her gown, she was overwhelmed by their exceptional aroma. When she came back to the entrance of the grotto, she wanted to leave by jumping across Deer. But who could have known that the latter would suddenly wake up from his slumber and dreams? He immediately shouted: "What kind of demon are you that you dare enter this grotto-mansion? Secretly stealing the immortal herb—what punishment do you deserve?" Lady Bai replied: "I am a disciple of Old Mother of Black Mountain.[40] But because my husband was struck by a disease and may die any moment, and because in the mortal world there is no magic herb to be found to save his life, I came here to seek this immortal herb. I would have asked Old Greybeard, but he has not yet come back, and I saw that you were still asleep and didn't dare disturb you, and therefore I had the temerity to go inside, and it is indeed a fact that I took two petals. Dear brother, I pray you to show some mercy. Since ancient times it is said that it is better to save a man's life than to build a seven-story pagoda. So please, brother Deer, do me a favor and inform Old Greybeard of my situation. I am sure he will show compassion!" Lady Bai implored him most piteously, and her tears coursed down like a flood. When Deer saw her in this sad condition, [he said:] "If you did it to save your husband's life, get out of here as fast as you can!" Lady Bai said: "Many thanks, brother, and good-bye!" Deer replied: "I am just afraid that brother Crane will come back, and then it will be impossible to escape, so get out of here now!" Just look how lady Bai kowtowed and left—she flew off, riding her clouds, like a bird escaped from its cage!

> At this moment lady Bai felt extremely relieved:
> She got the magic herb and was out of the palace.
>   She only thought bad fortune had turned to good,
> And she hurried back home to save her husband.
> But behind her brother Crane now loudly shouted:
> "You demon from nowhere, where are you going?"
>   Promptly turning her head, lady Bai had a look:
> Her heart was so scared her gall started to flutter!
> Riding on a cloud she suddenly lost her footing;
> Showing her original shape she fell into the dust!
>   When brother Crane saw this, he was filled with joy:
> All his life he never had tasted any savory meat.
> Widely opening his great beak he swooped down,

---

[40] Old Mother of Black Mountain (*Lishan laomu*) is a Daoist divinity with great magical skills.

Leaving no way for Suzhen to escape with her life!
In this moment of imminent danger what was best?
Who would be able to save her from certain death?

Now this White Crane had practiced self-cultivation for several thousand years, so when he saw this huge white snake, he was overjoyed and he spread his large wings, wishing to swoop down and swallow her! How could he know that Old Greybeard was looking all around him, and when he did not see brother Crane, he immediately took his leave of the other immortals, and once outside the grotto-mansion, he looked everywhere from his cloud. "Great! If I don't save her, for whom should she wait? I have known for quite a while that the white snake would come and steal the immortal herb, and that's why I ordered brother Deer to guard the gate, and ordered brother Crane to accompany me to the meeting. But just as I was expounding the classics and preaching the Dharma with the other immortals, that brother Crane suddenly disappeared, so I was afraid he left to hurt the White Snake. She and Xu Xian will later eventually achieve the fruit, so how can I not save her? I will have to get on my cloud and pursue him to save her!"

The immortal said good-bye to the other immortals,
And set off on his cloud in pursuit of brother Crane.
The White Snake had just shown her original shape,
And brother Crane was all set to gobble her down,
   When Old Greybeard loudly shouted the order:
"You're not allowed to commit such dire violence!
Set her free to go home so she can save her husband,
Whatever happened, take it easy—you have to relax!"
   When brother Crane heard this order, he could only
Settle down, show restraint, and not commit murder.

Old Greybeard said: "This White Snake and Xu Xian are united by fate as husband and wife. Her husband at home was frightened to death, and that's why she came to my palace to steal the immortal herb to save her husband's life. You will accompany me back home. At some later date she will be subdued by someone else." How did he know that the White Snake had collapsed in fright on the ground and still had not come to? So Old Greybeard nudged her with his staff, saying: "Don't be scared, but quickly go back to save your husband's life!" When she eventually slowly regained consciousness, she once again assumed a human shape, and left after having kowtowed to Old Greybeard.

Old Greybeard all along had known her intention;
He had divined the demon wanted to save her husband.
When lady Bai came to, having regained consciousness,
She kowtowed to thank the immortal for saving her life.
Tears coursed down her face at this moment in time;
The more she pondered this, the more she was pained.
"If this old immortal had only arrived one minute later,
I would have been destined to die and to lose my life!
I have been saved by an intervention of the bodhisattva,
By Guanyin who saves from suffering and from disaster!"
When Suzhen thought of this most heartrending event,
Her tears coursed down like a river, soaking her clothes.
We've spoken at length about lady Bai on her journey,
So let's tell again of Little Blue in the city of Suzhou.
"My mistress has been gone now for quite a few days,
So what is the reason she still has not come back home?"
When Little Blue thought of this heartrending situation,
Her eyes were filled with tears, which wetted her cheeks.
She turned around and showed her respect to Guanyin,
As she knelt down on her knees on the dust of the floor.
"I hope that the mahasattva will respond to my prayer
By protecting my mistress so she can come back home."
All of sudden she heard the sound of a gust of wind;
A strange fragrance hit her nose, in a quite scary way.
Just when she thought her mistress must have returned,
She heard someone outside the window call "Little Blue!"

When lady Bai arrived in front of the window, she put down her cloud and called: "Little Blue, I'm back!" When Little Blue heard this, it was indeed her mistress who had returned. She immediately opened the gate, and invited her mistress to come inside, as she asked: "Milady, how come your face looks like this?" Lady Bai replied: "I have suffered no end of tribulations! I have only barely escaped with my life, and I was almost not able to see you again!" When she thereupon arrived in front of the bodhisattva, she burned incense, lit candles, and expressed her thanks with a bow. She then hurried to the bed to see how her husband was doing, and exclaimed: "My dear husband, going to Mt. Song I suffered no end of tribulations,[41] and I

---

[41] Mt. Song in Henan province is the center of the Chinese world. The four directions and the center each were marked by holy mountains (also called marchmounds) that were widely revered as deities. For instance the deity of Mt. Tai in Shandong, the holy mountain of the East, was revered throughout China as a ruler of the underworld.

almost lost my life, but thanks to the protection of the bodhisattva I have been able to come home with the immortal herb, so now I am here to save you so you will revive!" She also said: "Little Blue, quickly heat some water!" And she handed the immortal herb to Little Blue, who looked at the herb in her hand and said: "This is indeed something divine!" She hastened to make a decoction of the herb, which she handed to her mistress.

When lady Bai had received this immortal elixir, she told Little Blue to come along, but the latter said: "Just wait a minute, Milady! Already earlier he suspected that we are demons, and now you have shown your original shape, which scared him to death when he saw you. When he regains consciousness, he'll surely be filled with suspicion toward the two of us. So what will we say to him to silence him? We must come up with a plan!" Lady Bai thereupon took out a white handkerchief, which she placed on the floorboards of the upstairs room. She loudly recited a magical formula, and once she had spit out a mouthful of blessed water, the handkerchief turned into a white snake. She then took out her precious sword and cut it into seven pieces, saying: "This plan will do, won't it?" and Little Blue replied: "Milady, that's a marvelous trick!"

When they arrived in front of the bed, they pulled the gauze bed curtains aside. "Little Blue, please support my husband." Lady Bai tasted the elixir, and then fed it into Xu Xian's mouth. You could see him slowly regain consciousness, and once his cheeks eventually had regained their color, he said: "Aiya! That really scared me to death!" Lady Bai voiced her gratitude to Heaven and Earth, and urged her husband to recover: "Your wife is here to save you!" But Xu Xian still seemed to be dreaming. When he opened his eyes wide, he only saw these two demons and shouted: "Leave me immediately!" Lady Bai said: "My dear husband, don't say things like that! I hurried to Mt. Emei to request help from my teacher. Old Mother of Black Mountain gave me an immortal herb that brings people back to life from nine deaths, and I sped back to save your life. If you talk about that white snake, then it is still to be found in the courtyard, but I have already cut it into seven pieces. If you don't believe me, my husband, you have only to go and look for yourself." Xu Xian replied: "I still don't believe you. Let me go and have a look." Lady Bai then said: "My dear husband, just take a good look." Xu stepped down from his bed, and supported by the two of them, he walked to the courtyard to have a look. Only then did he feel at ease, and he said: "Indeed, you are right!" He promptly called workers to remove the carcass and bury it, and he exclaimed: "My dear wife, if you had not come to my rescue, how could we have met each other again face to face?" Lady Bai said: "My dear husband, it's windy outside, so take a nap in your room. You must slowly recover."

Only then did Xu Xian finally feel at ease again,
And he exclaimed: "My dear wife, my precious darling,
I'm so grateful for your great favor and your deep love:
Risking your own safety you went all out to save my life.
   You were so kind as to go and fetch the long-life herb,
Suffering thousands, myriads of tribulations on the road!
When I will have fully recovered, am the old me again,
I will show my gratitude for this exceptional virtue."
   Suzhen addressed him then in the following words:
"My husband, there is no need at all to mention this.
As your wedded wife, I am not some ordinary woman,
It is only my proper duty to save my man and master."
   From this moment on the couple lived in harmony:
The husband led, the wife followed, devoted to him:
"My only wish is that divine Heaven will protect us,
So we may live together all our life till a ripe old age."

Our story goes that lady Bai computed yin and yang, and one day at night she went with Little Blue to the middle of the Yangzi and snatched three hundred loads of sandalwood, the full load of the large boat of some merchant. The next day she ordered workers to go to the bank of the river and transport all the sandalwood to the shop. The merchant wailed and wept, and wanted to commit suicide by jumping into the river, but he was saved by the monk Fahai of the Golden Mountain Monastery, who gave some money to the merchant so he would have enough to go back home. Now let's talk again about the monk. He then ordered his acolyte to go to the drugstore of Xu Xian, and there to sound his fish-drum[42] and ask for a donation.

   Xu Xian opened his mouth and came forward to ask,
Addressing the monk as reverend he came forward:
"May I ask you where your monastery is to be found?
Why do you go from house to house, asking donations?"
   The monk kowtowed and then addressed him thusly,
As he opened his mouth he addressed him as Milord:
"I want to erect full five hundred statues of arhats,
Of Good-in-Gifts, Dragon Daughter, and Guanyin.[43]

---

[42] The fish-drum is a hollowed-out piece of wood in the shape of a fat fish; it is used as a rhythmical instrument in Buddhist liturgy.

[43] Good-in-Gifts and Dragon Daughter are, in popular religion, the acolytes of Guanyin, and they often accompany her in popular iconography.

> I want these statues to be carved from sandalwood;
> The merit will be huge, the work's hard to accomplish!
> I've been begging for donations for over a month,
> But I still haven't met a man whose heart is good."

Xu Xian [said:] "I've been told that your monastery is an ancient institution, which was founded during an earlier dynasty, so why are there no officials and gentry who protect the Dharma?" The monk replied: "I am not allowed by my teacher to lightly open the register of donations. The person to be listed as the first donor has to be someone who has a karmic connection and agrees to sponsor the project all by himself." Xu Xian thought to himself: "It is no mean merit to carve the statues of the five hundred arhats and the bodhisattva Guanyin all from sandalwood, but where will one find such a great donor?" The monk said: "This can be accomplished if I only find a good man with the right karmic connection who can gladly donate three hundred loads of sandalwood." Xu Xian then thought to himself: "Now if he wanted silver, it would be a different matter, but if it comes to three hundred loads of sandalwood, I have the goods right here. We pulled them from the river, so as long as they are here in this house, it is illegally acquired wealth, so what is its use? But if I can donate them to the Golden Mountain Monastery to be carved into statues, they will create a huge merit. Now I should first discuss this with my wife, but I'm afraid she would not agree. So I will all by myself first put down the sandalwood in the register of donations, and later explain it to my wife."

> Lifting his brush with his fingers, he opened the register;
> Each character and every line was written quite clearly.
>   First he wrote that he hailed from Ningbo Prefecture,
> From Cixi County and that he was named Xu Hanwen.
> He gladly donated three hundred loads of sandalwood
> To be carved into statues of the arhats and of Guanyin;
>   He did so praying for ample good fortune for his family,
> So husband and wife would both enjoy health and peace;
> He did so hoping the Buddha's light would shine on him,
> So husband and wife would both enjoy health and peace.
>   When the monk saw this, he was overcome by joy, and
> Thanked this donor with a kowtow for his compassion.
> "On the many fields of blessing your merit will be great,
> Your sons and grandsons will become dukes and nobles!"
>   When the monk had said good-bye to return to his temple,
> Xu Xian turned around and went up to the upstairs room.
> There he explained to his dear wife what had transpired,

Which gave quite a start to lady Bai when she heard this.
"If we talk about three hundred loads of sandalwood,
The price easily amounts to several thousand of silver.
It's not easy at all to acquire such a large sum of money,
Why did you so easily give it all away to some monk?"

Xu Xian immediately replied in the following manner:
"My dear wife, please listen now to what I will tell you.
It's for the sake of Guanyin and the five hundred arhats;
He wants to have their statues carved from sandalwood.

In the conviction that you too love to do acts of charity,
I have shouldered this burden to show my compassion.
If in this life you have such fine and beautiful features,
It must be because you adorned statues in a prior life.

We, husband and wife, love goodness—don't be upset:
High Heaven never betrays those whose heart is good!"
When Suzhen had heard this, she could only smile:
"Whatever you do, think three times before you act."

If one makes a donation, it should be honestly done;
The Buddha will not fail sincerely devout believers.
Let's not expound on this oh-so-harmonious couple;
Let's return to the monk who entered the monastery.

He delivered the register of donations to the abbot;
The Chan master smiled as soon as he saw the list.
After waiting a few days he descended the mountain,
And transported the sandalwood to the monastery.

It came to the exact figure of three hundred loads;
A lucky day was chosen to start the carving project.
They started on the third day of the Ninth Month;
In the Third Month of the next year it was finished.

They settled on the first day of the Fourth Month
To open the eyes, and so they invited the sponsors.[44]
First of all they invited the most important donor,
The one who provided the sandalwood, Xu Hanwen!

They also invited the officials serving in the region;
They also invited the local gentry who were donors.
On the day of the ceremony it was quite a crowd,

---

[44] When new statues are consecrated, the final act of enlivenment consists in "dotting the eyes" (painting a black pupil in the white eyes).

As one after the other arrived outside the monastery.
Lady Bai knew about this already well in advance,
And she prohibited her husband from making the trip.
But our Xu Xian was repeatedly invited by the monk,
And his heart was set on going to Golden Mountain.
When he had espied a moment when he was alone,
He outwitted his wife and escaped from the house.
And when he arrived at the monastery for his visit,
The Chan master housed him in a hall at the back.
When the noon meal was over and all had dispersed,
Xu too said good-bye and wanted to go home.
But the Chan master insisted that he should stay,
And completely refused to allow him to go home.

Now the story tells that the monk Fahai told Xu Xian: "You originally were a disciple of the Buddha, so how come you have fallen into the hands of these demons?[45] Moreover, you have seen with your eyes how at the Double Fifth Festival she showed her original shape. Now you have arrived here, you should not go back!" But Xu said: "My wife knows many magic arts, so please be so kind as to quickly let me go home. If you keep me here for another minute, the two of them will follow me to this monastery and vent their spite by killing me!" Fahai then replied: "Mr. Xu, if you take me as your teacher, and shave your head to leave the household, I can protect you from all harm."

Now let's tell that lady Bai, when she didn't see her husband come home, computed yin and yang on the palm of her hand, and exclaimed: "Little Blue, a disaster! My husband is kept at the Golden Mountain Monastery by Fahai, who says that we two are demons and refuses to let him go home. What to do now?" Little Blue said: "What's the problem? You and I will hurry to the monastery and bring your husband back." The two of them thereupon by magic produced a boat and set off.

This couple of mistress and maid left the house;
Their heart was set on bringing the husband home.
On their back they carried two black-wind swords,
To fight a decisive battle against the monk Fahai!
Arriving at Golden Mountain they quickly debarked,[46]

---

[45] Some other versions relate that Xu Xian in his earlier incarnations had been a monk for seven lives, and that he had remained a virgin in each of these seven lives.

[46] Golden Mountain Monastery was built on a little island in the Yangzi River. In the nineteenth century the island became connected to the riverbank.

And walked as fast as they could to the monastery.
Little Blue then stepped forward, saying: "Master,
Please be so kind as to ask Mr. Xu to come here."

When lady Bai and Little Blue arrived at the Precious Hall of the Great Hero,[47] they stepped forward and exclaimed: "Reverend monk, I have been told that my husband Xu Xian is here in this monastery, so why do you keep him here? Quickly tell him to come here so he can go back with us." Fahai replied: "You evil monsters! Xu Xian is a disciple of the Buddha, but he was bewitched by you two, and against the rules you have harmed him! Now he is here, but as he has shaved his head and become a monk, he cannot go back anymore." Lady Bai replied: "Reverend monk, you make no sense. Even if my husband wanted to leave the household, he should first come home for a while and make provisions for his possessions and his family, and then it still would be early enough to leave the household. Now you keep him here and force him to leave the household, cruelly separating husband and wife, and decisively cutting off the Xu lineage. Is this the behavior of a proper monk?"

Lady Bai piteously implored the reverend monk:
"Quickly allow my husband to leave this temple!
　He is the sole heir of the Xus and still has no son;
Terminating a lineage is a crime against the norms!
I implore you, dear abbot, to show me some mercy,
Please forgive me my crime and let him go home!"
　The monk didn't pay any attention to her request,
He ignored her completely, he showed no reaction.
Lady Bai repeatedly implored him most piteously;
Suppressing her anger, she spoke with great humility.
　But when she had implored him in a heartrending way,
Suddenly the fire of blind rage set her body ablaze.
She now called him a demonic monk, a bald donkey,
Someone who wrongly recited the Buddha's name:
　"Now be a good boy and allow him to leave, and
Everything will be fine and I will forgive you here.
But if you dawdle yet another minute, you will die:
I will chop you to mincemeat and turn you to dust!"

Lady Bai and Little Blue implored the monk most piteously for his compassion, but after a number of times they could no longer suppress their rage, so they

---

[47] The Great Hero is a common designation of the Buddha. The Precious Hall of the Great Hero refers to the main hall of a Buddhist monastery, with its large statue of the Buddha.

loudly shouted: "You bald donkey, how come you refuse to change your mind? You are completely devoid of compassion!" And [lady Bai] said: "Little Blue, let's kill him!" The two of them grabbed their double swords, but Fahai promptly ordered his acolyte to counter them with his nine-dragon meditation staff. This meditation staff was a magical treasure of Buddhism: as soon as you started to wield it, the heavenly gods descended to come to your rescue!

  Upholding the Buddha the monk subdued the demons;
Magic of demons cannot defeat the Buddha's Dharma.
  The divine warriors descended from the empty sky,
Great heroes in their golden helmets and golden armor.
But Little Blue and lady Bai were terrible demons, and
The evil energy filling their breast angrily rose up high.
  The monks throughout the monastery were in a panic,
Each and every one of them had lost his soul and his gall.
Lady Bai commanded all demonic creatures of the water,
The shrimp troops and crab generals with their armies.
  Then she suddenly mobilized the Long River's waters
To swell up wide and far, and to rise in huge waves.
Millions of living beings were the victims of this flood;
This was determined by fate and could not be averted!
  The whole prefecture's population suffered this disaster,
As these two demons created evil they could not escape.
All the monks of the monastery ran to the abbot, saying:
"This flood will submerge the monastery with its waves"
  The Chan master thereupon took off his robe, with which
He covered the mountain's top, and the waters receded.
After a while the waves calmed down, no storm arose,
And the floods returned to their source, without waves.
  Then out of the blue one saw one flash of bright light:
The Pagoda-Bearing King subdued the White Snake![48]
A Guardian raised a demon-quelling pestle in his hands,
But the Star of Literature showed up to block his way.
  Now when the monk secretly pondered this matter,
He eventually noticed the tiny sprout in her sleeve—
The God of Letters had entered the womb of the snake:
Only after his birth would he be able to capture her!

---

[48] The Pagoda-Bearing King is Li Jing, a major general in the founding of the Tang dynasty (617–906), who was deified after his death as a mighty warrior god.

Lady Bai shouted: "Little Blue, ahead of us stretches one endless expanse of flooded houses, and no field or farm is anywhere to be found, so let us quickly by magic produce a little boat and row back. Let's collect our money and luggage and quickly make our escape back to Hangzhou. I've been told that my sister-in-law is a good woman, so let's go and stay with her. I could not have imagined that you and I today would suffer such an ugly defeat. Let's forget about him and get out!" Little Blue said: "Milady, in view of the situation there is no time for remorse or regret. Let us go to your sister-in-law in Hangzhou and then come up with some other plan."

Xu Xian was staying in the sutra building and filled with sadness, so he went to see Fahai and told the monk: "When I saw your acolyte who had left the monastery to beg for donations, I acted out of compassion and was the first man to write down his contribution so you could accomplish your great undertaking. I did so in the hope that I might live in ease and at peace for all eternity. I never imagined that once I had been invited to this monastery you would force me to leave the household, and separate me from my wife so we cannot be together anymore. When I come to think of this, I am overcome by sadness." Fahai answered as follows: "If that is the case, I cannot keep you here any longer. You still have evil karma that has not yet been paid off, but I am not at liberty to disclose it to you. Come and see me once she has given birth. Today your wife has returned to Wulin, and you will meet her at West Lake's Broken Bridge."

> The Chan master saw him off at the monastery gate;
> He helped Xu Xian out by employing a little magic.
> He had him ride on a cloud, with both eyes closed,
> And a favorable wind came blowing through the air.
>   He didn't know, he didn't notice he rode on a cloud;
> Only now did he know the master's magical powers.
> It did not even take him an hour to arrive in Wulin,
> And he stepped down from the cloud at Broken Bridge.

When Xu Xian opened his eyes and had a look, he said: "So here I am at Broken Bridge! This is strange. But I remember that Fahai told me I would meet her at Broken Bridge, so let me wait for her."

> As Xu Xian sat down, his heart was overcome by pain;
> As soon as he thought of his wife, his tears gushed forth.
>   "From Golden Mountain to here is quite a long journey,
> But in one quarter of an hour I've arrived at this bridge!
> The supernatural powers of the Dharma are unlimited;
> It's an extraordinary miracle which is really quite rare."

> He was pondering the power of the Buddha's Dharma,
> And then suddenly saw a little boat appear before him.
> When the two women in that boat walked up to him,
> It turned out that his darling had arrived at this bridge!
>   When Little Blue noticed him sitting on that bridge,
> She was at first sight overwhelmed by a towering rage.
> She promptly reported his presence to her mistress,
> And on these words the latter's eyebrows twitched.
>   "Why on earth has my lover now arrived at this place?
> Much better if all that transpired had long been erased!"

Xu Xian immediately stepped forward, and exclaimed, "My dear wife, today we are reunited by Heaven! A favorable wind brought you here. I have caused you so much trouble—it has all been my fault!" Lady Bai said: "My dear husband, how often didn't I warn you earlier? I told you not to go outside! But why did you have to keep us, mistress and maid, in the dark and sneak off to Golden Mountain Monastery, where you were bewitched by that evil monk? It even went so far that my maid and I had to fight him in battle. It was good for him that he had some magical skills, and so we did not kill him. He said that you wanted to leave the household and didn't want to be trapped in the red dust. If you indeed love the Gate of Emptiness,[49] why didn't you tell me earlier, so I wouldn't have had to confront him! Now Heaven has sent down a huge rain that drowned numberless people and animals. When I went back to the shop, nothing was left of our house, as it all had been carried off by the easterly stream. I could barely gather enough money to come to Hangzhou. On your account I have suffered time and again these many tribulations, but I will never hold it against you." She then asked Little Blue: "Which place is this?" Little Blue answered: "This is the meeting at Broken Bridge!"

> Suzhen was overcome by rage and anger this time,
> And awash in tears she wept in a heartrending way:
>   "I must conclude that you have a heart that is evil—
> A man who forgets love and duty, bereft of feeling!"
> Xu Xian urgently tried to comfort her, as he said:
> "My darling wife, please do not cry so profusely!
>   It was only that monk who was the root of all disaster,
> He invited me for the ritual of the opening of the eyes.
> How could I have known that that monk was so evil?

---

[49] The Gate of Emptiness is a common term for Buddhism, as it teaches that all beings are bound to change, to die, or to disintegrate, and therefore are insubstantial or empty.

He insisted on keeping me there and did not let me go!
My wife, we have been married now for three years,
How could I ever agree to be separated from you?
Every day again I bitterly argued with that monk,
And only then did he allow me to go back home.
He told me to stand on a cloud, and in a moment
I had arrived here in Hangzhou at Broken Bridge.
All other people were drowned in that huge flood,
But only we were lucky to be saved by that monk!"

Little Blue then addressed her mistress as follows:
"What your husband just said, is not mistaken at all!
Actually it is that old monk who has saved his life,
As otherwise he would have drowned in the flood.
I think that this must have been ordered by Heaven
In order to rescue the three of us and save our lives.
Now if he hadn't gone to Golden Mountain Temple,
He definitely would not have escaped with his life.
If it hadn't been for the monk and his clever trick,
How could he have guided us to that monastery?
It must be that the bodhisattva aids and protects us,
And guards the three of us from all kinds of danger.
It's not in vain that your husband does good deeds:
He who accumulates virtue will move the divinities!"

When Xu Xian had heard these words of Little Blue, he exclaimed: "Little Blue, what you are saying is right! If it hadn't been for the protection of Guanyin, we would not have gone to Golden Mountain Monastery, and we all would have lost our lives." Lady Bai said with a smile: "If you look at it from that angle, I wrongly blamed you. My dear husband, please don't be angry with me!" Xu Xian replied: "My dear wife, you and I are united in love as husband and wife, so why should I blame you? Shouldn't we be overjoyed now today we have met each other again?" Lady Bai then said: "My dear husband, if that's the case, where are we going to stay?" Xu Xian said: "My dear wife, let's all go to my elder sister and stay at her place for a few days in order to find a house. Tie the boat to the quay."

Xu Xian went ahead to the house of Li Junfu, and when he met his sister he told her everything that had happened. He then ordered a sedan chair to go and fetch his wife and her maid, and with their luggage and money they moved to the house of Mrs. Li. The latter came outside to welcome them and invited them inside. After they had formally greeted each other, they sat down as guest and host. Lady Bai said: "My dear sister-in-law, I will not hide from you that I went with your brother to Suzhou. For almost two years we ran a pharmacy, and we also made some money, but because of the heavy rains lately the whole city was flooded and everything in the shop was carried off by the easterly stream. Thanks to the protection of divine Heaven we were so fortunate as to escape with our lives, and that's why we have gathered some luggage and money, hoping to stay with you. You really must despise me." But Mrs. Li said: "Dear sister-in-law, why do you say that? It's thanks to you that my little brother could have his own business. Millionaire Wu from Suzhou often sent us letters, and also in the letters to Millionaire Wang he always said that you are such a capable wife. Now that we finally meet today, I can confirm that that is true. Ever since my brother suffered that injustice and had to leave, I have thought of him day and night, so now we are reunited today, I am filled with joy!"

> Mrs. Li addressed her then in the following manner:
> "When my brother left for Suzhou, it hurt my heart!
> Ever since I have been separated from my brother,
> I worried about him, every hour and every minute!
> But last year, on the occasion of Mid-Autumn,[50]
> The millionaire was so kind as to send us a letter,
> And now, thanks to the protection of Blue Heaven,
> Brother and sister fortunately are reunited again!"
> Xu Xian thereupon addressed her as follows:
> "My apologies, sister, for the worries I caused.
> Fortunately my dear wife is quite a smart woman,
> So we opened a pharmacy and made some money.
> The silver we saved amounts to a few thousands,
> And now Heaven has granted us to return home."
> Lady Bai once again wanted to add a few words:
> "Dear sister-in-law, I'm grateful for your concern.
> I lost my capital and suffered my tribulations,
> But good followed bad: I found this fine husband!
> Today husband and wife have come back home,
> And brother and sister are happily reunited again."
> Little Blue also quickly joined the conversation:
> "Our master that time was treated quite wrongly!"
> The two sisters-in-law got along marvelously:
> They agreed in all matters, and each was pleased.
> Junfu busied himself making all arrangements,
> And he found them a house where they could live.
> On a lucky day they moved into their new house;

---

[50] Mid-Autumn Festival is celebrated on the night of the fifteenth of the Eighth Month.

> The two families went there together, each happy.
> Inseparable during daytime, these sisters-in-law!
> Only at night each went back to her own apartment.
> They also bought a number of servants and maids:
> A formal hall and high rooms, a grand gate and wall!

A few months after Xu Xian had returned to Hangzhou, it happened to be the Mid-Autumn Festival. As the osmanthus flowers were blooming, they set out wine and food in the back garden. Junfu and Xu Xian shared one table, and lady Bai and her sister-in-law shared another table. While they were all talking, lady Bai said: "My dear sister-in-law, you and I have been pregnant since the same month. It would the greatest joy if we both would give birth to a boy. But if we would give birth to one boy and one girl, we should engage them to be married while they are still in the womb. In that case we would add kinship to kinship,[51] and they could continue the ancestral sacrifices of both families. How does that sound to you?" Mrs. Li said: "To be honest with you, I have had the same idea, and I have already discussed it with my brother, but I was afraid that you might object." Lady Bai exclaimed: "So we both had the same idea!"

> Lady Bai thereupon secretly was filled with joy:
> "In this way I will have accomplished my desire!
> And if this heir will be able to achieve success,
> Our families both will enjoy the emperor's grace!"
> Mrs. Li, her sister-in-law, addressed her, saying:
> "My dear sister-in-law, please listen to my words.
> If he can pass the examinations in the jade palace,
> He'll glorify the ancestors and enhance our status."
> Little Blue consulted the gods, asked an oracle:
> "Sister-in-law, the child you carry will be a girl.
> Yesterday at midnight I had a dream, in which
> Immortal Zhang came and delivered a boy to us.[52]
> My mistress hurried forward to receive the boy,
> And the little baby had a happy smile on his face.
> When I woke up, it had only been an idle dream,
> But my mistress, I'm sure, will give birth to a boy.
> And when he will have made a name in one try,

---

[51] Cousins of the same surname could not marry, but a marriage of cousins of a different surname was quite acceptable. In many parts of China this was even a preferred form of marriage.

[52] Immortal Zhang is venerated as a purveyor of children. He is depicted as a white-faced, long-bearded man with a little boy by his side.

> He will bring along as his maid this Little Blue!"
> When the ten months of lady Bai came to a term,[53]
> The little baby turned its body around in the womb.
> This pain in her belly felt as if carved by knives,
> But neither heaven nor earth offered her an escape.
> Little Blue served at her side and supported her,
> As she bit on her black hair during the labor pains.
> The Star of Letters descended to the earth below,
> And Immortal Zhang brought a boy to the gate.
> Innumerable gods and deities offered protection;
> Holding his brush, the Star of Literature appeared.
> Suzhen gave birth to a boy, and on the same day
> Mrs. Li gave birth to a girl. As a result of this
> Both families were filled with joy at this time
> As the lineage would be gloriously continued.

Lady Bai said to Xu Xian: "When I was about to give birth, I dreamed that a dragon encircled my body, so let's call the boy Mengjiao."[54] Her sister-in-law Mrs. Li on the same day gave birth to a girl, and they called her Bilian. The two families were overwhelmed by joy!

But light and shade pass by like an arrow, and soon the day of the Full Month had arrived, so the sister-in-law and the brother-in-law were discussing the head-shaving and preparing wine and food, as the next day they would sacrifice to the gods and entertain guests. When the fifth watch had come, lady Bai felt the blood in her heart well up. She hastily made a computation on her fingers, and exclaimed: "Alas, this is not good! Today my disaster arrives, and it will happen by my husband's hands. Oh my dear husband, the sky is not yet even bright, so why have you risen so early?" Xu Xian replied: "Today is the lucky day of our son's head-shaving, so I am afraid we will have visitors who come to offer their congratulations." Lady Bai said: "If there are guests, your brother-in-law can entertain them. Just stay here in this room, and wait till I will have done up my hair, and dressed our son in pretty clothes. Then we can go downstairs together with the baby to pay our respects to the deities and ancestors." Now lady Bai had computed yin and yang and learned that she would die by the hand of Xu Xian, and that's why she wanted to detain her husband, hoping in this way to survive the evil hour. But a servant came and said: "Outside a guest has arrived." Xu Xian called: "I'm coming!" Lady Bai said: "Your wife is waiting here. Please come back quickly!"

---

[53] In traditional China, a pregnancy was said to last ten months, counting from the month in which the woman became pregnant to the month in which she delivered the baby.

[54] A *jiao* is a kind of dragon and *meng* means "to dream."

When Xu Xian went outside to welcome the guest,
He discovered that Fahai had come to his mansion.
Fahai addressed him in the following manner: "Sir,
You are acting in a way that lacks all intelligence!
  You are a fine true disciple of the Buddhist school
To let your sorry life be harmed by a demon wife!
I now bring this begging bowl, given by the Buddha,
And it is my intention to capture your demon wife."
  Xu Xian thereupon secretly thought to himself:
"The actions of this old monk are inspired by evil!
Even if my wife may act like a witch or a monster,
It is absolutely of no concern to you, not even a bit.
  Don't try to come here today and to create trouble
By separating husband and wife, tearing them apart.
If I look at this little bowl, there's no reason for fear—
It definitely will be unable to harm my wife's body."
  As he stood firmly outside the door to her room,
She suddenly called from inside: "My dear husband,
I've been waiting for you now for quite some time,
So why have you still not come back to our room?"
  Xu Xian immediately answered her as follows:
"I am standing outside the gate for a good reason!
  You just stay in the room and keep waiting for me,
It is impossible right now for me to come inside.
If I would come inside, that might well harm you,
Because I'm afraid your star of disaster has come!"
  How did he know how terrible that bowl could be—
A ray of a golden light pierced and entered the gate!
Suddenly there had been a movement of her sleeves,
And as soon as it saw demon energy, it soared high.
  Lady Bai at this moment was terrified and scared,
So a white light escaped from the crane of her head.
The two lights, white and golden, battled each other,
But soon the golden bowl turned into black clouds.
  She loudly exclaimed: "This I cannot withstand—
The full weight of Mt. Tai is pressing on my head!"[55]
Xu Xian at this moment was at a loss what to do,
Scared out of his wits he hastily entered the room.

---

[55] Mt. Tai in Shandong is the holy mountain of the East.

Xu Xian saw that the flying begging bowl had entered lady Bai's room and now covered the top of her head. His wife loudly shouted: "Aiya, my dear husband, I'm done for!"

> Covered by the bowl she suffered unbearable pain:
> The Buddha's begging bowl was a thousand tons!
> Still polluted by blood, her computations were off:
> She had mistaken the hour of noon for the afternoon.
>   That's why she was well prepared for the later hour,
> But how did she know disaster would strike so soon?
> Immediately she called out to her darling husband:
> "Today is the day that I will be separated from you."

When Little Blue saw her mistress in this condition, she was overcome by sadness, and her tears gushed forth like a rain. But as there was nothing she could do, she scolded Xu Xian: "You depraved creature, how can you bear to see my mistress in this situation? It is all because of your vicious actions! How could I be willing to forgive you and let you off? I will have to take revenge on behalf of my mistress. That will be the only way to appease the rage in my bosom. Oh, my dear mistress!

> Xu Xian, you really are a man with an evil heart!
> This is all due to his evil and vicious machinations!
>   This whole bad situation is all due to your actions,
> You fully forgot the three years as husband and wife.
> My mistress treated you like some precious treasure,
> Attentive and considerate she wanted you to be fine!"
>   When Little Blue imagined this heartrending scene,
> She hastily shook her head a number of times, and
> Her head turned as big as a bushel, her eyes were bells,
> And she manifested her shape as a blue-tipped snake!
>   Xu Xian was so scared his souls were all scattered,
> But from under the bowl lady Bai loudly shouted:
> "My darling husband, now please don't be afraid,
> But just come and stand here by my side for a while."
>   With her left hand she grasped her husband's hand,
> And with her right hand she restrained Little Blue:
> "You have kindly served me with greatest devotion,
> Our love and affection far surpassed that of siblings.
> So I implore you not to do my husband any harm,
> As you still will have to take care of my little boy.

That monk Fahai, who is now seated in his study,
Also wants to harm you, so your life will decay.
I urge you to run for your life as fast as you can—
If you wait for another minute, you lose your life!"
   When Little Blue had heard her mistress' words,
She said good-bye to her mistress, weeping loudly.
Next all of a sudden a demonic twister arose, which
Soared into the distant sky, and she was gone.
   Let's not tell how Little Blue made her escape;
Let's return to the subject of lady Bai's sufferings.
   The begging bowl was resting on her shoulders—
When Xu Xian saw this, he was greatly afflicted.
He called "My dear wife!" but he got no answer;
Then his lovely wife had completely disappeared.
   Fahai, seated in his study, practiced meditation,
And his divine true nature penetrated the heavens.
A golden arhat appeared on an auspicious cloud,
And at the order of the Buddha arrested lady Bai.
   When Chan master Fahai came and lifted the bowl,
The bowl hung in the air, and it shook some times.
After a while it fell down on the boards of the room:
The body of lady Bai had completely disappeared!
   Xu Xian that moment was overwhelmed by grief,
But his throat was blocked and he could not speak.
All of a sudden he collapsed in the upstairs room,
A sigh escaped from his throat, his souls dispersed.
   If you'd want to know how she did at the pagoda,
Please read the next part, and I will explain it all.

From left to right: Lady White and Little Blue

ANONYMOUS

The Precious Scroll of Thunder Peak in Qiantang County of Hangzhou Prefecture in Zhejiang

Part Two

> He saved her life by a donation of a hundred coins,
> While she repaid him by a marriage of three years.
> The karmic debt is finished, and each goes his way,
> But it is her body that is crushed by sin and guilt!

The Chan master once recited "Amitabha Buddha,"[1] and once stamped his meditation staff on the ground, and suddenly lady Bai had disappeared. When Xu Xian lifted the golden bowl in both his hands, he only saw a tiny little white snake as small as a lamp wick, and he exclaimed: "My dear wife, this golden bowl has the unlimited power of the Buddha's Dharma, and it is a magic treasure from the Western Paradise, so how can I save you? I, this miserable wretch, have done you in, and the pain is killing me!"

> Xu Xian at this moment was wounded in his heart,
> He stamped his feet, beat his breast, awash in tears.
> He addressed the Chan master in the following words:
> "What you did here today was really too cruel by far!
> You and I shared no enmity in some earlier existence,
> Why did you have to hurt me today in this painful way?"
> Mrs. Li, her sister-in-law, did not yet know a thing,
> But one of the maids went and told her what happened.
> As soon as she saw this, her heart and gall shattered,
> And she collapsed on the dirt and the dust of the floor.
> She lifted the bowl of purple gold in both her hands,
> As she cried and wept, wept and cried, awash in tears.

---

[1] Amitabha Buddha is the Buddha of the Pure Land of the West. All who sincerely invoke his name will upon their death be reborn in his paradise, where they will live in bliss, awaiting the birth of the future Buddha Maitreya.

"Who was the person who played this vicious trick?
In just a moment he had her killed, leaving me alone!"
    Xu Xian addressed her in the following manner:
"That monk who came here was the root of disaster!
Who could have known that the bowl would fly off,
And force my dear wife to show her original shape!"
    When Mrs. Li had heard this story from her brother,
She reviled him in the following way: "You bastard,
    How did your wife treat you that you forgot her love
And betrayed her affections? You have no conscience!
My sister-in-law carried her karma from an earlier life,
And then in this life she married you, a lowlife scum!
    I've never known that you were such a lowlife scum,
Evil and vicious by nature, and far too cruel to boot!
Few men in this world sink so low as to kill their wife;
The Buddha's mouth, a snake's heart: you're no man!"
    Xu Xian then exclaimed: "My dear elder sister, please
Consider the love between siblings born of one womb!
I may have harmed my wife, but I did it unknowingly,
And now her pitiful death really wounds my heart."
    Mrs. Li promptly replied to him in the following way:
"What you have done here today shows no intelligence.
    If you behave like this even toward your own wife,
Who knows what love you have for your own siblings?
From this day on, I will cut all connections with you;
Like a sharp knife splitting bamboo: separated in two!"
    Hearing this, the Chan master addressed her as follows:
"Elder sister, there is no need at all for such blind rage!
Lady Bai was not a woman of the world of mortal men,
But a snake that practiced self-cultivation on Mt. Emei.
And when she had practiced for seventeen hundred years,
She changed herself into a girl so she could get married.
    Her sins are many as she created havoc for the people:
Golden Mountain was flooded, and many were drowned.
At the behest of the Buddha I have captured this demon;
I have no other intention at all, no desire to be cruel!"

Mrs. Xu said: "You evil monk, you don't follow the pure rules and show no compassion at all. The wife of my younger brother had no feud with you in an earlier life and did you no injustice in this existence, but you persisted in your desire to take her life. Even if she had been an evil demon, what concern was that of yours, a monk? I'd think that Blue Heaven's virtue is that of fostering life! But now you had to use your black magic and come up with false pretenses to snatch her away! You evil monk! You may be filled with wanton desire, but I'm afraid that she is an upright and virtuous woman, so she will not give in to your lust. All your effort will be in vain! Why should I be willing to let you go off?" When Fahai heard this torrent of abuse, he didn't know what to reply. After he had endured her curses for a while, he exclaimed: "Dear female patron, you don't have to be so enraged. True and false are so difficult to prove, and that's why you don't believe me. Please come with me to West Lake, and then I will let her out, so you can ask her yourself." Junfu said: "That's a deal!" They promptly hailed some sedan chairs, and Xu Xian and his elder sister, who carried Mengjiao, and the maids and relatives and neighbors, all went.

> When they got to the bank of the lake, they made a halt;
> At Thunder Peak Pagoda their sedans were put down.
> The Chan master stepped down from his sedan chair,
> He placed the golden bowl on the ground in the middle.
>   He allowed lady Bai to appear, that lovely woman,
> Just as before she was a beauty in hairpins and skirt.
> Having taken refuge in the Dharma, her heart was pure;
> Returned to the true root—not a trace of demonic rage!

She was reunited with her sister-in-law and her husband, and she also greeted her brother-in-law and his mother, and the relatives and the neighbors and all other people. They all came to see her and ask her what had happened. What a joy!

> Her sister-in-law addressed her as follows: "Dear sister,
> If I would tell you my feelings, my tears fill my cheeks!
> How sad that my little brother had no conscience at all,
> Committed this vicious deed, and killed you, a woman!
>   In my eyes you were such a smart and intelligent person,
> Yet you suffered deceit and abuse—I am totally baffled!
> How I hate that evil monk, who's totally bereft of reason—
> Why did he dare so abuse you and harm you, a woman?"
>   Lady Bai thereupon addressed her in the following way:
> "My sister-in-law, there's no need to harbor suspicions.
> I am not a human being, but in the four classes of birth
> I do belong to those creatures that are born from an egg.
>   I practiced self-cultivation for seventeen hundred years,
> And I came here to repay a favor, to compensate a virtue.
> That is why I became the wife of your younger brother,

> Due to his virtue I gave birth to a boy who will be his heir.
> But alas, in many actions I was reckless and disorderly,
> Creating havoc for the people who suffered a disaster.
>   I cannot escape from my crime that fills all of heaven—
> I never should have swerved from the rules of reason!
> When I flooded Golden Mountain, many lost their lives;
> I secretly stole the sandalwood, and so created disaster.
>   The Chan master came here at the behest of the Buddha;
> It was not his desire to pin me down, and bury me deep.
> The Buddha mind is compassion, saving us from suffering:
> He did not have any evil designs, seeking sex and money."

Lady Bai urged her sister-in-law: "There is no need to worry or grieve! Set your mind at rest, because at some later date we will be reunited again. As soon as I was subdued by the Buddha, I took refuge in Buddhism. He has laid his hand on the top of my head and given me the prediction of my future buddhahood, and so now the six roots are pure and clean,[2] and my mind, converted to the right Way, is free from any evil thought." Her sister-in-law said: "It's better to live for one day than to be dead for a thousand years. Even little ants love life, so how can you not be saddened by death?" Lady Bai said: "My body has not died at all!"

> Lady Bai addressed all present in the following way:
> "You all should cultivate the Buddha's lotus terrace.[3]
> If I today do not once again practice self-cultivation,
> How can I at some later day escape the three disasters?[4]
>   My body has not died but is buried deep in the earth;
> Quietly I practice self-cultivation, revering the Buddha.
> Today I must once again go the path of self-cultivation
> So at a later date I may visit the Isles of the Immortals.[5]
>   My dear sister-in-law,
> There is one thing that I would like to entrust to you:
> I have to ask you to feed and raise my little baby boy!

---

[2] The six roots are the six sense organs: eye, ear, nose, tongue, body, and mind. The attachments originating from the senses result in sin.

[3] The lotus terrace refers to the lotus-shaped seat of the Buddha. The expression here metonymically denotes the tenets of Buddhism.

[4] The three disasters refer to rebirth at the three lower levels of existence (in hell, as a hungry ghost, as a demon).

[5] The Isles of the Immortals are floating islands in the eastern ocean, on which the immortals spend their days in bliss.

If this son eventually achieves great glory and status,
That will comfort your heart and you'll smile for joy.
Husband and wife will be reunited at some later date:
My dear husband, you don't have to worry for me.
For this moment we will be separated, I must tell you.
Relatives and friends, we must part, please all leave!"

Lady Bai exclaimed: "My dear husband, please ask Mr. Buddha to tell you your own original identity.[6] I urge you to turn around quickly so you may soon achieve bodhi.[7] Your wife now has to take her leave!" Xu Xian said: "My darling, can't you come back?" Lady Bai replied: "How could I come back again now that I have arrived at this stage? My husband, there is no need for you to cry so sadly. Take good care of our son together with your sister, so he may grow up to become a man who will continue the ancestral sacrifices and ensure the survival of the Xu lineage."

She also [said:] "Mr. Buddha, can I ask you until when I will have to practice self-cultivation before I can achieve the true fruit?" Fahai replied to her: "From this moment on you must cultivate the true mind, remove the six roots and discard the three karmas,[8] and then you will be able to obtain a position among the immortals after twenty years. But if you don't change your nature and don't discard your passions and still give rise to evil thoughts, you will find it impossible to rise to a higher plane of existence even if the water of West Lake would dry up, Thunder Peak Pagoda would crumble, and the bore on the river would not rise anymore.[9] So please descend!" Lady Bai answered: "I will promptly obey your holy instructions!" The Chan master stamped his meditation staff on the ground, as he shouted: "Caverns of the earth, open up!" Slowly a hole opened up in the earth. Lady Bai once again said good-bye to everyone, and she also once again implored her sister-in-law to take good care of her child: "Don't worry about me! We will meet again later. I have to go!" And then Fahai pinned lady Bai down beneath Thunder Peak Pagoda. Xu Xian shouted: "My darling, I'll come with you!" But the Chan master said: "Mr. Xu, there is no need to be so sad! Husband and wife will meet each other again, so I urge you to practice self-cultivation and convert to the right Way. I now have to take my leave."

Xu Xian could only go back home with Mrs. Li and the others, and there he was once again reviled by his elder sister: "She was such a nice and capable woman! But you had the cruelty to play such a dirty trick! How can you live with yourself?"

---

[6] Mr. Buddha refers to the monk Fahai.

[7] Bodhi is the wisdom leading to enlightenment.

[8] The three karmas are the karmas originating from deeds, words, and thoughts.

[9] The bore on the Qiantang River to the east of Hangzhou was one of the city's great sights. The bore was supposed to be most spectacular on the fifteenth of the Eighth Month.

> His elder sister that moment again exploded with rage;
> She angrily reviled her younger brother as a scoundrel:
> "In what way and manner did your dear wife treat you?
> She honored her man and master like a fine guest!
>
> A wise and virtuous, smart and intelligent woman!
> Threefold obedient, fourfold virtuous, full of love![10]
> But you in your cruelty had to play this dirty trick,
> And wounded and harmed the life of a fine woman!
>
> Pinned down below a pagoda—when will we meet?
> If you want to find her, you must seek her in dreams!
> You're a cruel and vicious man—the heart of a wolf:
> How were you ever able to obtain such a fine wife?"

Xu Xian was reviled by his elder sister till he burst out into tears, and filled with sadness he returned to his room. When he saw the belongings of his wife, his tears gushed forth like a rain, and he thought to himself: "How can I show my face in this world? I can only shave my head and become a monk in preparation for a next life." He promptly cut off his hair, and sneaking out of the gate, he left.

> After seven lives of cultivation trapped in the red dust:
> One day he leaves the clan to go back to his true root!
> So Xu Xian cut off his hair and abandoned the family,
> Once he left the red dust, he practiced self-cultivation.
>
> His mind at peace he practiced the Way as a monk,
> Hiding at Zhaoqing Monastery, he lived an ascetic life.
> Inside the Gate of Emptiness he had no encumbrances;
> Practicing meditation he achieved true enlightenment.
>
> When Mrs. Li came upstairs, the baby in her arms,
> She wondered why she didn't see Xu Xian anywhere.
> But when she then walked over to the mirror stand,
> She saw his black hair, and awash in tears she said:
>
> "I only thought that my little brother was taking a nap!
> I'd no idea he might shave his head to become a monk!"
> His elder sister wept till all her innards were broken:
> "This feels as if random arrows are piercing my heart!"

---

[10] As a daughter a woman should obey her husband, as a wife her husband, and as a widow her grown-up son. The four virtues refer to chaste behavior, proper speech, modest appearance, and diligence in work.

Ever since Xu Xian had shaved his head and become a monk in the Zhaoqing Monastery, he strictly observed the pure rules and firmly cultivated the Way. When quickly three years had passed, he suddenly conceived the desire to roam like a cloud all over the world, so he said good-bye to the other monks, and left the monastery.

> Xu Xian said good-bye and left Zhaoqing Monastery;
> He took his leave of West Lake and traveled all over.
> Roaming like a cloud he visited the famous mountains,
> Both by day and by night he continued his journey.
>   Then unexpectedly he encountered the Chan master:
> Hair like a crane, cheeks like a boy, bones very clear.
> The Chan master long ago knew the meaning of this,
> And he came forward to guide him to his monastery.
>   When Xu Xian arrived at Golden Mountain Temple,
> Bells and drums harmonized with the voices of monks.
> He adopted the name of Daozong, and, seated in his cell,
> Revering the golden body, he took refuge in Mahayana.[11]

Our story goes that when Mengjiao had turned seven, he went to school and studied his letters. His intelligence was unequalled, and in smartness he surpassed all others. One day, when the teacher was not in the room, the older children at that school told him: "Mengjiao, you are the child of a demon, and, without knowing the truth, you call strangers your parents. Aren't you ashamed?" When Mengjiao heard these words, he had no answer at all, so he left the classroom and went back home, so he could ask his mother. When Mrs. Li saw her son come home, she said: "My son, at this time it is not even noon, so why have you been released from school so early? Or was the teacher perhaps absent?" Mengjiao answered her: "The others said something I didn't understand, so I have come back to ask mommy." Mrs. Li said: "So what did they say you didn't understand? Please tell your mother."

> Before he had said a word, Mengjiao was awash in tears,
> And then he informed his mother of what had happened.
> "When I, your son, had taken my seat in the classroom,
> The other kids over there at school started bullying me.
>   They said I was not a child that you had given birth to,
> And they even said that some demon was my mother!
> Dear mother, please tell me from whom I was born,

---

[11] The golden body is the golden body of the Buddha. Mahayana or the "Great Vehicle" refers to the type of Buddhism practiced in East Asia.

And who are the true biological parents of your son!"
When Mrs. Li heard this, she pondered his question,
As she silently reviled those damned kids at school.
She exclaimed: "How should I answer this question?
When I open my mouth, I will have to tell him a lie!
My dear boy, don't believe those slanderous words:
You and your sister and twins, both are my children!"

Mengjiao thought: "How come other people are telling these stories if what you tell me is right?" Mrs. Li said: "You rascal! I carried you in my womb for ten months, and nursed you at my breast for three years. I suffered a myriad of tribulations, raising you, this unfilial little rascal. Now you have turned seven, we sent you to a school to learn your letters, hoping that when you will have grown up, you will have success in the examination, so your mother will not have suffered in vain. But now you listen to the words of these mean people, and come home to speak ill of your own parents! If this is not a reason to give you a beating, I don't know what is! I'll call a maid to bring over the rod, so I can beat you to death, you little rascal!" A weeping Mengjiao cried out: "Aiya, dear mother!" And Mrs. Li also was awash in tears before she had ever hit him, and the two of them wept together.

Mengjiao cried and wept and knelt down in the dust:
"Dear mother, why do you have to become so angry?
It's not that your son believes all those idle words,
But it seems as if there is some reason in this case.
If your child is indeed a son who was born to you,
I should have the same surname, not another one.
If my true father and I have a different surname,
There must be a special reason for that situation.
My father is surnamed Li, and I am surnamed Xu,
So please, dear mother, explain how that happened.
Your child is happily willing to take responsibility,
Even if you beat me to death, I will not complain."

Mrs. Li said: "There's a good reason for that. Because you were beset by troubles in infancy, we were afraid you would not be able to survive, and that's why we had you adopted by the Xu family."[12] Mengjiao then replied: "If you had me adopted, how come I have never seen these adoptive parents?" When Mrs. Li had no ready answer to her son's question, she said: "Let's not discuss this any further!"

---

[12] Such feigned adoptions to fool evil ghosts were quite common in some areas of traditional China.

Mrs. Li had no idea how to answer this question:
He scrutinized her words and observed her actions.
She wished to speak but didn't, at a loss what to do,
While Mengjiao knelt down in the dust of the floor.

"As your child I am grateful for all your good care,
Never throughout my life will I forget your favors.
And if by chance I can achieve glory and nobility,
I'll repay your love with a phoenix cap and jacket.

Now who is the person who has given birth to me?
What is in birth and death my name and surname?
Please be so kind as to have consideration for me,
I hope and pray that you will show me compassion.

Whether by birth or by raising, we are one body,
I always will serve you with undivided devotion."

When Mrs. Li opened her mouth she reviled him,
She reviled him as a little rascal bereft of reason:
"How can your father and mother be fake or false?
How can you suspect your parents of being strangers?

Your father has never ever married a concubine,
Your mother has been his wedded wife till today,
And you refuse to believe the words of your mother,
But rather consider the words of others to be true!"

When Mengjiao heard this, his tears gushed forth:
"Dear mother, you still refuse to confess the truth!
If all my passionate pleading is of no use at all,
I'll have to leave home and travel to find them.

So, my dear mother, today I have to say good-bye,
To go looking for my parents in the world outside.
If Blue Heaven perhaps will manifest compassion,
I'll find my family and then come back home.

As long as I have not yet seen my parents' face,
Your child will rather die than come home again.
If I cannot repay the great grace of care and love,
I'll be reborn as a dog or horse to repay your love."

When Mrs. Li heard him say this, she got so scared that her souls left her body, and she hurried to say: "Mengjiao my son, you are still so little, who do you want to find in that wide world?" Mengjiao replied: "I will ask everyone I meet. If I can find my father and mother, we will come back together so I can serve both sides for the love of giving birth to me and raising me. But if I cannot find them, I also will not come back to serve you." Mrs. Li thought: "If I don't tell him, he will run away from home to go off on his quest, and if something unforeseen would happen, that would cut off the ancestral sacrifices of both these families." So she could only say: "My son, there is no need to be so sad! Let your mother tell you the whole story.

> Come with me, my son, to the upstairs room,
> And I'll tell you everything, from the beginning."
> With a complicated key Mrs. Li unlocked a chest,
> And from that chest she took a painted portrait.
> As she pointed to the painting she told her son:
> "These people in the painting are your parents!"
> Mengjiao looked at the painting very attentively;
> As his eyes were brimming with tears he thought:
> "This man and woman painted in black and white
> Plain to see are a couple, and still young in years."
> Mrs. Li then addressed him in the following way:
> "My dear son, now please listen to what I will say.
> But I'm afraid that you'll be saddened by my tale,
> Even a man of stone or iron would burst into tears.
> Your father's lineage originally is from Ningbo,
> And the family was settled there in Cixi County.
> He was my younger brother, we shared one womb,
> But our parents died early while here in Hangzhou.
> He was studying to be a manager of a pharmacy,
> And for some years he assisted in mixing the herbs.
> That year he had reached the age of twenty-three;
> His surname was Xu, Xu Xian; his style Hanwen.
> As it happened to be the Clear and Bright Festival,
> Your father went to West Lake to sweep the graves.
> And on the road he met the mother that bore you—
> Bai Suzhen was the name and surname she used.
> But by the origin of her body she was no mortal:
> She was a white snake spirit of a thousand years!
> The two of them fell deeply in love with each other;
> Based on this common desire they wanted to marry.
> Because your father was poor and lacked the money,
> Your mother gave him silver for the engagement gifts.
> But when your father wanted to exchange the silver,
> He was arrested by police officers and taken away.
> The silver had been stolen from the vault, these ingots,
> So he was accused of the crime and duly sentenced.

Mengjiao asked: "Mother, why did that happen?" Mrs. Li said: "This silver was silver from the Qiantang County strongroom, and it had been snatched away by your mother. Fortunately the magistrate was honest and pure. He noticed that your father was not a criminal type, and so he did not subject him to torture. He questioned him in great detail, and your father gave a truthful account. The magistrate immediately ordered the officers to arrest your mother. But as soon as she and her maid saw the officers come in, they miraculously disappeared, and that's why she is called a demon. Later the magistrate banished your father to Suzhou, and it turned out that your mother and her maid Little Blue were already in Suzhou, waiting for him.

> Your father then was banished to the city of Suzhou,
> And your mother had gone there and waited for him.
> In Suzhou they met with a certain Millionaire Wu,
> Who loved justice, and was free with his money.
> He urged your two parents to get together again,
> And so they celebrated their wedding a second time.
> They opened a drugstore, and called it Baohetang;
> The business was booming, so they had a good life.
> After they had run that shop for a number of years,
> They had amassed ten-thousands of ounces of silver.
> A monk from Golden Mountain asked for donations,
> And your father wrote down his name on that list:
> He alone gave three hundred loads of sandalwood
> To carve statues of the arhats and of Guanyin.
> The work was done, and the eyes were to be opened;
> He was invited to Golden Mountain—disaster struck."

Mengjiao said: "It is a huge merit to donate all by yourself three hundred loads of sandalwood, so why did this give rise to disaster?" Mrs. Li said: "My son, in this Golden Mountain Monastery you had a Chan master Fahai, who said that your mother was a demon, and therefore he kept your father in the monastery, not allowing him to go back. When your mother came to know this, she and Little Blue followed him to the monastery to ask your father to come home. But that monk refused to let him go, and that enraged your mother to such an extent that she engaged the monk in a battle of magic.

> A single drop of water cannot raise a hundred waves;
> One spark of fire can burn down thousands of houses.
> Suddenly the two of them engaged in a magic battle,
> And she harmed the people in a most distressing way.
> The population of the prefecture suffered a disaster,

And the sinful karma of this event was not minute!
   Later the couple came back to their old hometown,
And she was closer to me than my closest relatives.
And then a few months later you my son were born,
We were overwhelmed by joy over this rare jewel.
   But just when we were to celebrate the Full Month,
And when friends and relatives came to celebrate,
That monk Fahai appeared at the gate in person,
And said that your mother's sins were too many!
   In the Golden Mountain flooding people had died;
As she disobeyed Heaven, the sentence was heavy.
The Buddha had given him a bowl of purple gold
Under which to capture and subdue your mother."

Mengjiao asked: "So what happened eventually to my mother?" Mrs. Li said: "My son, that is chilling to tell. The golden bowl of that monk flew into her upstairs room, and when it covered the top of her head, your mother quickly changed into a snake, which was captured by the monk. So that's why we are not your father and mother. I am actually your aunt. When your mother was captured, I could not believe it, as I thought that that monk was deluding people with black magic, so I was not willing to let him get off that easily, but later I went with him to Thunder Peak Pagoda. There he allowed your mother to come out in human shape as before, and your mother explained everything to me in great detail. That's how I came to understand, and only then could I forgive the Chan master.

   So you should call me your aunt from now on,
And I in my turn should call you my nephew.
   At the suggestion of your mother you're engaged
Since before your birth to marry my dear daughter.
   But your father,
Overcome by suffering, departed for other regions;
He shaved his head and then left to become a monk.
   I now have raised you to the age of seven years,
And I love you more than I would a son of my own.
The ancestral sacrifices of the two families depend
On you, who will be the heir to continue the lineage."
   When Mengjiao had heard this, he spoke as follows,
Repeatedly addressing her as "my aunt" without end:
"Your nephew has been cared for and raised by you,
On top of kinship you have added still more kinship!
   Your love is as deep as the sea, and as high as heaven;

> If ever I achieve glory, you will receive a noble title.
> But because my mother is buried under a pagoda,
> > And I don't know
> Where my father may have gone for self-cultivation,
> > The karma of my sins is as heavy as a mountain—
> So how can I not be deeply pained in my heart?
> That detestable Fahai was totally bereft of reason,
> How could I be willing to forgive that evil monk?
> > A hempen cord of a thousand *zhang* still has a knot:[13]
> None measures the hatred for my parents' murderer!
> As long as I haven't taken revenge, I'm not a man—
> If I encounter him in a narrow lane, he is done for!
> > As long as I cannot revenge my father and mother,
> I have no desire at all to read books and writings.
> What is so special about the highest rank at court?
> A golden belt, a purple gown—just wasted effort!"

Mrs. Li said: "That Chan master Fahai roams like a cloud throughout the wide world, so where should you, still as young as you are, be able to find him? Don't be so sad, and diligently study your books. If one day your name is listed on the golden placard,[14] it's not too late to take revenge!" Mengjiao replied: "Your nephew is ridiculed by his classmates, so what face do I have to go back to that school?" Mrs. Li said: "If that's the case, your uncle will hire a teacher for you, so you can study at home."

> Mengjiao could only think of his father and mother;
> Tears coursed down his cheeks, such was his grief.
> His aunt urged him again and again to come down,
> And only then did Mengjiao walk down the stairs.
> > In his belly he secretly had come up with a plan;
> No one suspected that he had conceived this idea:
> While nobody noticed, he sneaked out of the house,
> As his burning desire was to meet with his mother.
> > He asked all he met for the road to West Lake,
> And where Thunder Peak Pagoda was located.
> By asking again and again he received directions;
> For an offering he now needed incense and candles.

---

[13] Ten feet equal one *zhang*.

[14] The golden placard refers to the poster on which the names are listed of those who have passed the triennial metropolitan examinations.

He said: "I have five copper coins with me. I will use three to buy incense and candles, and two to get some sugar cakes." Straightaway he arrived at the foot of Thunder Peak Pagoda.

> When he saw the pagoda, Mengjiao was afflicted;
> Sadly wailing and weeping, he cried out: "Mother!"
> Using earth to serve as incense, he deeply bowed;
> Sugar cakes and red candles he placed on the dust.
>   "I was not aware of your sufferings, dear mother,
> Because till this very day I was fooled by my aunt.
> But now the truth was disclosed by my classmates;
> When I questioned my aunt, she told me the facts.
>   My father shaved his head and became a monk,
> My mother suffers disaster here inside the earth,
> And I wrongly called other people my parents:
> Only today, alas, this all was made clear to me!
> In vain your son has grown till the age of seven,
> The crime of unfiliality weighs a thousand pounds.
> Kneeling down at the pagoda, I repeatedly call out,
> But you, mother, below the pagoda, will not know.
>   It is not because your son was slow or sluggish;
> It's because since my birth I didn't know a thing!
> When will I be able to revenge your cruel death?
> Only then will I have dissolved this great hatred!"
>   While outside Mengjiao was telling his tearful tale,
> His mother inside the pagoda heard him clearly.
> Raising her voice, she called out to her dear son:
> "Mengjiao, please listen to what I will say to you.
>   Even though I've been buried under this pagoda,
> I have spent these seven years in ease, at peace.
> Thanks to Fahai who came and enlightened me,
> I've taken refuge with the Buddha, his Dharma.
>   My son, no need to be sad and grieved at heart;
> Please allow your mother to explain the situation.
> You think that your mother suffers in darkness,
> But in pure stillness I practice self-cultivation.
>   So, my son, don't cry on behalf of your mother,
> But quickly go home, and read books and texts.
> If one day you are listed on the golden placard,
> Your mother too will not have suffered in vain.

You and Bilian will then be united in wedlock;[15]
The ancestral sacrifices of two families—it's you.
Great is the love shown to you by uncle and aunt,
Ten times as heavy as that of your own mother."
    While lady Bai spoke for this one long stretch,
Mengjiao heard her as clearly as clear could be.
"I only could think that you had lost your life,
I had no idea that you practiced self-cultivation.
    Fortunately, dear mother, you have not yet died,
Only now can I, your son, put my mind at rest.
But alas, I cannot get closer and hug your body,
I only hear your voice, but I do not see your shape.
    If mother and son are going to see each other,
I must topple Thunder Peak and save my mother.
The deities in the air will come to my assistance,
Clearly my filial piety will move heaven's court!"
    Again and again Mengjiao loudly cried and wept,
Hoping for a collapsed pagoda, to see his mother.
    Mrs. Li waited for her son, but he didn't return;
When she asked at his school, he hadn't been seen.
When Mrs. Li heard this, she grew quite concerned,
And she also informed her husband of the situation.
    Li Junfu wasted no moment and went out asking,
Asking the neighbors for news, then other people.
Some people who had met Mengjiao told him
That the boy had left through the Qiantang Gate.
    When Junfu heard this, he grew quite concerned,
Walking as fast as he could, three steps now two.
Hurriedly he walked out of the Qiantang Gate,
And arrived at the bank of West Lake to look.
    When he had passed all six bridges in his search,
He arrived at the pagoda and looked all around.

As soon as Junfu saw Mengjiao crying and weeping in front of the pagoda, he exclaimed: "My son, why did you come here all by yourself? Your mother at home is worried sick, and you had me worried too, so I hurried to come and look for you here. Just look, it's already getting late—aren't you scared? Come back home today with your daddy, and then we will return some other day to visit your mother."

---

[15] Bilian is the name of the daughter of Li Junfu and his wife.

Carrying the boy in his arms, Junfu returned home,
Where he blamed his wife for spilling the truth.
"When later he goes outside, we must take care
And have him followed by a servant at all times."
   Mrs. Li could only agree to what he told her,
And she urged the boy to set his mind at rest.
"When you have eaten dinner, go to your room,
And your mother will spend the night with you."
   But let's not talk about Mengjiao and his aunt,
But turn to the subject of Little Blue's revenge!

"Fleeing disaster I lived in hiding for seven long years,/ On Mt. Emei practicing self-cultivation in secret./ For the evil monk who killed my mistress my hatred runs deep:/ I have created throwing knives to take revenge. I am Little Blue. Today I have arrived at Golden Mountain Monastery. When I see Fahai, I will revile that bald scoundrel. I'm set to revenge my mistress!" Fahai exclaimed: "You evil animal, last time you escaped me, but today you yourself are seeking your death!" As soon as Little Blue heard these words, she battled Fahai with her throwing knives. The Chan master beat all her knives down in the middle of the River. When Little Blue saw that her throwing knives had all been undone, she tried to escape, but the Chan master suddenly got out his demon-binding cord, which he threw into the air. When he had tightly bound Little Blue, she manifested her original shape.

   Seeking revenge for her mistress is Little Blue,
But the work of seven years is undone in a day.
"It was for my mistress that I have been bound,
But do you know that, there under the pagoda?"
   Today her throwing knives had all been undone—
Could it be that someone would be her savior?
The very moment Little Blue suffered distress,
This alarmed Guanyin, who descended to earth.

The Chan master kowtowed and said: "Bodhisattva, may I ask you why you deign to descend to this place?" The bodhisattva said: "The White Demon has already been pinned down below Thunder Peak Pagoda. Now I have learned that you at the behest of the Buddha have subdued the Blue Monster. Please hand her over to me, so I can report to the Buddha." Fahai hastily handed her over, folded his hands and retired. Dragon Daughter took out the pure vase,[16] and magically made the snake smaller until she wormed her way into

---

[16] Dragon Daughter is one of the acolytes of Guanyin.

the vase. The bodhisattva exclaimed: "Blue Monster, you will have to practice self-cultivation with a proper mind, so you will be able to annihilate your earlier sins, and then you may be able to emerge again at some later date."

Now the bodhisattva had saved the Blue Demon, she went off to save Mengjiao from his disease.

> Longing for his mother Mengjiao became ill;
> For five years he suffered from a serious illness.
> Prayers to the gods and divinations didn't help;
> The medicines of famous doctors didn't work.
>   Mrs. Li again and again was awash in tears,
> When suddenly she heard a knock on the gate.
> She saw that a woman old in years had arrived,
> Who entered her house—her hair was all white!

Mrs. Li asked: "May I ask you, old woman, for what reason you have come here?" The bodhisattva said: "I have heard that you love to do good deeds, and that's why I have come here to ask for a vegetarian meal." Mrs. Li replied: "If you would like to have a meal, please come inside and sit there for a while." The bodhisattva then asked: "Who is this young master?" Mrs. Li replied: "This is my nephew. Because he lost his parents at a young age, he attracted this wasting disease. Prayers to the gods went unanswered, and the medicines he took had no result. He has been ill like this since he turned eight." The bodhisattva said: "I have here a cinnabar pill. He should swallow it with a cup of tea, and then he will be better." Mrs. Li took it in her hands, and said: "Many thanks!" But that old woman had disappeared—changed into a gust of wind, she rode off on a cloud!

> The bodhisattva Guanyin gave her a cinnabar pill,
> And that old woman had immediately disappeared!
> She unexpectedly had turned into a colored cloud,
> And straightway went to the Purple Bamboo Grove.[17]
>   Mrs. Li immediately knelt down on her knees,
> She kowtowed with eight bows to thank the gods.
> Mrs. Li then wasted no time to call for her son;
> Once he swallowed the pill, he was rid of woes!
>   Mengjiao's belly seemed suffused with fragrance;
> His whole body was purified, filled with energy!
> He smelled in his mouth a pure and fragrant taste,
> He was as before, fully recovered from his illness.

---

[17] The Purple Bamboo Grove is located on Mt. Putuo, a little island off the Ningbo coast, believed to be the Chinese Potalaka, where Guanyin lives.

When Mengjiao had recovered from his illness, he as before studied the books with greatest diligence in his study. He memorized poems and rhapsodies and prose essays at a glance, and when he had only turned twelve he passed the prefectural examination. And when he had turned sixteen, Mrs. Li told him: "My son, soon the metropolitan examinations will be held, so let me prepare your luggage, so you can go to the capital and sit for the examinations. If you pass and are listed on the golden placard and then come home, you will have repaid your mother's love in feeding and raising you." Mengjiao replied: "Your nephew will do as you say. But, my aunt, there is one thing I have to say. I will only set out on my journey if I first have visited my mother and offered her sacrifices." Mrs. Li replied: "My son, that is exactly what filial piety demands." The next day Junfu and his wife prepared vegetarian offerings. After they had crossed West Lake by boat, they disembarked, and went to Thunder Peak Pagoda, where they set out the offerings. Mengjiao walked up to the pagoda, and then wept and bowed and said: "At the advice of my aunt your son will go to the capital to seek fame. I have therefore come to offer sacrifices. Tomorrow I will set out on my journey.

> Your son is weeping here now, wounded at heart,
> And there is something that I'd like to tell you.
>   This hatred as deep as the ocean is hard to assuage;
> I cannot be called a man here in this mortal world.
> I'd rather see that mother and son are reunited
> Than that my name is listed on the golden placard.
>   My father shaved his head and then became a monk,
> And I have no idea where he may roam as a cloud.
> Please tell your son where I may find his traces?"
> He cried and wept, and piteously wept and cried.
>   When lady Bai, on the inside, heard this herself,
> She addressed her dear son with these instructions:
>   "Here below this pagoda I enjoy purest silence,
> I practice the Buddha's Way, cultivate my nature.
> My son, there is no need for you to be so grieved,
> Take good care of yourself and go to the capital.
>   Do not be worried at all times about your mother;
> Once at Golden Mountain, you'll find your father.
> Remember these words of your mother very well:
> When you return, I promise you, we'll be together."
>   Only when hearing this felt her dear son relieved,
> It diminished somewhat the sorrow in his innards.
> While he still thought his mother died a cruel death,
> He said: "At some future date we will be together!"

> He quickly ordered a servant to collect the plates,
> And with a deep bow said good-bye to his mother.
> Alas, he went with a heart that was hardened;
> Filled with grief he could only embark and go.

After Mengjiao had gone to Thunder Peak Pagoda to offer sacrifice for his mother and weep for her, he returned home and said good-bye to his uncle and aunt. Junfu saw him off at the quay, and then Mengjiao left.

After he had traveled for some days, he arrived at Golden Mountain Monastery. In his innocence the boatman said: "Young master, that place ahead of us is the Golden Mountain Monastery. This is the place where long ago lady Bai and Fahai fought their magic battle." When Mengjiao heard this, he remembered that his mother had told him to go and find his father at Golden Mountain, so he said to the boatman: "Please moor your boat here. I want to burn incense at this monastery."

> Mengjiao walked up to the gate of the monastery,
> Hoping to find his father here at Golden Mountain.
> With lowered head he entered the temple's gate,
> Bowing to the many buddhas, the numerous gods.
> Maitreya in the middle was laughing out loudly;
> The four great heavenly kings stood in two rows.[18]
> Weituo, protecting the Dharma, raised his pestle;
> In golden helmet and armor he showed his might.[19]
> Thereupon he entered the Hall of the Great Hero:
> Three great Buddhas were seated in the middle.
> And on both sides he saw the five hundred arhats,
> Statues made of sandalwood, adorned with gold.
> Mengjiao there knelt down on a cattail hassock,
> And kowtowed eight times with sincere devotion,
> He then prayed to the Buddha to guide his way
> And grant him that he might find here his father.

As soon as some monk there saw him, he asked: "May I ask you, sir, where you are from?" Mengjiao replied: "I hail from Qiantang County, and I have come here to visit a famous reverend." The monk asked: "Which reverend are you looking for?" Mengjiao said: "There is a 'fa' in his name." The monk replied: "That must

---

[18] Maitreya is the Buddha of the future. He is often depicted as a fat monk who is laughing loudly. The four heavenly kings are fearsome divine warriors who protect Buddhism; they are usually depicted as huge statues in a monastery's entrance gate building.

[19] Weituo is another protective Buddhist deity. He is often associated with Guanyin.

be the monk Fahai. He left three years ago to travel to other places, roaming like a cloud." Mengjiao then said: "Then there is still another monk, but I forgot his religious name." The monk said: "He will be difficult to find if you have forgotten his religious name. In our monastery we have over five hundred monks, and each has his own cell, so how could we check them one by one?" But Mengjiao suddenly came up with a solution: "Am I telling you to check individually on each of these more than five hundred people? This monk hails from Hangzhou and was surnamed Xu. That should be enough to identify him?"

Now our story goes that Xu Xian, who was now called Daozong, had lived for three years at the Zhaoqing Monastery after he had entered the Gate of Emptiness, and that he now had been living for thirteen years at Golden Mountain Monastery. Suddenly he thought to himself: "Alas! How painful it is that lady Bai is captured and pinned down under Thunder Peak Pagoda! I remember that the Chan master three years ago told me that I would be reunited with my son in this year, in this month! When I left home, the boy was just one month, and now he must have turned sixteen. If this time father and son would meet each other face to face but be unable to recognize each other, it would all be in vain. So let me go to the Great Hero Hall to pay my respects to the Buddha." He also bowed before the bodhisattva Guanyin. When he lifted his head, he suddenly saw a young man whose features were extraordinary, and whose appearance was impressive.

> He stepped forward, bowed deeply, and then asked:
> "May I ask where you live and how you are called?
> And what kind of business brings you to these parts?
> Please tell me all the details, sir, so I may hear them."

Mengjiao returned his greeting, and said: "Reverend, I will tell you truthfully. I hail from Qiantang County in Hangzhou. Because I am on my way to the capital to seek fame, I passed by your monastery. I had heard that the Buddha images at this ashram are magnificent, so I came here first of all to admire the statues, and secondly to pay my respects to the monks." Daozong said: "That is too kind of you. Please let's have some tea in the guest room so we can have a better conversation."

> In earlier years father and son has been separated;
> Today flesh and blood were to be reunited again!
> While Daozong walked in front, leading the way,
> Mengjiao followed behind him, walking together.
>   The two of them entered into the meditation hall,
> And sat down, taking their seats as host and guest.
> Following an exchange of courtesies, a cup of tea,
> Mengjiao opened his mouth, asking this question.

Mengjiao asked: "May I ask you, reverend, where you do hail from? And what were your surname and name? Did you leave the household as a child, or did you shave your head as an adult?" Daozong replied: "Dear sir, it's a long story if I have to tell you how I left the household." Mengjiao said: "Reverend, please take your time."

> "When I was a layperson I hailed from Ningbo;
> Our family originally is from Cixi County there.
> But my parents moved to the city of Hangzhou,
> Unfortunately they passed away when still young.
>   They left behind the two of us, my sister and me:
> I am surnamed Xu, Xu Xian, my style is Hanwen.
> My elder sister became the wife of some Li Junfu,
> Who works at the Qiantang County as an officer.
>   Because our financial situation was very bleak,
> I worked as an assistant at a pharmacy for a living.
> And on the day of the Clear and Bright Festival,
> I went to West Lake to sweep my parents' grave.
>   On the road I met lady Bai, such a smart woman!
> Becoming a couple we were united in marriage.
> But my wife was not a woman of the mortal realm,
> But a thousand-year-old miraculous snake-spirit!
>   Hardships and reunions—we shared three years,
> And she gave birth to a boy to repay an old favor.
> But many died when she flooded Golden Mountain;
> As she broke Heaven's rules, her sins were great.
>   Thus she is buried below Thunder Peak Pagoda—
> When I come to this point, I'm killed by sadness.
> Because my wife was captured under the pagoda,
> I abandoned that one-month-old baby and I left."

Mengjiao said: "Reverend, to whom did you entrust that one-month-old baby when you left the household?" Daozong replied: "I have an elder sister who is married to Li Junfu. Because I secretly left the house, I never entrusted the baby to anyone, but I am sure she will have raised the kid." Mengjiao then asked: "What was the name of your son? And how old would he be by now?" Daozong said: "Sir, please let me tell you.

> Before she gave birth my wife had a strange dream,
> In which she saw a *jiao*-dragon encircling her body.
> Because of this lucky sign, she settled on his name,

And the name she chose for my son was Mengjiao.
If I count the years, he must be sixteen by now,
But I do not know whether he grew up to be a man."
   Upon hearing these words, Mengjiao, awash in tears,
Immediately knelt down in the dust on both knees,
Exclaiming: "My father, I am your son Mengjiao!
I came here in the hope of finding my dear father!"
   When Daozong realized that this was his own son,
He embraced him and wept in a heartrending way:
"My son, how much you suffered without parents!
You haven't seen your own father for sixteen years!

Aiya, my son! Thanks to your uncle and aunt you have been raised! You never are allowed to forget that—they surpass a mother!" Mengjiao said: "I am on my way to seek fame. If my name will be listed on the golden placard, I will return to Golden Mountain, and take you with me back home, so I can serve you as a son at dawn and at dusk, and exhaust the way of a son." But Daozong said: "My son, as I have left the household, I cannot return to the laity."

   "Today father and son have been reunited again,
This is more unexpected than a bolt from the blue.
But one sires a son as an insurance against old age,
Escorting you in old age to the hills is a son's duty.
   If you, my father, refuse to return to the family,
Then your son will be guilty of unfilial behavior.
If you, my father, stubbornly refuse to return,
I, your son, will stay with you in this monastery.
   You will be a monk and I'll serve as an acolyte;
Father and son, we will practice self-cultivation.
Why should I painfully chase glory and fame?
Without a care or a worry we'll lead our lives!"
   Daozong addressed him in the following way:
"My son, what you say makes no sense at all!
All in vain you would have studied the books!
All in vain you would have gained your degree!
   Only because the Xu lineage still lacked an heir,
Did your mother descend to this mortal world.
Alas, after experiencing hundreds of sufferings,
She was buried under a pagoda—for your sake!
   My son, there is no need for you to be grieved,
Glory and fame are important—don't stay here!"

At this moment Mengjiao truly was at a loss,
But he didn't dare disobey his father's order.
   They talked heart to heart throughout the day—
Till the sun went down and the moon appeared.
I cannot tell you all they said during that night:
At the crowing of the golden cock, dawn broke.

Daozong said: "My son, the date of the examinations is not far away. The winds are mild, the sun is warm, so the weather is invigorating. So quickly off by boat to go to the capital and sit for the examination." Mengjiao said: "My father, I will follow your advice, and say good-bye right now." Daozong exclaimed: "My son, let me recite a gatha![20]

> On this journey you will be able to travel like a cloud;
> Passing as top-of-the-list, you'll enjoy imperial favor.
> Both your parents will one day be reunited once again;
> Together at the ancestral sacrifice, showing old fame."

Mengjiao took his leave of his father with a bow,
Daozong accompanied him till outside the temple.
Outside the monastery's gate they said good-bye;
As father and son separated, tears soaked gowns.
   On the wide and open road he met no obstacles;
No waves rose on the sea, the skies stayed clear.
Fortunately a favorable wind accompanied him,
And after a smooth journey he came to the capital.
   By imperial edict all students were summoned:
In crowds they entered the examination grounds:
On the second of the Second for the first session;
On the Birthday of Flowers for a second session.[21]
   The chief examiner was imperially appointed
To select the best men for the sake of the state.
On the fifteenth the three sessions were finished;
On a dragon-phoenix day the placard was posted.
   The first name, the top-of-the-list: Xu Mengjiao,
An inhabitant of Qiantang County in Hangzhou!
His Majesty granted him three cups of fine wine;

---

[20] A *gatha* is a Buddhist poem.
[21] The Birthday of Flowers is celebrated on the twelfth day of the Second Month.

> At Crying Deer Banquet high rank was bestowed.[22]
> Mengjiao thanked his teacher and chief examiner,
> Then he paraded through the streets for three days.

After Mengjiao had passed the examinations as top-of-the-list, he expressed his gratitude the next day at the third quarter of the fifth watch,[23] and kneeling down, he reported: "Your Majesty, by your grace I have been allowed to pass the examination. My mother is [a snake spirit] that practiced self-cultivation for over a thousand years, and she was united in wedlock to my father who had shown her a favor in a former life. Alas, he relied on relatives who operated a pharmacy in Jiangsu and spent his days in very modest circumstances. Who could have known that my father would become the victim of rumors, and that he would be enticed to his monastery by the monk Fahai of Golden Mountain, who pressured my father to leave the household and become a monk. When my mother came to the monastery to fetch my father, he was hidden by the monk Fahai who addressed her in a most abusive way, whereupon the two of them engaged in a battle of magic, which resulted in a flooding of Golden Mountain and a great loss of human life, all because of this Fahai. When my parents had returned to their hometown, and I had been born and reached the age of one month, Fahai unexpectedly again showed up to pester them. In his hand he held a magic bowl and he loudly declared to act at the behest of the Buddha. Claiming that the crimes of my mother filled heaven, he captured my mother and pinned her down under Thunder Peak Pagoda. When my father saw this, he was so distressed that he became a monk at Golden Mountain. I have been raised by my aunt Mrs. Li. Now I have passed the examinations with highest distinction, I request that she may be ennobled with an official patent as a repayment for her love and care in feeding and raising me. As my mother is still buried under the pagoda, I humbly request that Your Majesty will give the order to destroy Thunder Peak so as to free my mother from the pagoda. I also hope that Your Majesty may give an order to command my father to return to his family, so I may serve my parents and give full expression to my filial devotion. I humbly beg you to graciously agree to this request.

> Your Majesty, weeping blood I expound my feelings,
> As I hope to save my mother from her bitter suffering.
> Please order Thunder Peak Pagoda's destruction,
> To free my mother from disaster, so she may be saved!

---

[22] At the Crying Deer Banquet the emperor feasted the students who had passed the metropolitan exam (and the subsequent palace exam). The name derives from an ode in the Book of Songs, in which the host celebrates the fine quality of his guests.

[23] In imperial China, court audiences started at break of dawn. As the night was divided in five watches, the third quarter of the fifth watch refers to the opening of the audience session.

I also hope that you will order to award a noble title
To my aunt, as a reward for feeding and raising me."
The emperor personally drafted the imperial edict,
Which was read out at the palace gate for all to hear.

The emperor's edict read: "The new top-of-the-list Xu Mengjiao has reported that his mother, upon practicing self-cultivation for a thousand years, entered the world of the red dust, and inappropriately wounded and harmed living beings, so how could Blue Heaven not be roused to anger? He has requested the destruction of Thunder Peak, but as this is an ancient monument dating from an earlier dynasty, it cannot be torn down, so he will have to wait till her merit is fully accomplished, when she will be able to free herself and soar off. Now the son she gave birth to has achieved fame, We issue an edict that a memorial arch may be erected in front of the aforesaid pagoda, and We also ordain that she be granted a full spread of imperial offerings in sacrifice, so she will not have borne a famous son in vain. As his father Xu Xian has already left the household, he should be allowed to follow his own preference. We order that he be awarded one monastic cap adorned with the seven jewels, one red woolen cassock, one dragon-head meditation staff, and one pair of cloud-climbing shoes. We command the local officials to set aside one thousand *mu* of good fields to provide for all his needs.[24] Mrs. Li, the aunt of our beloved servant, has great merit in feeding and raising him, and We raise her to the noble rank of Lady, and officials will issue her a patent. We order that she be provided with a phoenix cap and dawn jacket. The wife of our beloved servant will be raised to noble rank and receive such patents depending on his functions. We allow our beloved servant to return home so he may offer sacrifice to his ancestors, expecting him to return to the capital within a year in order to be appointed to a suitable office." Mengjiao thanked the emperor for his grace by shouting: "May Your Majesty live a myriad of years, and a myriad of years, and a myriad times myriads of years!"

Once the edict had been read, the orders were executed;
Mengjiao accepted the decisions, his eyes awash in tears.
While wearing the black gauze cap,[25] he wasn't yet happy—
By passing at the first try, famous throughout the world!
He took his leave of the civil and military officials at court;
He said good-bye to his fellow students, and left the capital.
Mengjiao traveled throughout the night, as fast as he could;
He passed prefectures and counties without ever stopping.

---

[24] Sixteen *mu* make up one acre.

[25] The black gauze cap was the typical headgear of an official.

But when the top-of-the-list arrived at Golden Mountain,
He had his boat tied up at the quay to visit the monastery.
All the monks of the monastery came out to welcome him;
To the sounds of bells and drums they received the edict.
　　As he welcomed the edict, Daozong deeply knelt down;
An incense table was quickly arranged—what a bustle!
"What an exceptional event that you achieved this rank,
Let's express our gratitude for the ample imperial grace!"

Mengjiao said: "My father, please be seated, and allow your son to express by a bow his gratitude for your grace in siring me." Daozong said: "My son, today, now your name has been listed on the golden placard and you also have received such ample favors from His Majesty, your mother's sufferings have not been in vain, and even though she may be buried under the pagoda, she can close her eyes in peace."

　　At the monastery father and son were filled with joy
When suddenly a monk entered to announce to them
That the officials of the whole prefecture had arrived
To pay their respects, and now had entered the gate.
　　Mengjiao went out in cap and girdle to receive them:
"Allow me to thank you for showing such kindness!"
And the assembled officials replied as with one voice:
"Sir, we have come here to offer our congratulations!"

Mengjiao replied: "Thank you very much for taking such trouble. I have come here at the behest of the emperor, whose sagely order and edict commands you gentlemen to set aside one thousand *mu* of good fields for this monastery as an investment to provide for its needs." The assembled officials answered as if with one voice: "As this is an imperial order it truly has to be respected. Upon our return to our offices, we will convene the local gentry and make arrangements for this donation." Then the assembled officials took their leave and departed.

As soon as Mengjiao had seen them off, he hurried to write a letter to his family to erect a memorial arch in front of Thunder Peak Pagoda. He also sent his servants to Zhenjiang to buy red silk and have more than five hundred cassocks made for the monks. In this way Mengjiao stayed for a month at Golden Mountain Monastery. One day Daozong said to him: "My son, you are staying here, but your uncle and aunt at home must be eagerly awaiting your return, so you should go back home, offer sacrifices to the ancestors, and celebrate your wedding with your cousin. Don't waste your time."

Hearing these words the top-of-the-list replied thusly:
"Lacking in filial piety, your son deserves punishment.
I, your son, receive this salary from the imperial house,
So I should fully practice both loyalty and filial piety.

But when serving one's lord, it is difficult to be filial,
So I have to abandon my father, leaving you all alone.
How can I be told to depart from my father's presence?
It is impossible for me to tear me away, be separated!"

But Daozong immediately called his son, and argued:
"We, father and son, each have our own road to travel!
I advise you, my son, to go back home with all speed;
Please convey on my behalf my greetings to your aunt.

Celebrate the wedding-night with your cousin Bilian,
The engagement while yet unborn should be honored.
I hope you will live in harmony throughout your life;
May your marriage be blessed with the birth of sons.

As an official you must always be loyal and righteous,
Serving the dynasty with true valor and a loyal heart.
Love the people like children, be strict in inquiries;
Don't covet the people's wealth, be pure and honest!

There is no need to worry about your father at all—
Now quickly go home, don't dawdle here any more."
Mengjiao promptly addressed his father by saying:
"Following your fatherly advice I'll take my leave."

Mengjiao thereupon took leave of his father, and Daozong said: "My son, when you return home please inform your uncle and aunt that I am quite happy here in the monastery, and tell them not to worry about me. Make sure to inform them of that, and tell them to take good care of themselves."

The top-of-the-list said good-bye to his dad and left,
Seen off at the gate by all monks of the monastery.
With a favorable wind all the way, he traveled fast,
And within a few days he had arrived at Hangzhou.

Overcome by joy Junfu and wife hung up lanterns
And decorated the house—what a crowded scene!
They promptly set out an incense table in the hall:
By imperial edict they were awarded title and gifts.

The top-of-the-list then sacrificed to the ancestors,

Offering sacrifice to both the Li and the Xu lineages.
He then asked his uncle and aunt to take their seat,
And thanked the couple for all their love and care.
   "My son, now you have passed the exams so young,
Your aunt's worries haven't been wasted in vain!
   You've discarded the blue gown, now wear purple,[26]
And the flowers on your cap sparkle as they shake.
Today the whole family enjoys this brilliant glory,
And my daughter is blessed that she now is a Lady!
   My son and son-in-law: on both counts I'm happy;
Thanks to the emperor the whole family's ennobled!
If one son becomes an official, all enjoy his salary;
Three generations of ancestors are raised to heaven!"

The top-of-the-list told his aunt: "Your nephew has reported to the emperor and received these patents of nobility for you. Uncle and aunt, please receive this official girdle and the phoenix cap and dawn jacket, and then allow me to express by bowing my gratitude for your love and your raising." Mrs. Li said: "Your filial piety is truly exceptional! All my care has not been in vain!" Mengjiao also said: "Then there is still something else I have to tell you.

   My father has become a monk at Golden Mountain,
And I wanted to urge him to return and come home.
But he said that he has left the household for good,
On no account will he return to the life of a layman."
   When Mrs. Li heard this, she was filled with joy:
"It is truly rare to find a son with such filial piety!
Your father is fully devoted to cultivating the Way;
The emperor in his grace has given him treasures."
   The top-of-the-list addressed her again, and said:
"My father also sternly enjoined me to listen well,
To transmit his message which I had to remember,
And to convey his best wishes to the two of you.
   Don't be worried, he says, and have no concerns:
I live thanks to your blessing at ease and in peace.
May you all upon hearing this message be happy,
And each and all live in harmony, filled with joy!"

---

[26] Students who have not yet passed the highest examinations wore a blue gown, while the highest officials were allowed to wear purple.

Now let's tell that at West Lake the construction of the memorial arch had been completed. They then selected a date and prepared the three kinds of vegetarian offerings, and the whole family went to West Lake to offer sacrifice. That was quite a crowded scene!

> Three offerings at Thunder Peak: filled with filialty;
> Lady Bai's disaster is finished: she leaves the dust!
> The top-of-the-list, together with his uncle and aunt,
> Arrived then at West Lake to sacrifice to his mother.
> With twenty-four bows he kowtowed most deeply;
> The top-of-the-list wept tears in a heartrending way.
> Imperial offerings, sacrificed at the emperor's order;
> In official cap and official girdle: something special!

Mengjiao said: "Your son has passed the examinations with the highest honors, and I had hoped to destroy Thunder Peak Pagoda and save you, my mother, so I could take care of you for all the years of your life and give full expression to the feelings of a son. But alas, the emperor did not grant my request, so there is nothing I can do."

As the top-of-the-list was presenting the sacrificial offerings while sadly crying, one suddenly saw the Chan master Fahai descend from the sky, and exclaim: "Sir top-of-the-list, here I am!" When Mengjiao heard that Fahai had arrived he was only too eager to crush his body into a pulp, but then again he thought to himself: "Let's see what he will say or do, and then decide on a course of action." So he asked: "Dear reverend, what's the holy teaching you are bringing us? You must be filled with kind compassion and feelings of sympathy and save my mother from this pagoda. Please take my intense obsession into account, first of all because of her virtue in giving birth to me, secondly because of her effort and care on my behalf, and thirdly because of the love for our parents. As a Confucian son, I must make loyalty and filiality my first duties." The monk replied: "Sir top-of-the-list, your words exemplify loyalty and forgiveness and filial piety. Because your filial piety has moved the heavens, I have come here at the behest of the Buddha to allow your mother to leave the pagoda, so mother and son, oh top-of-the-list, may meet!" The Chan master stamped his staff on the ground, and shouted: "Underworld, open your gates!" Suddenly you saw the earth split in two.

> The Buddha's Law is limitless, the Law's sea is deep![27]
> By stamping his staff he opened the gates of the hells.
> All of a sudden a girl in skirt and hairpins appeared:
> None else that Bai Suzhen in the years of her youth.

---

[27] The name Fahai may be translated as "Ocean of the Dharma" or "Sea of the Law."

Her features were indeed not those of mortal women,
She now was even far more beautiful than formerly.
Fahai then addressed him in the following manner:
"Sir top-of-the-list, here please meet your mother!"
    The top-of-the-list promptly fell down on his knees,
Loudly he wept at the top of his voice, saying: "Ma,
It is sixteen years since you gave birth to your son,
But only today am I allowed to see my dear mother!"
    As soon as lady Bai saw him, her tears gushed forth;
Embracing him, she loudly wept in a heartrending way.
She threw both her arms around her son's shoulders,
And her tears coursed down, soaking her garments.
    "Fortunately you now have passed the examinations,
And your filiality has moved heaven, saving my life.
My son, you can untie your knotted sorrows and cares;
Please forget your hundred and thousands of worries!"

Mengjiao told his mother: "My mother, while you were living below this pagoda, I cried sad tears from morning till night, as I was thinking of all the endless sufferings you must be experiencing! Father had already shaved his head and is at Golden Mountain Monastery. I have repeatedly tried to change his mind, but he stubbornly refuses to come back home." Lady Bai said: "My son, I have only myself to blame from my disaster, so don't blame him. While living below the pagoda these last sixteen years, my heart was at peace and I practiced the Way, with greater results than if I would have practiced self-cultivation throughout my life in the hidden chambers and high lofts of this mortal world. Why should your father be willing to return to the laity now he has entered the Gate of Emptiness? Still your filial piety is exceptional, and your parents are happier than if they were in heaven!"

Lady Bai also addressed his uncle and aunt: "Please allow me to thank you for raising my son! It must have cost you so much care and effort! If my son has grown up to manhood, it is all thanks to your love and care. Even though I may be living here below this pagoda, this gratitude is engraved on my heart!" Mrs. Li said: "My dear sister-in-law, once you had entrusted him to us, we gave it all our care and effort. On top of that you also mentioned that the continuation of these two families completely depended on this one drop of blood and bones. So first of all we had to consider the ancestors, and secondly there was your love. Now your son has grown up and achieved fame, your and my labor in giving birth to him and raising him has not been in vain. He has brought glory to the ancestors, and the ancestral sacrifices now have a root and source to rely on. Remembering, sister-in-law, all your problems in those earlier years, I cried sad tears by night and by day, and in waking and dreaming my thoughts were with you, right till this very day! Who could have known that today we would meet each other again—how that gladdens my heart!"

>Mrs. Li addressed lady Bai in the following manner:
>"How well do I still remember the events back then!
>When I had only met you for a few days, we already
>Were the best of friends, feeling likewise at all times.
>Each of us was pregnant, we were heavy with child,
>And we engaged the unborn children to be married.
>Then one day we gave birth to both a boy and a girl,
>But who could know that disaster would strike you?
>Once back home after seeing you off to this pagoda,
>Frost fell atop of snow—such were my sufferings!
>I had no desire at all to eat any rice or drink any tea,
>And throughout the night I cried and wept till dawn.
>At all times of the day I carried the baby in my arms,
>Nursing and spoon-feeding him for a full three years."

>When she had heard this, lady Bai spoke as follows,
>"Dear sister-in-law," she exclaimed, and she said:
>"I left behind this little boy of only one month old,
>So I caused you, dear sister-in-law, no end of trouble.
>I suffered the pangs of the ten months of pregnancy,
>But the three years of nursing drew from your blood.
>If it hadn't been for your kind care in raising him,
>How could he have made it to the golden placard?
>My son,
>You must serve your uncle and aunt with respect,
>Because they surpassed your mother's care by far!"

>The top-of-the-list promptly answered as follows,
>Repeatedly exclaiming "Dear mother" a few times:
>"Dear mother, I'll remember your instructions well;
>These words like gold and jade I'll store in my heart.
>I pray you, dear mother, to come back home with us,
>So we may together enjoy a life of glory and riches."

Lady Bai said: "My son, I have already taken refuge in Buddhism, so I am not my own master." The top-of-the-list exclaimed: "Reverend, allow my mother to come home so I may wait on her throughout her life in order to give full expression to the Way of a son." Fahai replied: "Sir top-of-the-list, when your mother earlier tumbled down into the world of red dust, she caused herself these tribulations. Fortunately, the roots of her self-cultivation went deep, because otherwise she would have been annihilated. For these sixteen years under Thunder Peak Pagoda she has peacefully practiced self-cultivation, dissolving her sins and crimes. Moreover, your filial piety, top-of-the-list, has moved heaven, so now I, this old monk, have received the command of the Buddha to come here and liberate her from the pagoda so mother and son may meet, and then to take your mother, who has a place in the ranks of the immortals, with me to heaven to enjoy eternal bliss. Such joy! But how can she ever be reborn in heaven if you keep her here in your mansion to enjoy glory and splendor?" When the top-of-the-list heard this, he loudly wept and sadly wailed: "Aiya, my mother! From the moment I entered this world, I have never seen the image of my parents, so how can I bear to be separated now I barely have seen your face? If I hear the words of the reverend, we will not be able to meet again in this life and in this existence!"

> The top-of-the-list knelt down in the dust in tears;
> Loudly weeping and lamenting, he cried: "Mother,
> The heart of your son feels as if carved by knives,
> Is it perhaps only in a dream that I see my mother?"
> Lady Bai immediately exclaimed: "My dear son,
> Please do not cry, as there is no need to shed tears.
> Pursuing glory and fame, you're the top-of-the list;
> Practicing self-cultivation I ascend to high heaven.
> That joy and pleasure are truly without compare,
> Surpassing those of the mortal world many times!
> My dear son, now quickly go back to your home,
> And celebrate the marriage with your dear cousin.
> As an official you must act with honest loyalty,
> Don't covet riches and power, harming the people.
> Practice self-cultivation also while serving in office,
> Instruct the people well, and inquire into the facts.
> May the two of you, rich and noble, live in harmony,
> And may you and your heirs practice self-cultivation."

Lady Bai then asked the Chan master: "Did Little Blue achieve liberation?" Fahai replied: "Little Blue's merit was shallow, and her sins were heavy, so her sufferings have not yet come to an end. But after ten years she will join you in the ranks of the immortals!" Fahai then pointed to the sky, and after a while two colored clouds descended from above. Lady Bai said: "Dear sister-in-law, I will have to leave!" Mrs. Li replied: "Dear sister-in-law, may you enjoy eternal bliss now you go to the palaces of heaven!" Lady Bai then said: "Many thanks for your golden words!" And she also said: "Mengjiao, your mother must go!" And Fahai said: "Sir top-of-the-list and all you other gentlemen, good-bye!" As soon as the auspicious clouds touched down, Fahai and lady Bai each stepped on a cloud to disappear into the distant sky.

> She had suffered many tribulations for twenty years
> Because of entanglements from an earlier existence.
> Stilling her heart she cultivated the fruit of bodhi,
> And in clear daylight she soared into the clear sky!
>   Now lady Bai had fully suffered her many sorrows,
> Her ascension to heaven this time was fully perfect.
> Riding a cloud she returned to Ultimate Pleasure;[28]
> Unencumbered and free, she became an immortal!

The top-of-the-list lamented and wailed and loudly wept, and then he returned home with the others.

Junfu selected a lucky day, and the top-of-the-list and Bilian were married. Husband and wife lived in harmony, like fish and water.

> All too soon one year of light and shade had passed;
> By imperial edict he was appointed to a higher rank.
>   The emperor appointed him as governor of Henan,
> So he invited his aunt and uncle to his official palace.
> With his wife, a cousin but not of the same surname,
> He went and took up his post, governing the people.
>   Pure and honest, husband and wife lived in harmony,
> And four sons were born to continue two families.
> Each had a pair of heirs, practicing self-cultivation:
> Honestly practicing cultivation, protecting their soul.
>   The essays of all four sons were of stellar quality,
> So they all passed the examinations with high rank.
> They displayed loyalty, filiality, and righteousness;
> Talented and capable, each of them loved goodness.
>   From generation to generation they were high officials,
> And for all eternity the family will produce great men.

Now let us tell that Xu Xian had retired to Golden Mountain Monastery where he practiced self-cultivation. He had the background of having been a monk for seven generations, but because he had not yet cut off himself from love and desire, he suffered these entanglements in the mortal world. Because he now received the instruction of Fahai, an elder fellow-monk from an earlier life, he could achieve perfect enlightenment and return to the Pure Land.

---

[28] Ultimate Pleasure is one of the many names of the blissful Pure Land of the Buddha Amitabha.

When Daozong had reached the age of sixty-three,
He one day closed his eyes and went off to the West,
To be reborn in the Western Paradise in a golden body—
The husband now was a Buddha, the wife an immortal.
   If people of this world are willing to do good deeds,
It turns out that above their head there is blue heaven!
Just look at the loyalty and filiality of the Xu family:
They enjoyed riches and status, glory and splendor!
   So I urge all good men and also all devout women
To widely practice good deeds—blessings will follow!
Families accumulating goodness will be amply blessed,
But people who commit evil will suffer punishments.
   To be filial and obedient to your parents comes first;
Accept your lot, guard yourself, and enjoy your lifespan!
Do not commit any evil but practice many good deeds,
Be of benefit to other people in whatever you may do.
   To try to accept indignities is the true way of the sage;
To shut your mouth and keep silent surpasses mediation.
Filially obeying your parents-in-law is Buddha-worship;
If you stick to the Five Norms, you will go to heaven![29]
   Eat vegetarian food, refrain from killing living beings;
In studying the Way you must try to outperform others.
A gentleman guards his nature, preserves his position—
Pure and clean like sages and saints, nourishing his soul.
   The Precious Scroll of Thunder Peak has been performed,
May you all imitate its perfect loyalty and its filial piety.
May you, good men and devout women, remember it well:
If you'll not become a bodhisattva, you'll be an immortal!
   Cultivate virtue both in your heart and also in your body;
And both as a mortal or a sage, you can achieve perfection.
Cultivate your mind and your body, cultivate your mouth—
If so, never did man or woman not achieve transcendence.
   If upon cultivation mind and body are freed of hindrances,
You will without a worry ascend to the Western Paradise!

---

[29] The Five Norms refer to the proper relation between lord and official, father and son, husband and wife, elder brother and younger brother, and friend and friend.

FOUR ANONYMOUS YOUTH BOOKS

From left to right: The Immortal Greybeard of the Southern Pole and Chan Master Fahai

FOUR ANONYMOUS YOUTH BOOKS
(ZIDISHU)

The United Bowls

The magic of Buddha and Dharma has always been unlimited;
The body of the Way is empty, based on its inherent suchness.
If your spiritual intelligence is not deluded, then who is this me?
Once the four elements are an empty nothing, then that is Chan!
    Sweep away all demonic air, return to the road of enlightenment;
Share in the correct enlightenment and leave for Spirit Mountain.[1]
People at present love to tell stories of the subjugation of demons,
But who knows it's the demon in his heart that is hard to dislodge!

Xu Xian said: "My master, what object will you use to subdue the demon?"
Fahai replied: "These bowls may be small, but can contain even the heavens![2]
Our Lord the Buddha, the Tathagata, personally gifted me with these:
Their marvelous shape is empty on the inside and round on the outside.
    The original shape of all evil demons will immediately show itself—
If you don't believe me, take them into your room, and there try it out!"
Xu Xian received them in both his hands, carrying them high in his hands;
Straightway he entered the fragrant room, lifting the pearly curtains.
    Lady Bai was sitting there in that room, with the baby in her arms,
When she suddenly saw that magic Buddhist treasure show up in front of her face!
Her gall aflutter, her heart all frightened—she had lost all human color;
Her soul had gone, her spirits scattered—her cheeks looked like ashes.
Even though she had those smart supernatural powers, she now could not use them,
All secret formulas and magic mantras she might want to recite now would be in vain.
    "Well, damn it! That monk of Golden Mountain has come once again,
And this time around I definitely will not be able to save my own life.

---

[1] Spirit Mountain refers to Spirit Vulture Peak near Rajagrha. The Buddha is said to have pronounced the *Lotus Sutra* here. In later literature it often stands metaphorically for enlightenment.

[2] The bowls are begging bowls that fit together perfectly.

My dear husband, your heart and innards are truly way too cruel—
In vain was our love and companionship during these many years!
　Let me not talk about the silk gowns and jade food I provided you with;
Let me not talk about the piles of gold and stacks of jade, all that money.
Let me not talk about the playful frolics of phoenix and *luan*, those joys of the bedroom;³
Nor let me talk about the shared wine and clear songs, those pleasures of moonlit nights.
　On your behalf I racked my brains while sharing your troubles;
On your behalf I courted disaster and raised suspicion in others.
On your behalf I risked my own life to fetch the cinnabar herbs;
On your behalf I suffered panic and fear and I almost had died.
　All I hoped for was to grow old together, without any changes,
Not knowing you'd dump me halfway, creating these tribulations.
It all must be due to my settled fate, so there's no way to escape—
But you're also to blame for your vicious heart and ruthless hands!
　Even though I may be of a different kind, you should protect me—
We are husband and wife, so how come you show me no love?
You may have been enticed to do this by that mean-spirited monk,
But still you should have begged him on my behalf to show pity!
　You are not just idly standing by, watching which side will win,
But you even want to assist him from the side as I sneak to death.
Thank you very much for watching with wide-open eyes as I die,
Without a thought for the fated bond of our meeting in the rain!"
　Just when lady Bai was recounting all that had happened before,
The little baby in her arms woke up with a cry and started to weep.
With his two little eyes he looked up,
And grabbed for his mother's breasts, wanting to drink some milk.
　When lady Bai saw this situation, she grew even more distressed,
As if her tender innards were pierced by a knife, her organs torn out,
And she exclaimed: "My cute little boy, how bitter your fate will be!
Never will it be possible for you to see your own dear mother again.
　If I think back on those ten months of pregnancy and on your birth,
How many tribulations did I suffer, how many moments of misery!
I hoped that once you grew up as an adult you would be at my side,

---

³ The *luan* is a mythical bird very much like a phoenix. In Chinese mythology the phoenix (*feng*) is not a solitary bird but it lives in pairs. Frolicking of the phoenix and the *luan* is a conventional symbol of happy sex.

And would wait on your father in bright clothes, with playful antics.[4]
I also hoped you would pass the examinations at your first attempt,
So I would be ennobled by a five-colored imperial patent of nobility.
Who could have known that today I'd have to abandon my dear son,
That only after one month the bond between mother and son
 would be broken?
  These events all are brought about by that callous and cruel father of yours,
Who shows no consideration for his wife, and no consideration for his son!
Who will take care of you from now on when you are hungry or cold?
Who will love you and pity you when you have the measles or the pox?
 When you wake up in the morning to look for someone to play with,
  who will hold you?
And who will cuddle you when you sleep at night on the bed?
Just look at his two little eyes with which he observes his mother—
Sucking on my breast he is drinking and seems so cheerful and happy!"
 Just while lady Bai found it impossible to part from her little son,
That magic treasure suddenly soared up and then hovered in the air:
Her bones grew weak, her muscles grew soft—she had to sit down;
Her mouth went mute, her eyes just stared, as if she had a seizure.
 When she heard the terrifying weeping from the master bedroom,
Little Blue hurried over and then looked in through the window,
To see Xu Xian idly standing by the side of the bed and watching,
While lady Bai was bereft of all energy as if she had passed out.
 That magical treasure flew about in the air, in circles, without ever stopping,
And involuntarily her towering rage rose up to heaven like a flame!
But just when she stepped forward and was about to kill Xu Xian,
Lady Bai hastily grabbed her, blocking her with her last strength.
 And she said: "This is not the fault of my husband, he isn't to blame,
It is all the fault of that monk, who persuaded him to act this way.
Anyway, this was predestined from an earlier life, it has to be,
So it would be all in vain if you would now kill my husband!"
 So Little Blue could do little else but to let go of Xu Xian—
Then suddenly she saw that Chan master right in front of her!
Three times he stamped the ground with his nine-ringed tin staff,
To the effect that the earth was shaking, scaring the heavens!
 Little Blue's heart and gall were shattered that very moment,
And she turned herself into a whirlwind and a whiff of smoke.

---

[4] Lao Laizi, a famous exemplar of filial piety of ancient times, dressed up in children's clothes in order to convince his senile parents they still were young.

She fled to a mountain forest in order to save her own skin,
Without any consideration for the love between mistress and maid of these years!
 When lady Bai saw that Little Blue had fled, she grew even more distressed;
As she fixed her eyes on her husband, her tears gushed forth like a fountain,
 And she said: "I will not harbor any grudge against you even now,
There is no way to escape from my fate, I cannot change Heaven.
I may have grown up in the wilds as a monster from the woods,
But I managed to practice self-cultivations for thousands of years.
 I achieved perceptive intelligence and came to the world of man,
And only then was I capable of tying the marriage knot with you.
All my life I never conceived any desire to do you harm—
I'll swear to Heaven I never had even the slightest idea to do so!
 Little Blue was quite enraged by the way in which you behaved,
And would say that I was soft on you and always took your side!
But now it all has come to pass exactly the way she said it would—
Never in all my life did I suffer greater injustice, but whom can I tell?
I don't have many things to say to you as my final instructions,
But please take care of this little baby who now loses his mother.
If you will marry once more and bring home some lovely bride,
Don't look with disdain on this child!
 As long as you are willing to promise you will never do so,
I will be at peace and close my eyes below the Yellow Springs.[5]
Alas, I cannot even protect myself, how much less than others—
Even if I would blabber on without end, it would all be in vain!"
 She turned around and exclaimed: "Oh my son, oh my darling,
In a moment we will be separated for ever, in life and in death!
 In all this hurry I did not have the time to leave you a souvenir,
But this belly-cover you are wearing was made by your mother.
When you see this piece in the future, it will be like seeing me,
But don't be deeply moved in your innards, vexed in your heart!
 I have computed that you are predestined for riches and glory,
But I'm afraid that when you obtain office, my flesh and bones will have decayed.
So when you offer sacrifices for your mother following your examination success,
Who will know where my intelligent soul may be hanging out?
 When the mother thinks of her son, a heavy grudge buries the full ten miles;[6]
When the son thinks of his mother, continuous tears clamor to the nine heavens.

---

[5] The Yellow Springs refer to the realm of the dead below the earth.

[6] West Lake is often said to be ten miles square. The miles in this context are the Chinese mile or *li* of c. 600 meters.

You will have no way, I'm afraid, to remember my face and my features,
And even if you have a painted portrait, it will be hard to call me to mind.
  So if you will want to burn paper money, in which direction should you turn?
And you'll also be unable to sweep my grave on some southern or northern hill.
My dear child, quickly drink a little bit more, and then I'll have to let go..."
Just watch as she cannot lay him down, and also is incapable of speech.
  When she wants to hand him to Xu Xian, she again clasps him to her bosom,
And rustling tears gush forth from her eyes, as if from a fountain!
The little top-of-the-list was strangely perceptive and intelligent,
And he likewise wailed and wept, crying at the top of his voice.
  He wept till heaven and earth were darkened by somber clouds,
Till gods and ghosts cried and groaned, all moved to compassion.
As soon as Xu Xian had taken the top-of-the-list in his hands,
That magic treasure came down on her head with the weight of Mt. Tai!
  In one soaring flash one big flame shot up to heaven, ten thousand meters of red;
With a tumultuous crash the thunder roared, shaking the passes of heaven.
Lady Bai could not hold out any longer and showed her original shape,
She was a huge snake of a hundred meters, coiled up below the pagoda!
  The assembled gods displayed their magical powers all together;
The Chan master, with palm pressed to palm, recited his mantras.
Then all of a sudden a roaring whirlwind arose, moving rocks and sucking up sand,
And in that pitch-black darkness you couldn't see the sky because of layered clouds.
  Xu Xian was so scared that he trembled all over his body,
And as he thanked the reverend he said: "You have saved my life—I was stupid,
  But now your disciple has seen through the eye-deceiving image of this world,
From this day I want to make a clean break, and jump out of this realm of dust!
I want to turn away from the path of delusion and go the road of enlightenment;
I want to escape from the ocean of suffering and want to ascend Spirit Mountain!"
  The Chan master touched the top of his head and listed the precepts,
With a "Buddha Amithaba" he three times circumambulated the Buddha.
The Chan master said: "Take the Buddha as your teacher, there is no other way;
Return to the root, rediscover the source—they are found in your heart!
  Your son is destined by fate to outperform the whole world in the examinations;
Later he will glorify his ancestors and establish his fame throughout the world.
Even though she was an evil demon, cultivating a heterodox way,
She carried him for ten months, and gave birth to this top-of-the-list!
  Hand him over for now to your elder sister so she can raise him;
In whatever you do, you are not allowed to go against High Heaven.
If you can cultivate the right fruit and achieve the Great Way,
You yourself will become a Buddha, and all your relatives will go to heaven!

By saving your suffering wife from the prison in the earth,
You will glorify the unlimited magic of Buddha and Dharma.
At that time the whole world will bathe in light and go to Ultimate Bliss,
And all heavens will rejoice and successfully establish good karma.
  In this way my little compassion in converting you will not have been in vain;
Only then I'll be able to report on my mission to the Buddha on Spirit Mountain."
Xu Xian did as the reverend told him to do, and entrusted his son to his sister,
So cutting off all love and affection, and all attachments to the world.
  Later the boy occupied the head of the turtle, and sacrificed to his mother;[7]
That must be counted as the reunion of husband and wife and of mother and son.
The Buddha had said that the White Snake could only reappear in this world
If West Lake would dry up till the very last drop.
  To this day the pagoda loftily soars up beyond the highest clouds,
As the sinking light of the setting sun dazzles one with many colors.
This has left us the fine scene of Thunder Peak in the Setting Sun,
And it makes a beautiful tale for ten thousands and thousands of years.

---

[7] The person who passes the metropolitan examinations with highest honors as "top-of-the-list" is said to occupy the head of the turtle.

The Sacrifice at the Pagoda

    The West Lake's Ten Sights are beautiful and well worth viewing;
Thunder Peak in the Setting Sun has been famous till this day.
The pagoda's upside-down image is reflected in the water below,
While the pagoda's pinnacle soars up high, touching heaven above.
    The scenery from morning till evening hides even sun and moon;
Under a clear or cloudy sky it shifts its shape as fog or clouds arise.
Upon leisurely discussing past and present with a rustic greybeard,
I wrote this chapter of the old affair below Thunder Peak Pagoda.

Because the young top-of-the-list was extremely concerned about his mother,
He went to Thunder Peak in order to set out sacrificial offerings.
Wailing and weeping with every step he arrived at West Lake,
And soon observed the precious pagoda majestically soaring into the sky.
    As his eyes observed the pagoda, his heart was shattered by pain,
And he said: "My mother's corpse is resting here inside the pagoda!"
With eager heart and hasty steps he came to the foot of the building,
But the sight that he saw was chilly and bleak and extremely distressing.
    He only saw somber clouds thickly surrounding and covering the pagoda,
While a black fog all around was hiding its foundation from view.
A sad wind was howling from all directions so the bronze bells chimed;
A fine rain was falling on the thirteen stories, so the green tiles felt cold.
    The heavy shade of a myriad of pines with their swaying branches made
       it impossible to see the sun,
And in the dark shadows of a thousand bamboos with their rustling leaves
       one could not see the sky.
Without interruption the many hills had surrounded this place for a thousand years,
While the single lake with its constant stream for all eternity had never been idle.
    By the side of the road rampant weeds had grown into shrubs as tall as a man,
While atop the pagoda strange birds sadly sang as if complaining of an injustice.
The glazed green tiles after all these many days and years now had lost their luster,
While on the painted beams, exposed to wind and rain, the fresh colors had faded.
    Sideways throwing its squat shadow in the last rays of the setting sun
Over a cold spring at its foot as the evening mists were rising—
Even ordinary passers-by would feel moved to tears at this sight,
How much more so the son she had borne—how could he not be distressed?

The young top-of-the-list knelt down before the pagoda, and wept: "Dear mother!
Only today your son has come here to make his bows in front of your grave.
Alas, never since my birth have I seen the figure and face of my mother;
Imagining you without any support, I tried to recall your loving features.
　How could I form myself an idea when I wanted to call your face and voice
　　to my mind?
And I am even more at a loss when one mentions your banter and laughter.
No orphan in this world is suffering such a bitter fate as this son of yours,
As I have become the most unfilial son since the beginning of heaven and earth.
　Long ago, I recall, when it was barely one month since my birth,
My mother was punished by Heaven, and suffered this strange injustice.
I never will know how many tears you must have shed at that moment—
Holding your son you must have felt as if your flesh was cut off, your heart
　was ripped out, and your organs were pierced.
　Cruelly I was taken from your bosom—your own flesh and blood was stolen away,
And you followed those fierce gods and evil ghosts to the mountains of shade.
As determined by fate it is a son's duty to guard and protect his mother,
But all because of me you died an early death to be buried below the sources.[1]
　If I at that time would have only been able to speak,
I would have wept and prayed before the throne of the Buddha.
And in case the Buddha would not have accepted my prayers,
I would have been happy to kill myself and die in your place!
　The proverb says: 'The compassionate Buddha comes to your aid!'
So how come he refuses to show compassion only in the case of my mother?
As a result I look in vain on this pagoda, not knowing how I may save you.
How could this not cause myriads of sufferings to congregate in my heart?
　Dear mother, if you have intelligence and power, snatch me away from here,
So mother and son on the roads of the sources both may be freed from attachments.
Otherwise, my innards are definitely bound to break!
Each and every day shattered to smithereens my wounded heart longs to see you.
　In all other families, I notice, mother and son are united and stay together;
Playing in colored clothes the son expresses his filiality at his parents' feet.
Even in the poorest families a son still has his father and mother,
And despite the simple diet they live in pleasure all the days of their life."
　"Overcome by sadness," he said, "your unworthy son has come to offer sacrifice,
But my mother's soul has long since dispersed and cannot return.
Below the still and silent double sources she doesn't hear my weeping;
From the black and dark prison in earth none answers my questions.

---

[1] The sources refer to the Yellow Sources, the realm of the dead.

During your lifetime, dear mother, your supernatural powers were so extensive,
So upon your death you still should be grand and imposing.
If it is true that you don't exist and enjoy your sacrifices in vain,
Then you truly have no shape and body, so I never will see you.
  Oh, how I would like to order to the Five Nail Giants to push over this pagoda![2]
Oh, how I would like to command the Six Scale Gods to pull down this pagoda![3]
Your voice and face are clearly so near, but still I cannot see you,
So even if I would erect a stele and build a mound it would all be in vain.
  The best I can do is to commit myself to goodness and practice charity;
On your behalf I can also sponsor a mass of remorse to absolve your sins.
But alas, my allotted blessings are few, and my hidden karma is shallow,
So how can I bring my mother back to life again like erstwhile Mulian?"
  The young top-of-the list wept till heaven and earth both turned dark,
And all he could do was offer the rice, pour out the soup and libate the wine.
A twister sucked the ashes of the burned paper money up into the sky, whirling,
And it seemed as if lady Bai's soul really received the paper cash.

Eventually Xu Xian obtained the Way and achieved the right fruit,
And he liberated his wife so she could become a terrestrial immortal.
This is the exceptional scenery of Thunder Peak in the Setting Sun—
For a myriad of years, for a thousand springs this will be a fine story.

---

[2] The Five Nail Giants were servants of the king of Shu (modern Sichuan). At the behest of their king, they hauled a golden ox from Qin (modern Shaanxi) across the steep mountains that up to that time had formed an absolute barrier between the two states, and in this way they created a road that allowed the king of Qin to invade and conquer Shu.

[3] The Six Scale Gods are among the most fearsome divine warriors at the command of a Daoist priest.

Weeping at the Pagoda

I

What can be told about the golden hills of ocean isles?
The monument of Thunder Peak still sighs about Xu Xian!
Why talk about the karmic cause and later consequences?
Why tell about the joy and pain of partings and reunions?
   As soon as thoughts of love arose, this lady Bai showed up;
But he was haunted by Fahai when proper longings sprouted.
No word about the double bowl by which he caught the monster—
A chapter now on Little Blue who came to the pagoda!

Lady Bai originally was an immortal maiden residing in heaven;
Following the Queen Mother she served in the ranks of immortals.
Because her carnal desire was aroused, she suffered a karmic fate:
Together with the incense boy she descended to this mortal world.
   Who could have known she'd take the wrong womb and end up as a snake?
But once she had obtained the Way she turned into a dashing beauty!
Then there was Little Blue, also a snake, who became her companion;
She too was a miraculous animal of many years and a master of magic.
   Mistress and maid lived in hiding at West Lake, looking for her lover,
There they ran into the reincarnated incense boy, now called Xu Xian.
Following this chance encounter these two people became a couple,
Not knowing that their fine marriage would be doomed from the start!
   Now in the school of the Buddha there was a monk named Fahai—
Originally a scabby turtle that had obtained the Way after a thousand years!
Because he had seen the immortal maiden serving the peaches of immortality,
This evil monk had conceived a secret desire that was anything but proper!
   Because these two people now had been reborn on earth and had become a couple,
His jealous heart was all too visible in his fiercely bulging eyes.
The rage that filled his heart could only be assuaged if he could separate this couple,
So he started to spread rumors before the throne of the Buddha!
   He said that in the present world there were too many monsters,
Creating havoc throughout the cosmos so there was no peace;
And that if not subdued these monster would become a plague,

Just like that monkey that long ago had upset the Western Sky![1]
Because of this he talked the Buddha into entrusting him with a magic treasure:
This evil monk was dispatched to the world here below
To capture inside this bowl all evil creatures that had achieved power,
So all ten thousand dharmas would take refuge in good causes.[2]
Having obtained this treasure the monk came to Golden Mountain Monastery,
Just when Xu Xian went there to repay a vow he had made.
This Fahai talked to Xu Xian till he had become scared,
And the two of them conspired to use a secret trick.
With the aid of an amulet they pinned lady Bai down,
So she was captured in the golden bowl and couldn't move.
Alas, this immortal beauty who was destined to suffer disaster,
Was imprisoned under Thunder Peak Pagoda like a crushed jade, a damaged pearl!
I will not tell what happened to Fahai and to Xu Xian,
And I also will not mention how that suffering beauty survived all these years.
Let me tell you about the escaped Little Blue, now without her mistress:
She was just like a fluttering petal, a falling leaf, borne by the wind!
Hiding herself deep in the mountains on a distant isle where no man ever came,
Overcome by myriads and thousands of worries and sorrows she could tell none,
She mourned, filled with longing, her former companion on moonlit nights,
And recalled, alone and lonely, her old friend whenever the flowers bloomed.
So she thought: "Lady Bai all by herself is suffering this disaster inside
    Thunder Peak Pagoda—
Alas, how can her lovely frame and weak body continue to carry this burden?
If I consider it carefully, that monk Fahai is truly detestable:
What kind of a feud did my mistress have with you that you acted this way?
You messed with a loving couple till they became strangers to each other!
And even more pitiable, the little baby who lost his mother was still in his
    swaddling clothes!
Come to think of it, it was also Xu Xian who was in the wrong:
He should not have lent his ears so easily to that slander!
Had it not been for Xu Xian who trusted the words of the monk,
How could the latter so out of the blue have created such mayhem?
As a result this fine couple turned into a couple of archenemies,
That bald donkey scared you so much your mind was lost, your reason gone![3]

---

[1] This line is an obvious reference to the first chapters of the sixteenth-century novel *Journey to the West* (*Xiyou ji*), which narrate the rebellion of Monkey against the heavenly authorities.

[2] The ten thousand dharmas refer to the elements from which all beings are formed.

[3] "Bald donkey" is a common curse word for monks.

Alas, my mistress in her innocence was trapped by his vicious scheme,
When will she ever be liberated and see the light of day once again?
Mother and son, husband and wife, and mistress and maid all are eagerly
Hoping for that one day when the whole household will be reunited!"
   As Little Blue was thinking backward and forward, her heart was shattered,
And pearly tears, dripping drop by drop, turned into streaks of red blood.
Then suddenly she thought: "Why don't I secretly go off to Thunder Peak
To see what her situation may be and whether she is still in one piece?"
   Little Blue silently used a magic trick to work her miraculous power;
Releasing wind and clouds a thousand miles were covered in an instant.
Straightway she hastened to the West Lake;
There the dimly remembered mountains and streams were still the old scenery.
   The Five Willows Dike was bathing in the light of the setting sun,
While an autumn mist was lying down on each of the Six Bridges.
Her innards all racked by pain Little Blue arrived at Thunder Peak Pagoda;
When awash in tears she looked out from one of its windows she saw a dark
   fog spreading all around.

II

> The autumn light above the lake: the green so lush grows cold;
> A scenery that breaks the heart as silence fills the hills.
> The Bridges Six are now deserted, visitors are few;
> The Willows Five are desolate, as leaves fall from the trees.
>   Some strands of discontinuous fog now hide the distant peaks,
> And longer bands of evening mist surround the setting sun.
> How can one ask about this sad and chilly situation?
> The many pains that wound her heart show clearly on her face!

When Little Blue saw the scenery of West Lake she felt deeply distressed,
And involuntarily pearly tears gushed forth as she sadly tweaked her mouth.
When she hurried to have a look inside the pagoda, she was struck in the face
   by a cold wind;
Fog was everywhere; no human being was to be found, only black darkness.
   Terrified she thought: "How come there is nobody here—could something
have happened?
My mistress most likely must have died and lost her life!"
In her panic her tears coursed down, and in a sad voice, full of distress,
   She said: "My mistress, where are you? I've come to see you—I'm Little Blue!"
   Let's not tell how Little Blue outside the pagoda called to her in a sad voice,

But let's talk about lady Bai, whose energy had been reduced to almost nil.
Ever since she had entered Thunder Peak Pagoda,
She was, alas! not the bewitching beauty of before anymore.
   Her coiled-up body was lying down flat inside the bowl—
How could she endure the chilly air of the cold well below the pagoda?
Fortunately her former karma was not yet finished and her foundation was strong,
Because if she would have been a mere mortal her life would be in danger!
   Yet even so she was gradually losing her Three Flowers and Five Energies,[4]
But captured by the golden bowl all her magic was now of no use.
There were only the chilly fog that penetrated her and the piercing cold wind—
Never did she see the sun in the sky in this deep darkness without night or day.
   She could not be bothered by her somber resentment and limitless sufferings,
And with the little bright intelligence she had left she harbored her right energy.
Alas, she spent all day in a dark haze as if in a drunken stupor,
And only when Little Blue kept on calling did she seem to return from a dream.
   "This is the result of all your passion because you were so filled with passion!
Now you nurse your deep hatred in vain, dear mistress, and all for whom?
I still remember those early days when we were hiding at West Lake:
The two of us had such a great time—we could do what we wanted!
   But from the day that you were married to that Xu Xian,
The arena of love was unexpectedly filled with problems.
How could I have known that now I wouldn't even know whether you're dead or alive?
You've become a sunken pearl, a shattered jade, a fading moon, a ravaged plum!"
   Little Blue cried tears of blood, and sighed as she spoke like an oriole;
Her throat was choked by her weeping, and her breathing went heavy.
When lady Bai inside the pagoda heard that it was truly the voice of Little Blue,
It moved her so much she was choked by grief and collapsed on the ground.
   In her charming voice she said: "Little Blue, is that you outside? This hurts me to death!
Just look at me: the thin thread of my life is almost all gone!"
When Little Blue heard this voice calling from inside the pagoda,
Her eager heart was both overjoyed and filled with sadness.
   Suddenly she heard: "Who is the person who has come here to see me?"
As she listened carefully, the voice was familiar as it said: "Who are you?"
As she listened again she was deeply distressed by that sad voice so mournful,
And she said: "Dear mistress, how come no trace can be seen, so where do I find you?
   You and I were of the same kind and our feelings surpassed those of siblings;
Our hearts were glued together and we never left each other for even an inch.

---

[4] The Three Flowers are essence, energy, and spirit. The Five Energies here probably refer to the energies of the five internal organs.

I had hoped that the two of us would flourish like intertwined branches,
But who could know you would all day be pestered by this evil dew and chilly wind?
   I have no idea what kind of evil karma we, mistress and maid, had committed,
But too bad that we had to encounter by chance that traitorous bandit!
That Xu Xian should not have believed the words of that evil monk,
And turn a loving couple of husband and wife into nothing but ashes.
   How often didn't he come up with schemes to harm the two of us,
But, alas! in your innocence you never turned back from your folly.
For the sake of Xu Xian you risked your life to find recipe and medicine,
And but for the kindness of the Queen Mother of the West, you would've lost your life!"
   She said: "Dear mistress, where are you hiding so I cannot see you?
I have been here for quite a while—this really scares me out of my wits!
Your supernatural powers were not insignificant,
So how come you now willingly allow yourself to be imprisoned by a clod
   of earth and a pile of bricks?
   Lady Bai said: "It is not that I am incapable of leaving this pagoda,
But the miraculous power of the bowl gives me no leeway.
If I want to escape from this bowl, one must implore the Buddha:
Once I can get out of this golden bowl, I won't fear anyone!
   My only problem is that I have no one who will go for me to Spirit Peak,
Who else do I still have as a close friend apart from you?"
Little Blue said: "I have wanted to save you now for many days,
So if that's what it takes, that's a duty I'll be happy to perform!
   I will be only too happy to step in boiling water or walk across a burning fire
As long as you are freed from disaster and spared from all danger!"
She said: "Dear mistress, put your mind at rest, take good care of yourself,
And let me make this journey to the Western Paradise!"

Leaving the Pagoda

I

Wounded by all limitless emotions of the world of dust,
Her heart, once so hot and passionate, had turned to ice.
Opening her eyes she awakened from the dream of love,
So, turning her head, she discarded the tangle of luxury.
    Solid earth and high heaven in the end are but an illusion,
And oaths and promises like mountains and seas are a lie.
If a person who has come back is looking for the road of return,
It has to lead to the highest peaks on the isle of Penglai.[1]

As the young top-of-the-list was thinking of his mother, his sadness increased;
Alas, overcome by pain from morning till night, he was awash in tears.
With sincere devotion he piteously implored Fahai to set her free,
And his pure and undiluted filial piety moved the holy monk.[2]
    Thereupon he promised to come to Yue in the middle of the current month,[3]
In his compassion he would aid mother and son to meet with one another.
The filial son, now filled with joy, repeatedly thanked him,
And Fahai told him he didn't need to wait but should go ahead.
    Overcome by joy the young top-of-the-list now left the monastery,
And when he came home he informed his father how he saved his mother.
On the appointed day father and son arrived together at West Lake,
Just at break of dawn on the day of Clear and Bright.
    At this moment it happened to be the scenery of the end of spring,
And everywhere the fine sights had been woven together naturally:

---

[1] "A person who has come back" is a person who is destined to achieve enlightenment in his or her present existence. Mt. Penglai is one of the paradisiacal floating islands of the immortals in the Eastern Seas.

[2] We learn later in this text that Xu Mengjiao had learned the truth about his background after passing the examinations, and had then traveled to Golden Mountain Monastery. In this version of events, Xu Xian has not become a monk.

[3] Yue is the region to the east of the Qiantang River. It often is used to refer to its most important city Shaoxing, but here it must refer to Hangzhou.

Covered by pearls of morning dew fine flowers and strange plants collected thousands of reds;
Glowing in the light of dawn emerald willows and dark pines displayed a myriad of hues of green.
　In pair upon pair yellow orioles and purple swallows twittered with artful voices;
Couple upon couple of butterflies and roaming bees danced on their light wings.
The breeze was pure and clouds were light in a pleasing sky of deepest blue;
No billows arose and no wave was stirring on the mirror-like lake so widely white!
　The young top-of-the-list hurried toward the pagoda and hastily knelt down,
Exclaiming: "Dear mother, today we, mother and son, will finally be reunited!"
And as he spoke, he could not stop his tears from coursing down;
Filled with eager anticipation he was waiting for the monk's arrival.
　Now just as the young top-of-the-list was waiting, his heart in a whirl,
He saw a woman who arrived as if floating, of most gracious mien:
Her face, he saw, was like a lovely flower, her waist like a tender willow;
You'd say her makeup was like painted jade, her features toppled a wall!
　After she had kowtowed in front of the top-of-the-list, she said with a smile:
"Young master, it has been some years since I left and now you're grown up!"
The top-of-the-list had no idea who she might be and he became nervous,
But as soon as Xu Xian had seen Little Blue, a blush had reddened his face!
　He could do nothing else but step forward, force a smile, and say: "Little Blue,
What is the fortunate coincidence that we can meet each other again today?"
Little Blue answered: "Since we were separated more than ten years have passed,
And I've been hiding on immortal isles to practice again heaven-repairing skills.
　Understanding all mysteries I have found that my mistress' distress will end today,
And that's why I've come here today for the purpose of serving my mistress."
Only now did the young top-of-the-list realize that this was Little Blue,
So he hastily stepped forward and greeted her as his tears coursed down.
　And he said: "Sister Blue, please accept my apologies for this late greeting,
I hope that you will forgive me for not recognizing you in my foolishness!
Ever since you and my mother each went their different ways,
For more than ten years you were gone with nowhere a trace to be found.
　And when I had grown up and was thinking of my mother,
Where oh where could I find and see her face?
You, sister Blue, also never came by to visit me,
So there was no one whom I could ask for news about my mother!"
　Little Blue heaved a heavy sigh and nodded her head, and said:
"Young master, the situation now is different from that in the past!
Ever since that disaster I've grown cold toward the world of dust.
Understanding all mysteries, I'm about to achieve the Great Way.

That's the reason why I never had opportunity to come and visit you,
It's not that my heart had grown cold or that I was bereft of feeling!"
While the two of them were talking about the events of those years,
They saw that over there the ruddy-faced monk of Golden Mountain had arrived!
   Xu Xian and his son hastened to welcome him,
And Little Blue also stepped forward and kowtowed to thank the monk.
Fahai nodded his head and exclaimed: "How wise is this woman!
She turned around and very soon the Way will be achieved!"
   The young top-of-the-list again knelt down in front of the monk,
And implored him: "Dear Master, display the magic of the Law and show
   your supernatural powers!"
When the Chan master together with all other people had arrived at the foot
   of the pagoda,
He started to recite his mantras and to employ his mysterious skills.
Then you heard a clap of thunder and saw a flash of golden light,
And all of sudden the gate of the pagoda swung open from east to west.
Slowly swaying her fragrant body lady Bai emerged from the pagoda;
As she leisurely cast glances all around, her appearance was confident.
   Even though her body had been incarcerated in darkness for over ten years,
Her jade features were as before, and she still was her old beautiful self.
She deeply bowed toward Fahai, and said: "Revered teacher,
Many thanks for your grace in enlightening and restoring stupid me!"
   The Chan master said: "Self-awakening far surpasses enlightenment by others,
Only she who eagerly ascends the other shore is fully intelligent."
Lady Bai kowtowed and repeatedly said: "I am grateful for your instruction,
I thank you, master, for striking me over the head with your staff and
   awakening me from my ignorance with your shouts!"
Master Fahai repeatedly said: "Great! Great! It's time for me to go!"
And you saw him rise into the sky like one shaft of auspicious light.
Father and son expressed their thanks by bowing toward the sky,
And when Little Blue and her mistress met again they said how much they
   had missed each other.
   The young top-of-the-list hastily turned around and bowed to his mother;
As he held on to her lapels he knelt down, so moved he lost his voice!
He said: "By this cruel longing for you you almost killed your child!
How difficult it has been to finally achieve this day of reunion of mother and child!
   For more than ten years you have been suffering all kinds of bitter tribulations!
Alas, as I, your child, was longing for you, I wept tears of red blood.
Ever since your child reached the age of understanding, I've been looking for you,
But alas, there was nobody who was willing to give me a full explanation.

Only this spring, when I had passed and came home covered in glory,
Was my aunt eventually willing to tell me the full inside story.
Alas, I fainted a number of times and repeatedly came to again;
Thinking of you, I neglected to sleep and forgot to eat and then fell ill.
  All I could do was to go to Golden Mountain and find Fahai,
And implore him to show pity for mother and son and leave his mountain.
Fortunately he displayed compassion and was moved in his heart—
Only thus could our family be reunited, mother and son see each other!
  So, dear mother, I invite you to come home so we can all be together,
Allow your son to filially serve you at dawn and dusk as one happy family!"
Filled with sadness and joy the young top-of-the-list knelt before his mother—
Since ancient times it is said: It's the nature of women to be ruled by attachment.

II

As she faced her own son, lady Bai fixed her eyes on the top-of-the-list,
And while she put her hands on his shoulders she scrutinized his face.
With his white teeth and red lips, she saw, he was sophisticated and elegant,
With his pure spirit and brisk energy he by nature stood out from the crowd.
  As he faced his mother, speechlessly taking her in, his tears gushed forth—
A thousand kinds of attachments, together with limitless painful emotions!
Lady Bai's cold heart that already had turned to ice was shattered once again,
And as she watched her darling son, involuntarily tears filled her eyes.
  And she said: "My son, ever since that day on which I abandoned you,
I have suffered endless disasters and tribulations of uncommon severity.
This limitless blackness is as dark as eternal night and knows of no dawn;
This shivering cold is partly due to chilly wells and partly due to the winds.
  In deepest darkness I passed my years one way or another;
As if lost in a trance I allowed the days and months to go by.
Longing for my loved one I eventually saw you once in a dream,
But when I woke up, that only doubled the gut-desire for my son.
  If I had not by practice achieved this Dharma-body to suffer these tribulations,
My soul long ago would have turned into a firefly amidst the lakeside grasses.
Fortunately I now have this filial and obedient son who saves his mother,
So it is not in vain that I fell into this world and spent half a lifetime there.
  Even though now I once again see the light of day and meet with my son,
Your mother, dear son, has something she has to tell you.
Ever since I suffered that calamity, I achieved enlightenment,
And I've come to see that all attachments of this mortal world are empty.
  Don't talk to me about a purple seal and golden sign thanks to my son's scheming;

Don't talk to me about a phoenix jacket and cap of pearls thanks to my son's glory!
Don't talk to me about making me happy by child-like antics here at my feet;
Don't talk to me about five tripods and three slaughtered animals for every banquet!
    Even if you would serve me filially in a thousand ways to my limitless joy,
After my death it would all boil down to a three-foot wall and a horse-mane mound.[4]
It cannot compare to this obstacle-free state now I have achieved the Great Way,
Which allows me to wander at will across the blue skies and azure heavens.
    Now I go to the moon palace to visit White Maiden;
Then I go to the immortal isles to meet with Qiongying.[5]
Elder and younger sisters enjoy themselves with poetry and wine beyond the Three Isles;
Old acquaintances early and late accompany me amidst a myriad of clustered flowers.
    And then I can collect simples and dig out roots to while away the time,
Or I move freely back and forth between the many peaks of Mt. Penglai.
This kind of free and easy roaming without any restriction or hindrance,
Isn't that far better than fully suffering sweet and sour in this mortal world?"
    Lady Bai had seen through the red dust, and her deeply emotional words
Scared the top-of-the-list to such an extent that his filial heart was shattered
    and his eyes were filled with tears.
After quite a while he said: "Dear mother, we were separated for over ten years,
    and we have met for only a moment.
Alas, I even haven't had the time to fix your features in my mind.
    With great difficulty flesh and blood have been reunited, the greatest joy on earth!
Why do you want to abandon your son once again, going off in a different direction?"
The young top-of-the-list held on to his mother as he was overcome by grief,
While Xu Xian stepped forward and greeted her, his face partly showing his shame.
    Forcing a smile, he said: "My dear wife, don't blame me for what happened then,
But please show some consideration for the sincere feelings of your filial son!
Moreover, thanks to your great virtue his endowment is exceptionally intelligent;
Occupying the turtle's head, he has snatched away the prize of top-of-the-list!
    So I hope, my dear wife, that you will show forgiveness for your son and husband,
And that you will come home with us so we may together enjoy peace and glory."
On the one hand Xu Xian bowed to his wife, on the other he pronounced
    this speech,
But lady Bai heaved a heavy sigh, and then said: "Now please understand:
    Once I left, I fathomed in stillness all mysteries, so my heart resembles a mirror,
And I deeply regret how I wrecked my career once I had fallen into this world.

---

[4] A horse-mane mound refers to a specific style of grave mound; a wall would surround the area of the grave.

[5] Both White Maiden (*Sunü*) and Qiongying are well-known female immortals.

I only cared for the common flight of lovebirds, lost on the sea of delusions,
And so I lost my place in the immortal ranks, a quick arrival at Mt. Penglai.
  I only cared for a love as lasting as mountains and peaks, as heavy as a thousand years,
And so I lost my companions like mist and sunset-clouds, as light as a single leaf.
  I only cared for sweet harmony of zither and lute, for intense love and longing,
And so I lost my free roaming over hills and streams, this great passion for the fields.
  I only cared for the joy of hearts united behind green embroidered curtains of gauze,
And so I lost my freedom to wander at will in the Cassia Mansion and the
  Toad Palace.[6]
I only cared for spring flowers and autumn breezes from morning till night,
And so I lost the wild crane and idle clouds that are moving east and west.
I only cared for the friendship of phoenix and *luan*, for minds intertwined,
And I lost the freedom to come and go on ocean isles and immortal mounds!
Alas, being lost I entered this darkness without any understanding,
And my brightly shining heart of ice was covered by my infatuation!
  Enticed by attachments I all of a sudden followed the lead of the silkworm,
And it was clear that I encaged myself in the threads that I myself had spun.[7]
Alas, for half a life I was entangled by my own infatuation—
My body had almost turned to yellow sand, and my breath to air.
  With great difficulty I one day awakened from that dream of yesterday,
And in one *salto mortale* I jumped out off the bottomless pit of the human world;
In truth, now the debt of karma has been repaid, the threads of dust have been cut.
From now on we will say good-bye, and all will be more empty than empty.
  To my joy the grotto-mansion of earlier times is still standing,
And I don't have to fear that after all this time I will not know the way.
I've decided on this course of action, so we will not be reunited,
And why is there any need for you to talk about love at this time?"
  Addressing the top-of-the-list, she exclaimed: "My dear son,
Your mother would like to say a few words which you must remember.
You are blessed with intelligence, and your fate holds great fortune;
If you act well, you will with every step advance in a fine career.
  As you are capable of such display of filial piety in front of your mother,
You must remember to manifest loyalty while serving your ruler at court.
As a human being your gall should be large and your heart should be small,[8]
Your ambition should be well-rounded, and your trust should be sincere.

---

[6] The cassia tree is said to grow on the moon, which is believed to be inhabited by a toad.

[7] In Chinese the word for thread (*si*) has the same pronunciation as the word for thought/longing (*si*).

[8] The gall is the seat of valor and courage. To be "small-hearted" (*xiaoxin*) means to be careful, paying attention to the smallest detail.

If you can govern the state and order your house so you will bring glory to
    ancestors and descendants,
I will not in vain have been a wife in the Xu family for my whole life.
Once I will have gone you should not harm your body by your sad thoughts,
So I will not have to worry even though I am living among the immortals.
    From now on your mother will roam freely, forever without any anxiety,
So you, my son, should rejoice—why would you have to be depressed?
Just think: yesterday and today are for me as different as heaven and hell;
The realms of the Yellow Springs and the azure skies are not the same!
    Moreover, I have achieved the Great Way, and wander unencumbered;
Of course there will be a day when mother and son will meet again."
When lady Bai had finished speaking, she turned around and said: "I have to go!"
But the young top-of-the-list grasped his mother and clutched her tightly.
    Loudly weeping he said: "Mother, one way or another take pity on me, don't go!
I still have a thousand things and myriad words that I want to tell you!"
As lady Bai watched her son, her innards were rent,
But she clenched her teeth, suppressed her tears, and hardened her heart.
    Stretching her jade-white hands she pushed away the hands of the top-of-the-list,
Then quickly turned around and called for Little Blue.
As she said: "Follow me!" they shared one flash,
And one white cloud soared up into the sky.
    Availing itself of an easterly wind it sailed as stably as a little boat, and as fast
    as an arrow;
It went off to the edge of heaven—in a blink of the eye it had disappeared without a trace.
Overcome by emotion the young top-of-the-list collapsed on the ground as if
    in coma or in a stupor,
And alas, the tears that fell on his gown drop by drop colored the sleeves all red.

APPENDIXES

Appendix I

Li Huang *and Other Classical Tales of Bewitching Snakes*

Stories of young men encountering bewitching beauties who turn out to be demons are a frequent topic in the rich literature of classical tales (that is, short stories written in the classical language). The young men often, but not always, are students away from home. The demons may be female ghosts or animals or even objects that because of their advanced age have acquired the power to change their appearance and take on human form. Their aim in having sex with a young man is to rob him of his essence (viz. his semen, of which man is supposed to have only a limited supply). Their victims soon take on a sallow appearance and eventually will die, unless they are saved in time by the intercession of an exorcist.

The demon may be any animal, and stories of bewitching white snakes are actually rather rare in view of the thousands upon thousands of stories of this kind of story that have been preserved. One of the best-known examples is the story simply entitled Li Huang. *This story derives from the ninth-century collection* **Many Marvels** (Boyi ji) *by an author who hides his identity behind the pseudonym "Master Spirit of the Valley" (Gushenzi); it has been preserved in the* Taiping guangji, *a large late-tenth-century compilation of classical tales.*[1] *The two other classical tales in this selection, "The Wife of County Magistrate Sun" and "The Student Qian Yan," are found in the* Records of the Listener (Yijian zhi), *a large late-twelfth-century compilation of miracle tales by Hong Mai (1123–1202).*[2]

---

[1] The translation is based on Li, 1961, 3750–52.

[2] The translations are based on Hong Mai, 1981, 1062–63; 1755–56.

Li Huang

In the second year of the reign-period Yuanhe (807) Li Huang from Longxi, a nephew of the Commissioner for Salt and Iron [Li] Sunzhi, while [at the capital] awaiting his reassessment for appointment, was enjoying his free time at the Eastern Market of Chang'an. There he espied an oxcart, with some servant girls offering goods for sale on the cart. When Li peeked inside the cart, he saw an elegant woman dressed in white and of an extraordinary beauty. When Li asked who she was, a servant girl said: "Our lady is a widow, and her original surname is Yuan. She earlier served the Li family, and at present she is wearing mourning for her husband. But as the period of mourning is about to end, she is selling these articles." When he further inquired whether she might be willing to marry again, she replied with a smile: "Who knows!" Li thereupon gave her cash to buy brocades. The servants then relayed her words as follows: "Allow me to borrow your money to make some purchases. Please follow me to my house to the left of the Zhuangyan Monastery where I will return your money to you without fail."

Li was very pleased. At that time it was already getting late. He thereupon followed the oxcart, and only after nightfall did it arrive at its destination. When the oxcart had entered the central gate, the woman dressed in white descended from the cart by herself and entered the house as she was screened by her servants with a curtain. When Li descended from his horse, he suddenly saw a servant come out with a bench, inviting him to sit down. The servant said: "How could there still be time tonight to receive your money? If you would perhaps know someone here with whom you could stay, you might want to go to his place to settle your business tomorrow morning." Li replied: "It's not that I want my money back right now, but I also know no one where I could stay, so why do you want to keep me outside?" The servant went inside, and came back out again, saying: "If you have no one else, you also of course can stay here, as long as you don't criticize us for our sloppy hospitality."

After a while the servant said: "Please, sir, follow me." Li straightened his gown and entered. In the courtyard stood a woman of a certain age who was dressed in blue, and who greeted him with the following words: "I'm an aunt of the one dressed in white." He sat down in the courtyard, and after some delay the one dressed in white came out. Her white skirt was dazzling, and her pure skin was lustrous, while the simple elegance of her words and bearing was not different from the divine immortals. After they had exchanged some courtesies, she quite suddenly went back inside. The aunt sat down and apologized, saying: "The colored fabrics you so kindly sold to her are far superior to what she bought these last few days. But she is deeply worried and ashamed about the amount of money she borrowed." Li replied: "These gaudy textiles are too crude and coarse to serve as the garments of a lady. How would I dare mention a price?" She replied: "She is shallow and lowly and not worthy of serving you as your maid. Also, living in poverty she has accumulated a debt of thirty thousand coins. But sir, if you do not reject her, she is delighted to serve you." Li was very pleased and bowed at her side, and as he got up, made his arrangements. Now Li happened to have a warehouse quite nearby and he ordered one of his own servants to go and fetch thirty thousand coins. When these had arrived in the blink of an eye, a small gate to the western side of the hall was thrown open with a loud sound. Rice and dishes had already been laid out in the western room. The sister-in-law invited Li to go inside and sit down, as she cast flashing glances at him. When the beauty also arrived, she was told to sit down, but she did so only after bowing to her sister-in-law. Six or seven people brought in the food, and when they were done eating, they called for wine and drank to their heart's content.

Li stayed there for three days in a row, and their drinking and merry-making knew no bounds. But on the fourth day the sister-in-law said: "Sir, you should go back to your own place, because otherwise your uncle the minister may be wondering where you are staying for so long. You can come back later without any problem." As Li also wanted to go back, he followed her advice, took his leave, and left. When he mounted his horse, his groom noticed that Li smelled strongly of rotten meat. When he then arrived back home and was asked where he had been for all those days, he came up with some made-up story.

But then his body felt heavy and his head felt dizzy, so he asked for a coverlet and lay down. He happened to be married to a daughter of the Zheng family, who was at his side and said: "You have already been appointed to a new office. Yesterday you had to report to the authorities, and because we couldn't find you, my two elder brothers reported to the authorities on your behalf." Li thereupon answered in a very apologetic manner. When shortly thereafter the two Zheng brothers arrived and questioned him where he had been, Li had already started to be delirious, and could only mumble some excuse, and he said to his wife: "I will not recover!" Even as his mouth was still speaking, they noted that the body under the blanket was gradually melting, and when they lifted the coverlet, they only saw a puddle of water—all that remained was the head!

The whole family was greatly terrified, and when they questioned the grooms who had accompanied him, they learned the whole story. When they went to look for the old house, they only found an empty garden, and in it a honey-locust tree. From its branches hung fifteen strings of cash, and at its foot they found another fifteen strings of cash.³ Otherwise there was nothing to be found. When they questioned the neighbors, these said: "One often sees a huge white snake at the bottom of the tree, but nothing else. If she called herself Yuan, she must have used the empty garden as her surname."⁴

Hong Mai, *The Wife of County Magistrate Sun*

The gentleman County Magistrate Sun lived ten miles outside the county capital of Danyang. He had married the daughter of a certain local family. Of the three siblings, Sun's wife was the youngest. Her appearance was exceedingly seductive. She loved to apply a few *taches de beauté*. Whether it was freezing cold or oppressively hot, she would always wear a white gown and a red jacket. Her posture and expression were just like those of a woman in a painting! But whenever she would take a bath, she would hide herself behind double screens, and she would not allow the maids to come near her—even when rubbing her back, she would not call for their help. Sun had repeatedly asked her why she behaved in this manner, but she would only smile and never provided an explanation.

But after ten years, when she was approaching thirty, a slightly tipsy Sun noticed that she was having a bath and made a little hole to spy on her for the fun of it. But all he saw was a huge white snake coiling in the tub, her eyes darting around in a most terrifying manner. As fast as he could he ran to his study, where he made up his own bed to sleep, intending from now on to live apart from her. His wife was well aware of this, and as soon as she had left her bath, she went over to his study and said to him: "I may have been at fault, but you also made a mistake! Please don't harbor any suspicions. Come tonight to our bedroom and share my couch—you won't be hurt!" Even though Sun was filled with fear, he did not know how he could refuse, and so he slept with her as before, and their close intimacy and happy love was just as in old times.

But deep in his heart Sun remained suspicious and fearful, as if pricked in his side by a thorn. Tossing and turning, he could find no rest. Depressed and morose he fell ill, and within a year he had died. This happened in the *dingwei* year (1187) of the Chunxi reign period (1174–1189). When Zhang Sishun was in charge of Jiangkou Township in Zhenjiang County, the prefect ordered him to serve as acting magistrate, and so he learned all the facts. In the third year of the Qingyuan reign period (1195–1200) this woman had turned forty and was still alive.

---

3 One string of cash is made up of a thousand coins.
4 The family name Yuan and the word for garden (*yuan*) have the same pronunciation.

Hong Mai, *The Student Qian Yan*

Qian Yan was a student from Guangzhou and lived in the Qingfu Monastery to the south of the city. He was devoted to study and, never slackening in his resolve, would only go to bed each night after midnight. One evening a beautiful girl in a crimson skirt and green sleeves entered his room while holding a candle. She greeted him with a smile and said: "I was born in a noble family, but unfortunately I have fallen into the windy dust.[5] I have long admired you, and that's why I have decided to come to you." Yan was living all by himself in direst poverty, so when he suddenly saw such a beauty, he deemed her a gift from heaven: he invited her to spend the night with him and swore her his eternal love. At daybreak she left, but he didn't dare follow her out on the streets, so he could not know where she went. The girl excelled in song, and she had such a pleasing personality that he never had enough of her. From that moment on Yan completely neglected his earlier studies as if he had a mental disease and was out of his mind. After quite some years and months had passed the girl became pregnant.

Zhou Zizhong, a geomancer from the city, was a good friend of Yan. When he came by to visit him, he was astonished at how emaciated he had become, and when he asked him what had happened, Yan told him everything. Zizhong said: "The only rational explanation is that you are the victim of a demon! Liu Shouzhen, the priest of the Shouyi Temple, practices the correct method of the Five Thunders of the Heart of Heaven of the Ultimate Supreme, and his effectiveness in supporting and aiding those in danger and need have been spectacular. I will take you with me to see him, and we will ask him for his holy water in order to save your life. If not, you may die any moment, and then your remorse will be too late." Yan was frightened, and did not want to waste any time, so they immediately went to Liu's place. Liu quickly fetched a bowl of water, and when he looked into it after Liu had worked his magic, he saw as his reflection a huge serpent, which seemed to be recoiling in fear. Liu ground cinnabar and wrote an amulet, which he handed to Yan with the words: "Show this to the creature as soon as it appears!"

Yan went home and when he had gone to bed in the second watch of the night, the girl arrived, just as amorous as ever. But Yan said: "I now know that you are a snake spirit!" and showed her the amulet. The girl kept silent and did not utter a word, but in a while she turned into two snakes: one very large and the other still small, and these two snakes slowly made their way out of the door. Yan was frantic with fear. At break of dawn he ran to Liu to inform him of what had happened, but still he insisted on moving to another place.

The monster never appeared again.

---

[5] "The windy dust" is a common metaphor for prostitution.

APPENDIX II

West Lake Monsters

Whereas classical tales tend to be written in a laconic and factual style, vernacular stories, written in a language closer to the shared spoken language of late-imperial China and often mimicking the performance of a professional storyteller, indulged in attention to detail and exhibited a remarkable representational realism. The genre of the vernacular story had already flourished in the tenth century as we know from texts discovered at Dunhuang, but then disappeared from view again for the next few centuries. The later development of the genre can be traced from the thirteenth and fourteenth century onward. Originally, vernacular stories would appear to have been printed individually. From the seventeenth century onward vernacular stories were printed in collections. The model for such collections was set by Feng Menglong's three collections of forty vernacular stories each, published in 1620–1627, and of which Stories to Caution the World (Jingshi tongyan) *was the second. Feng Menglong's collections included both recent stories and stories that had been composed during the preceding centuries. Feng Menglong's collections, however, were not the first. In the middle of the sixteenth century the Hangzhou bibliophile and publisher Hong Bian had put out a collection of sixty stories. Hong Bian's collection is known by two titles,* Sixty Stories (Liushijia xiaoshuo) *and* Vernacular Stories from the Qingping Mountain Studio (Qingping shantang huaben). *The contents of this collection are heterogeneous in character, style, and quality, and it does not appear that the collection was a commercial success. Today only about half of its contents remain.*

One of the preserved stories is West Lake's Three Stupas (Xihu santa ji). *This story has been dated to the thirteenth or fourteenth century, and so would seem to belong to an earlier period than the story of the White Snake included by Feng Menglong in* Stories to Caution the World. *One feature that distinguishes* West Lake's Three Stupas *as an early story is its use of a poem-chain prologue. In this case the poems and lyrics all describe West Lake and its attractions, serving as a fitting introduction to the main story.*[1]

---

[1] The following translation is based on Hong Bian, 1957, 22–32. I have also consulted Chen Yizhong, 2000, 295–312.

West Lake's Three Stupas

> The glistening gleam on the lake is at its best under a clear sky,
> But mountain colors in mist and haze are even rarer in the rain.
> If you compare West Lake to the well-known beauty named West,
> Both a light makeup and many layers become her equally well.

This is a poem by Su Shi on the beauties of West Lake.[2] As these words did not fully express his ideas, he also wrote a lyric to the tune of "Charming Eyes":

> Climbing the tower I stare ahead, deep in my cups,
> And talk to a guest about the travails of travel.
> Even though you, sir, may have seen all
> Famous mountains and surpassing sights,
> None of them can compare to West Lake!
>
> The bright sky of spring,
> The rains of summer and autumn's frost
> Are followed by the snow of winter.
> The glistening gleam of the lake,
> The mountain colors all around,
> Are nowhere found in this world.

Because that still had not fully described the beauties of West Lake, let me recite a descriptive set piece:

> Since earliest times the champion scenery of Jiangnan:
> Qiantang has prospered since the beginning of history.[3]
> It doesn't only have the famous scenes of days bygone—
> You only have to look at the landscape of West Lake:

---

[2] The famous statesman and poet Su Shi (Dongpo; 1036–1101) served as prefect of Hangzhou from 1089–1091. During this time he oversaw the building of a long dike, still known as "Su's Dike," which crosses the lake from north to south and contains six bridges. The "well-known beauty called West" is better known as Xi Shi.

[3] Jiangnan refers to the region to the south of the Yangzi, roughly corresponding to the southern part of Jiangsu and the northern part of Zhejiang. Qiantang is the name of the river to the east of Hangzhou city; it is also the name of one of the two counties that share the administration of Hangzhou city.

You see a thousand *qing* of transparently blue rippling waves of glass,[4]
Surrounded by thirty miles of graciously green halcyon hills and peaks.
On the fields in the spring breeze
  Light peach and dark apricot resemble makeup;
On the lake during summer days
  Green leaves and red flowers look like a painting.
When the light of autumn has aged,
  Tender chrysanthemums by the fences amass gold,
And when the winter snow has melted,
  Sparse plum trees on the hilltops open their jade.
Flower nurseries border on wine shops;
Banner pavilions encircle fishing villages.
At the quays of willow islands
  Painted boats halt their oars and call for passengers;
In front of Prosperity Tower
  Blue linen flutters high to advertise the sale of wine.
The lofty pines for nine miles are dark green as they soar up;
The flowing water under the six bridges is blue as it ripples.
The distant sunset glow shines on the three Tianzhu Monasteries;[5]
At night the moon rises high above the southern and northern hills.
Clouds arise at the entrance to the grotto for calling the gibbons,
And birds fly across the top of the mountain of the Dragon Well.
Before the Hall of the Three Braves a thousand fathoms of blue;
In front of the Shrine of the Four Sages one mirror that floats.[6]
Observe the ancient traces of Dongbo on Su Shi's dike,
And see the old dwelling of Hejing on Orphan Island!
The monk with his tin staff has gone off to Lingyin Monastery,
And the flower seller arrives to sell his wares on Willow Bank.

Here at West Lake you have true mountains and true streams, which may be visited and enjoyed in each of the four seasons of a year. There are a few other places in this world with true mountains and true streams:

---

[4] A *qing* corresponds to roughly 6.66 hectares.

[5] The three Tianzhu Monasteries are the Lower Monastery, the Middle Monastery, and the Upper Monastery.

[6] The Hall of the Three Braves was a shrine dedicated to the memory of the poet Bai Juyi (772–846), who had once served as governor of Hangzhou; the recluse Lin Bu (Hejing; 967–1028), who lived on Orphan Island in the middle of West Lake; and Su Shi. The Shrine of the Four Sages had been established in the middle of the twelfth century in honor of the four heavenly generals.

The Golden Mountain Monastery in the Yangzi in Runzhou;
The Pavilion of the Drunken Greybeard in the Langxie Hills of Chuzhou;
The waterfall of Mt. Lu in Jiangzhou;
And the Glistening Rock in the Brocade-washing River in Sichuan.

These few places may have true mountains and true rivers, but how can they compare with the beauties of West Lake? For instance, when a storm rises, there are toppling waves of a thousand feet, and when a rain pours down, there's a heaven-scouring flood of a hundred fathoms. Even when it rains heavily for a full month, the lake never overflows, and even if there is a severe drought of more than three months, the lake never dries out. Indeed:

The one mirror of bright waves is a glistening blue;
The mountain colors all around are layers of green.
The rocks that are produced are just like fine jades;
The plants growing here are numinous mushrooms.

The visitors who arrive at spots deeply hidden by clouds and hear roosters crowing and dogs barking, the spinning of thread and the weaving of linen, believe themselves in a grotto-heaven here on earth, on the isles of the immortals in this world!

All scenery of West Lake is out of the ordinary:
Green hills layer upon layer, water overflowing.
From behind the wood one vaguely hears a shuttle,
As if people are living on those verdant slopes.

West Lake is equally lovable at dawn and at dusk, under a bright sky and in the rain, and in the moonlight:

A clear morning startles your eyes:
  The transparent and glistening
    Gleam of the whole lake;
At dusk and leaning on a balustrade
  One sees one boundless expanse
    And mountain colors in layers.
When snows falls down,
  Towers and terraces on both banks spread out their jade;
And on a moonlit night
The whole sky with its stars and planets floating like pearls.
A pair of peaks rises opposite each other in north and south;
The three Tianzhu Monasteries are hidden on verdant slopes.
When all monks and their followers have gone back home,
Flower sellers arrive to sell their wares below the willows.

Whenever it is spring there are voluptuous grasses and the rarest buds, red flowers, purple blooms, tender greens, and charming yellows. There are golden apples, jade plums, Yuexi peach trees, Xiangpu apricots, herbaceous peonies from Luoyang, and crab apples from Chengdu. There's the red bushcherry, the white tuberose, the purple lilac, and the yellow climbing rose. There's the cap-shaped tree peony and the jasmine you wear in your hair, and these are only the flowers. Then there's the water: one moment it is trembling with a color like glass, and the next moment it is rippling and gleaming with a blue sheen. If you use the water of the lake to make wine, it will be sweet; if you use it to cook your rice, it will be fragrant; if you use it to make vinegar, it will be sour; and if you use it to wash your clothes, they will be sparklingly white. As for the products of this lake: the water chestnuts are sweet, the lotus roots are crisp, the lotus flowers are tender and the fish is fresh. When the artisans who decorate bells fetch this water to create their blue and green, it will give these colors an exceptional clarity. When the owners of dye shops fetch this water, it will impart to their purple and pink an exceptional freshness. On this lake there are over a thousand painted boats that go back and forth like arrows and little craft that speed in all directions like a shuttle. If you would paint this on a fan, there are two lines of verse:

> Here was dug-out a place where fish and birds forget all sorrow;
> This unfolds the heavenly paradise of supreme joy of West Lake.

West Lake is not too deep and not too shallow, not too wide and not too distant:

> Its deepest spots can't be fathomed with a bamboo pole;
> In shallow spots one cannot move about a painted bark.
> When boating at the widest spot one does not meet,
> For coming and going the most distant spot is too far.

There is still another short descriptive set piece, which only tells the beauties of West Lake:

> The sagely monuments of the capital;
> The exceptional scenery of West Lake:[7]
> The water emerges from a deep aquifer,
> The waves fill even the most distant banks.
> A wide expanse of white waves:
>   A bounteous harvest for the whole region for a thousand years;
> Layer of layer of green mountains:
>   A source of joy for the common people during all four seasons.
> Then there are

---

[7] Hangzhou served as capital of the Southern Song dynasty (1127–1278).

The ten miles of the Long Dike,
   Where flowers shine on painted bridges,
      And willows sweep the red balustrades;
The two peaks, south and north,
   Where clouds enclose tower and terrace,
      And mists enshroud Buddhist monasteries.
Peach-blossom creeks and apricot fields;
Exceptional plants and strange flowers.
Ancient grottoes and hidden rocks,
And white stones and pure sources.
One remembers the fine lines of Su Shi,
   Who left a pure reputation for all eternity,
   Or imitates the fragrant mind of Du Fu
      To repay the charming scenery of late spring.[8]
Scions of princes and sons of dukes,
Maidens of Yue and beauties of Wu,
Sit on precious horses with silver saddles,
Ride in sedan chairs decorated with ivory;
The fine sun warms their red and green,
The tender breeze moves silk and gauze.

If it was not for the setting sun and the closing of the city gates,
They'd pursue their pleasure all through the night without end.

Below the branches of the red apricot
   And in the shadow of the green willows,
      The scenery surpasses that of Penglai and Yingzhou;[9]
Rare fragrances carried by the breeze:
   Orchids are right now in full bloom.
      As far as the eye can see peach flowers amass brocade.
All along the dikes fragrant grasses spread their carpet.
When the wind arises, the small waves are white;
When the rain is gone, the far mountains are green.
Mists enshroud the banks with their willows,
While flowers weigh down on the wall of Wulin.[10]

---

[8] The Tang-dynasty poet Du Fu (712–770) dedicated numerous poems to the scenery of the Serpentine Pond in Chang'an.

[9] Penglai and Yingzhou are two of the three floating islands of the immortals in the eastern ocean.

[10] Wulin is another name for Hangzhou.

Today I will tell you a story about a young man who had quite an adventure, all because he visited West Lake for pleasure on Clear and Bright. To this very date the monuments on West Lake still remain, and the legend has been told and retold without end.

These events happened during the Chunxi reign-period (1174–1189) of Emperor Xiaozong (reg. 1163–1189) of the Song dynasty, when outside the Yongjin Gate of Lin'an Prefecture there lived a man who had been a commander general under the command of His Excellency Yue [Fei].[11] His surname was Xi, so people all called him Commander General Xi. He had one son called Xi Xuanzan.[12] After his father the commander general had passed away, the family consisted of four people, as there was only Xuanzan's mother and his wife. And then there was an uncle, who had become a priest and studied the Way on Dragon Tiger Mountain.[13] This Xi Xuanzan was just over twenty and he never had cared about wine or sex, as he only loved to fool around. That day it happened to be the Clear and Bright Festival. What did it look like?

>The weather is now rain, then sunshine;
>The temperature is not cold and not hot.
>The delicate tender greens
>   Look as if cut from oh-so-thin light silk;
>Those graceful light reds—
>   Aren't they like made from oh-so-bright fine brocade?
>While the yellow orioles, wagging their tongue, sing in the next garden,
>The powdered butterflies, following the scent, circle carved balustrades.

Xi Xuanzan thought: "Today is the day of the Clear and Bright Festival. All beauties and poets are enjoying the sights of West Lake, so let me go there too and take in the scenery of the lake and have some fun." So he went to the hall and told his mother: "Today I want to go to West Lake to have some fun. Is that fine with you?" His mother replied: "My son, that is no problem as long as you make sure to come back early."

---

11   Yue Fei (1103–1142) was one of the major generals supporting the Southern Song dynasty. When the central government decided to abandon its attempts to recapture Northern China and pursue peace with the Jin dynasty, Yue Fei was recalled to the capital and killed. In later centuries Yue Fei would be venerated as a great patriot.

12   Xuanzan, though used as if it were a personal name, actually may well be a designation of a low court functionary.

13   Dragon Tiger Mountain (*Longhushan*) was the location of the main temple of the Zhengyi Daoist lineage, headed by members of the Zhang family.

When Xi Xuanzan had obtained his mother's permission, he left the house all by himself, carrying his crossbow. After he had left the city though the Qiantang Gate and passed the Zhaoqing Monastery, he went to the location of the Water Mill. And when he passed in front of the Temple of the Four Sages at Broken Bridge, he saw a bustling crowd of people, all standing in a circle. When Xuanzan pushed those people aside, he saw a girl. How was she dressed?

> The hair on her head was done up in three tufts,
> Which were tied up with three strips of red silk.
> In them she wore three short hairpins of gold.
> From top to toe her whole body
>   Was dressed in an outfit of mourning white.

This little girl had lost her way. When Xuanzan saw this, he stepped forward and asked her: "To which family do you belong, and where do you live?" The girl said: "My surname is Bai and I live on the lake.[14] I came here with my grandmother for a walk, but my grandmother has disappeared, and now I've lost my way." She promptly stepped forward, grasped Xi Xuanzan by his clothes, and said: "I know this gentleman! He lives next to us!" All she did was weep, and she refused to let him go, so Xuanzan could only take this girl with him, board a boat, disembark at the Yongjin Gate, and tell his mother when he got home. His mother said: "My son, you went out for some fun, so why are you bringing this girl back with you?" Xuanzan told his mother the whole story: "I did this out of charity. If people come and claim her, we will return her."

This little girl was called Maonu, and from that moment on she lived at their house. Soon more than ten days had passed. Then one day when Xuanzan was having his meal, he heard quite a commotion outside the gate of the house, and he saw that in a sedan chair carried by four carriers an old lady had arrived. When he observed the old lady, this is how she looked:

> A chicken skin covered her body;
> Her crane hair resembled silver.
> Her hazy eyes resembled slightly muddied autumn streams;
> Her white hair was like the thin clouds on Mt. Shamanka.
> Her body resembled the faded flowers of the Third Month;
> Her fate was like the late autumn's frozen chrysanthemum.

When the old woman stepped down from her sedan chair, Xuanzan noticed that she was dressed all in black. When Maonu from behind the screen saw this old woman, she called out: "Granny, I'm here!" The old woman said: "You had me worried sick! Asking from door to door I got here. But who was the one

---

14   The surname Bai is written with the character *bai* (white).

who saved you?" Maonu replied: "This gentleman was so kind as to save me and take care of me." The old woman then greeted Xuanzan, who asked her inside to have a cup of tea, but the old woman said: "Now he has been so kind as to save you from great danger, we should invite Xuanzan to our house and treat him to some wine in order to express our thanks." The old woman ascended the sedan chair—after she had thanked his mother, she ascended the sedan chair with Maonu. Following the sedan chair, Xi Xuanzan arrived at a small gate-building to the side of the Temple of the Four Sages. When Xi Xuanzan stood before the gate, he saw:

> Golden nails covered the door
> And green tiles filled the eaves.
> All around the place red paint and plastered walls;
> On both sides carved balustrades and jade steps.
>   It was exactly like
> The grotto-mansion of immortals,
> The palatial dwelling of a prince!

The old woman took Xi Xuanzan inside, and once inside he saw a woman dressed in white, who came out to welcome him. When Xuanzan observed her carefully, she truly looked like this:

> Dark clouds amassed as hair;
> White clouds congealed as skin.
> Eyes like wide waves of autumn streams;
> Eyebrows like the rising jet of spring hills.
> Peach buds—the light makeup on pink cheeks;
> A cherry pearl—the small dot on her red lips.
> Her linen shoes set off her oh-so-small golden lotuses;[15]
> Her jade fingers showed oh-so-slender bamboo shoots.

As soon as this woman saw Maonu, she asked the old woman: "Where did you find my daughter?" The old woman then told her the whole story of Xuanzan and Maonu. The woman then exchanged some courtesies with Xuanzan, and they sat down as guest and host, while two girl servants dressed in blue provided them with wine. In a little while all dishes of land and sea were set out. What did it look like?

> In goblets of transparent glass drops like pearls dripped down;
> Dragon and phoenix were cooked and roasted: the jade lard cried.
> Gauze curtains and brocade screens engendered a fragrant breeze;
> While iguana drums were struck and dragon pipes were blown.

---

[15] Bound feet are often referred to as golden lotuses.

At the banquet he was urged to drink till too drunk to stand;
Brilliant teeth sang their songs while slender waists danced.
In truth, a day of greening spring when the sun was setting:
Peach blossoms were swirling down just like a rain of reds.

One cup was then two bowls, and a third cup of wine had been served. When Xi Xuanzan looked more closely at the woman, she was as beautiful as a flower and as white as jade, so his heart and mind were shaken and moved. But when he asked the woman for her name, he saw someone step forward and ask: "Milady, can we exchange the old one now a new groom has arrived today?" The woman said: "Yes, that is fine. Set to work quickly so Xuanzan will have a snack to go with his wine." That very moment he saw two giants grab a young man, remove his cap and girdle, unbind the hair on his head, and tie him to the general's pillar,[16] with in front of him one silver basin and one sharp knife. In a flash they cut open the skin of his belly and took out his heart and liver, which they presented to Her Ladyship, scaring Xuanzan so much that his souls left his body! Her Ladyship poured out some hot wine and invited Xuanzan to taste the heart and liver. Xuanzan could only pretend that he had had enough, but Her Ladyship and the old woman ate with gusto. Her Ladyship then said to Xuanzan: "I am deeply grateful that you saved my little daughter. Now my husband has passed away, I would like to become your wife!" Indeed:

Spring is the connoisseur of flowers,
And wine is the matchmaker for sex.

That night the two of them went hand in hand to the orchid chamber.

When that night had passed, Her Ladyship kept Xuanzan with her for over half a month. His face became sallow and his body lost weight, so he became homesick and said: "Milady, let me go home for a few days, and then I'll be back." Before he had finished saying this, someone entered and reported: "Milady, can we exchange the old one now the new groom has arrived?" Her Ladyship said: "Yes, please do so!" A number of giants arrived before her, escorting a young man. How was he dressed?

His eyebrows wide, his eyes brilliant;
His energy vibrant, his spirit so pure!
Like Ma Chao of the Three Kingdoms;
Resembling Guan Suo from Huaitian;[17]

---

[16] Upper-class Chinese men wore their hair long. The "general's pillar" is a standing post to which a condemned person is tied when he or she is to be executed.

[17] Ma Chao is one of the generals who served under Liu Bei. Guan Suo is the son of Liu Bei's sworn brother Guan Yu, and a great warrior.

> Like a living Avalokitesvara from Sichuan,
> The Fiery Spirit Lord in a Taishan Temple![18]

Her Ladyship invited that man to sit with her and have some wine, and ordered the giants to take out Xuanzan's heart and liver. At that time Xuanzan's three souls were dispersed in all directions, and he could only go and beg Maonu: "Little girl, I once saved your life, please now save mine!" Maonu went up to Her Ladyship and said: "Dear mother, he once saved my life, so please forgive him." Her Ladyship said: "Lock him up in that thing!" You then saw a giant get out an iron cage, and place it over Xuanzan, who felt as if pressed down by a mountain. Her Ladyship and that other young man went off to become man and wife.

Maonu said from the outside of the cage: "I will save you!" She lifted the iron cage up and said: "Now close your eyes, because if you open your eyes, you will die a cruel death." When she had said this, Xuanzan closed his eyes, and Maonu took him on her back. Xuanzan heard the sounds of wind and rain, and with his arms around her neck he felt that she was covered in feathers, so he thought to himself: "This is strange!" One moment later he heard Maonu shout: "We have landed!" But when he opened his eyes and looked around, she was nowhere to be seen and he found himself on top of the city wall at the Qiantang Gate just before daybreak. How did it look?

> The Northern Dipper was tilting sideways,
> And the eastern sky was slowly brightening.
> The neighbor's rooster crowed three times,
>   Waking the beauty to apply powder and make her toilette;
> The precious horses whinnied repeatedly,
>   Urging people to hurry toward the arena of fame and profit.
> A few morning clouds stretched along the azure welkin,
> While a single red sun ascended the supporting mulberry.[19]

He oh-so-slowly followed the road to the Yongjin Gate, and arrived in front of his own house. As soon as his wife opened the gate, she said: "Xuanzan, how come you only come back more than half a month after seeing that girl off? Your mother was worried sick all day!"

When his mother heard them, she came out. Seeing how sallow his face was and how much weight he had lost, his mother said: "Why did you stay away for so long?" Xuanzan said: "I almost never would have seen you again!" And then

---

[18] In his male manifestation, the bodhisattva Avalokitesvara is usually depicted as a handsome young prince. The equally handsome Fiery Spirit Lord is the third son of the Grand Thearch of the Eastern Marchmound (the divinity of Mt. Tai and a ruler of the underworld).

[19] At dawn the sun ascends by the sky by climbing the supporting mulberry tree.

he told the whole story to his mother from the very beginning. She was very scared and said: "My son, I understand what is going on. This place here is the water outlet of the Yongjin Gate. It must be that the water outlet is blocked, and that's why this has happened. You take your rest to recover, and I will find us another house where we can move to." Soon one day she had found an empty house at the Zhaoqing Monastery bay, and after they had selected a lucky day and a good hour they moved there. Xuanzan recovered completely.

Light and shade quickly sped by, and soon another year had passed, and the Clear and Bright Festival was approaching. What did it look like?

> Every family prohibits fire now the flowers contain flames;[20]
> Each and every house hides smoke as willows spit out mist.
> Horses with golden bridles whinny—fields of fragrant grasses;
> On jade towers people are drinking—an apricot-blossom sky.

Xi Xuanzan thought: "Last year when I went out for some fun I ran into that woman, and now another year has passed!" That very day Xuanzan took his crossbow and left his house through the back door to look for birds by the willows. In one of the trees he saw a creature call, and when he looked, it was that bird that all people hate when they see it. How did it look?

> When the hundred other birds sing, people are pleased,
> But what happens when the crow starts to raise its voice?
> Those who see the bird all hate it, those who hear it spit,
> Because in earlier days it has been jabbering too much.

So it was a crow. Xi Xuanzan placed an arrow on the bow, and after he had taken aim, the arrow flew off and hit that crow! It made some violent jumps, and once on the ground it transformed itself into an old woman dressed in back. The old woman said: "Xuanzan, you escaped, and then you moved to this place!" Xuanzan shouted: "A ghost!" Turning around, he ran away, but the old woman said: "Xuanzan, where are you going?" And she shouted: "Come down!" A cart fell down from the sky, together with some ghost servants. The old woman said: "Grab him and put him in the cart. Close your eyes! If you do not close your eyes, I'll make sure you die a violent death!" The fragrant cart rose from the earth like a leaf, and straightaway he arrived again at the earlier gate building near the Temple of the Four Sages, where they descended.

The old woman escorted Xuanzan to the hall, where he saw the woman dressed in white come down from the hall, saying: "Xuanzan, you managed to escape!"

---

[20] Clear and Bright coincides with (and eventually replaced) the Cold Food Festival, which was celebrated on the third day of the Third Month and following. On the Cold Food Festival people would not light a fire for cooking for three days, hence the name.

Xuanzan said: "Your Ladyship, I beg you to forgive me!" Again she kept Xuanzan with her to have sex with him.

After over half a month Xuanzan said: "My Lady, I am afraid that my old mother will be filled with worry, so let me go and see her and then I will come back again." When Her Ladyship had heard this, her willow-eyebrows were drawn erect, and her starry eyes bulged with rage, as she said: "You still long to go home!" And she shouted: "Demon servants, where are you? Get me his heart and liver!" She gave the order to have Xuanzan tied to the general's pillar. Xuanzan cried at the top of his voice for Maonu: "I saved you once—why don't you save me now?" Maonu begged her mother: "He saved me once, so don't have him killed!" Her Ladyship said: "You little slut, there you come again to talk me around. Have him placed under the chicken coop. That will finish off his life!" The demon servant untied him and placed him under the iron cage.

Xuanzan called on Heaven which did not respond, and called on Earth which did not listen. But when he was overcome by despair, he saw Maonu at the side of the cage, saying: "Brother, I will save you once more!" She then lifted the iron cage and said: "Close your eyes, and throw your arms around me." Xuanzan once again threw his arms around Maonu, and heard the sounds of wind and rain. After a moment Maonu shouted: "You're landing!" She threw down Xuanzan, who fell into a water chestnut patch. As he opened his eyes he shouted: "Save me!" You quickly saw two people pulling Xuanzan from the water. As he told them his whole story, these two men said: "That's too weird! This young man must be bewitched! Where do you live?" Xuanzan told him he lived near the Zhaoqing Monastery bay, and the two men took him back home. When his mother heard about this, she came outside to greet these two men, and the water chestnut growers told her how they had saved Xuanzan. His mother was overcome with joy and got some wine to reward these two men, whereupon they left. Xuanzan once again told his story to his mother, who said: "My son, now don't go outside anymore!"

After a few days, on a day when Xuanzan's mother was standing behind the screen, she saw that the screen was lifted as someone walked in, and a Daoist priest entered. How was he dressed?

> His crown was divided into two buffalo-horn hair-tufts;
> His body was wrapped in a short brown Bashan jacket.
> His facial expression was dignified,
> And his bearing was awe-imposing.
> You'd think he was one of the Three Purities of the world above;
> He must be a transcendent visitor from the Isles of the Immortals.[21]

She looked him over and said: "Brother-in-law, it has been quite some time,

---

[21] The Three Purities are the highest divinities in the Daoist pantheon.

so what brings you here today?" This Daoist priest was indeed the younger brother of Commander General Xi, the Immortal Xi, who had just returned from Dragon Tiger Mountain, and who said: "Sister-in-law, how come you have moved to this place?" Xuanzan also came out of his room to greet his uncle. The priest said: "I saw some black ether rising to the west of the city of an evil demon pestering someone, and when I came to pursue it, it turned out to correspond to your house!" Xuanzan's mother told the full story of what had happened, and the priest said: "Nephew, these three demons are really pestering you." Xuanzan's mother had a vegetarian meal prepared, and invited the immortal to dinner. Afterward he said: "Tomorrow I will be distributing amulets in the Temple of the Four Sages, and you should also come and ask me for some. Also write a statement of formal accusation for deposition at the altar. I have to sentence these demons." Then the immortal left.

The next day Xuanzan and his mother bought incense and paper images and wrote out a statement of formal accusation for deposition at the altar. After they had closed the gate, they asked the neighbors to keep an eye on their house and went straightaway to the Temple of the Four Sages. Once the immortal had submitted the accusation and consulted [the divination blocks], he said: "Wait till tonight, and then I will deal with them." First he had Xuanzan drink some holy water and give up the demon's spittle. When evening fell, the priest lit lamps and candles, lit incense and again and again recited his incantations. He also wrote out magical amulets which he burned in a candle. Then suddenly a black wind arose. What did it look like?

> The wind,
> The wind:
> It moves the leaves;
> It scatters the petals.
> Now it comes from south or north;
> Then it comes from east or west.
> In spring it makes the willows sprout;
> In fall it robs the wutong of its foliage.
> Cooling, it enters the doors of rich mansions,
> Chilly, it also penetrates the humblest homes.
>
> Even Chang'e hastily closes the gate of her Toad Palace;
> Master Lie rides up to the sky, asking to save the people![22]

When that wind had passed, a divine warrior appeared. How was he dressed?

---

[22] Chang'e, the goddess of the moon, lives in a world of ice. The moon is also inhabited by a toad. Master Lie (Liezi) is able to ride the wind.

> His face had the dark color of the double date;
> Shooting stars brilliantly flashed from his eyes.
> His gown of black silk was encrusted with clustered flowers,
> His red headband was embroidered with a fierce tiger in gold.
> In his hand he carried a sword decorated with the seven jewels,
> Around his waist he wore a belt of the green jade from Lantian.

The divine warrior reported for duty, asking for his orders from the priest. The immortal said: "Arrest those three demons in the lake!" The divine warrior said, "Yes, sir!" and he had not been gone for long, when the arrested granny, Maonu, and the woman dressed in white all appeared before the immortal.

The immortal said: "You are demons, so how do you dare harm the son of a duly appointed official?" The three of them answered: "They should not have blocked our water gate. We beg you, sir, to forgive us, as we never harmed his life!" The immortal said: "Manifest your original shape!" Maonu begged Xuanzan: "I never did you any harm, so please don't force me to show my original shape!" The immortal ordered the divine warrior to give them a beating, and everything was fine as long as he had not yet beaten them, but as soon as he had hit them a few times, that Maonu turned into a black chicken; the old woman turned out to be an otter, and the woman dressed in white a snake! Immortal Xi said: "Get me some iron jugs, and lock these three demons in them!" When the warrior had done so, he sealed the opening with an amulet, and sank the jugs in the middle of the lake.

Immortal Xi then collected donations and had three stone stupas constructed to keep these demons captured in the lake. To this day these ancient monuments still exist. Xuanzan became his uncle's disciple, and with his mother he lived like a cleric while staying at home, and lived till the age of one hundred.

> Because three demons emerged in the lake,
> The immortal was induced to visit this place.
> Today they are captured and hidden in a jug,
> Ensuring a safe peace for thousands of years.

The Three Stupas, the end.

APPENDIX III

The White Snake on Stage

The legend of the White Snake is to this day a very popular subject for traditional Chinese drama. It is found in the repertoire of almost all genres of regional opera of recent centuries. Its revision as a Peking opera by Tian Han (1898–1968) enjoyed great popularity in the 1950s in the People's Republic of China, and greatly influenced the dramatic versions in other genres as well. Tian Han's adaptation, which is available in at least two English translations, follows the tradional plot up to the White Snake's imprisonment under Thunder Peak Pagoda. Tian Han turns the White Snake into a fierce warrior against traditional patriarchy and religious authority in the pursuit of free love. The final scene of Tian Han's play depicts the destruction of Thunder Peak Pagoda and the liberation of the White Snake by the united army of water creatures under the leadership of the Blue Snake.

The Legend of the White Snake probably was adapted for the stage as early as the sixteenth century. He Xuejun mentions three titles of play scripts dating from the sixteenth century,[1] citing as his authority an article by Shen Zu'an, but Shen Zu'an mentions only one of these three titles in the article concerned, claiming that the manuscript concerned belonged to Dai Bufan.[2] Dai Bufan, however, does not mention this play in his own writings on the legend of the White Snake,[3] and if the manuscript does still exist, its present whereabouts are unknown. We are on safer ground when it comes to Chen Liulong's Thunder Peak (Leifeng ji). *This play, now lost, is listed by Qi Biaojia (1602–1645) in his* Classification of Plays from the Far Mountain Hall (Yuanshantang jupin). *From the eighteenth century we have three different plays, all entitled* Thunder Peak Pagoda (Leifeng ta): *one by Huang Tubi (1700–1771), which closely follows the story as printed by Feng Menglong; one as performed by the famous Yangzhou actor Chen Jiayan and his daughter, which includes the birth of Mengjiao and his liberation of his mother; and one more by Fang Chengpei, who provided a more literary version of the popular stage version. It is this latter*

---

[1] He Xuejun, 1995, 64 note 4.

[2] Shen Zu'an, 1983.

[3] Dai Bufan, 1956.

version that is highly praised by many critics in the People's Republic of China, as it almost completely does away with "the demonic air" of Bai Suzhen and stresses her pure love for Xu Xian.

The following three summaries of these eighteenth-century plays, together with the short biographies of the authors, and the discussion of the sources of the plays and their interrelations, have been translated from Guo Yingde's A Comprehensive Record of the Chuanqi Plays of the Ming and the Qing Dynasties (Ming Qing chuanqi zonglu) of 1997, pp. 933–36; 1019–20; 1010–11. Whenever possible, Guo Yingde precedes a discussion of the play proper with a summary of the available biographical information on the author. The discussion of the play itself starts with a listing of early references, proceeds to a detailed summary of the plot, and is concluded by further comments. I have inserted subtitles in the translations in order facilitate reading. I have also added some notes.

I

Huang Tubi's *Thunder Peak Pagoda*

About the Author

Huang Tubi. Style Rongzhi. Pseudonyms: Banana Window Layman; the Master Who Guards the Truth. A person from Songjiang (now part of Shanghai City). He was born in the thirty-ninth year of the Kangxi reign (1700) and died after the thirty-sixth year of the Qianlong reign (1771). He was a student by hereditary privilege. In the sixth year of the Yongzheng reign (1728) he visited the capital to apply for selection to a post and was appointed as the vice prefect of Hangzhou prefecture and reassigned as assistant prefect of Huzhou. In the fifth year of the Qianlong reign (1740) he was upon evaluation appointed as vice prefect of Quzhou and reassigned as vice prefect of Weihui prefecture in Henan. In the nineteenth year of the Qianlong reign (1754) he came to the capital upon the completion of his term to be received in audience by the emperor. He was skilled in poetry and prose and excelled in lyrics and arias. He composed seven *chuanqi* plays: *Leifeng ta, Xiyun shi, Mengchai yuan, Jie jindiao, Wenrouxiang,* and *Shuangzhi ji,* which have been preserved, and *Meihua jian,* which has not been preserved. Collectively they are known as the *Complete Collection of the Depression-Dispelling Studio (Paiminzhai chuanqi)* or *Musical Plays of the Pavilion for Seeing the Mountains (Kanshange yuefu).*

Thunder Peak Pagoda (Leifeng ta)

Editions

This title is listed in *Catalogue of the Ocean of Plays (Quhai mu,)* where it is classified as an anonymous *chuanqi* of the Qing. The same is the case in the *Inquiry into Plays (Qukao)* and the *List of Plays (Qulu,)* so I am afraid these listings may not refer to Huang's play. The edition of the play included in the *Kanshange quanji,* which was printed in the Qianlong reign of the Qing has been preserved, and is found in libraries such as the Tianjin tushuguan. It is titled *Leifeng ta,* and lists the author as the Banana Window Layman of Fengmao. It is preceded by a preface by the author (*zixu*) which is stated to have been "written in the Ergui Studio at Qiantang by the Banana Window Layman of Fengmao on the twelfth day of the Eighth Month of the third year of the Qianlong reign (1738)." The play consists of thirty-two scenes divided over two *juan*.

Summary

The play tells that Xu Xian from Hangzhou on the basis of his birth ranking is also called Xiaoyi (Little Two). His father and mother both have died. He lives therefore with his brother-in-law Li Ren who is serving as a clerk of the Southern Corridor Cabinet Vault, and works as a first assistant in the pharmacy of his uncle Li Jiangshi. At the Clear and Bright Festival he goes to Baoshu Monastery to make offering for the well-being of his parents, and on his way back home he hires on West Lake the boat of Zhang Agong to take him to the Yongjin Gate. At that very moment a thousand-year-old snake spirit of the Eastern Main who has transformed herself into a young widow and calls herself Ms. Bai, and who has ordered a blue fish (black carp) to change into a servant clad in blue whom she calls Little Blue, arrives at the West Lake. She waits till Xu's boat passes by, and asks to be taken on board. In the boat they fall in love with each other and Ms. Bai makes an appointment with Xu to meet her at the entrance of Double Tea Lane at Jian Bridge. When Xu arrives, Little Blue acts as the matchmaker, and they agree to get married, wherupon she gives him two ingots of silver. It happens that fifty ingots have gone missing from the vault of Commander Shao, and posters are put up for the arrest of the criminal. When Li Ren sees that the silver Xu is bringing home is part of the missing silver, he reports the matter to the authorities. When interrogated by the prefect, Xu provides a detailed account of the facts, whereupon they set out to arrest Ms. Bai. The government's silver is recovered, but Ms. Bai and Little Blue suddenly disappear. Ms. Bai returns to the West Lake, where all water creatures complain about being netted by a fisherman. When Ms. Bai strongly berates the fisherman, he is saved by the intervention of the Chan master Fahai.[4]

Because of this case of the stolen silver Xu Xian is banished to Suzhou, where he becomes an assistant in the shop of Mr. Wang, and the latter and his wife treat him very well. Then one day Ms. Bai and Little Blue suddenly arrive and come up with a convincing explanation, whereupon Ms. Bai and Xu get married. When a Daoist priest of the Sleeping Buddha Monastery sees Xu, he says that he is bewitched by demons and gives him an amulet. Ms. Bai asks to be allowed to eat the amulet but nothing weird happens, so Xu harbors no suspicions anymore. But Little Blue kidnaps the priest and chases him away. Already earlier the crab spirits and turtle spirits of West Lake had stolen the precious goods in the vault of the lombard of Zhou Jiangshi, and offered these to Ms. Bai. On the Day of the Bathing of the Buddha, Xu goes to the Chengtian Monastery to

---

[4] The episode of lady Bai's return to West Lake and Fahai's intercession of behalf of the fishermen is one of the few additions of Huang Tubi to the plot provided by the vernacular story. He probably inserted this episode in order to enable Fahai to appear relatively early in the play, in accordance with the genre requirements of *chuanqi*.

amuse himself, carrying a coral fan-pendant that had been given to him by Ms. Bai, whereupon he is arrested by police officers. Ms. Bai quickly orders the crab spirits and others to return the stolen goods, and claiming that she goes looking for Xu, she disappears from the shop.

The government clerks at Suzhou thereupon banish Xu Xian to Zhenjiang, where he becomes an assistant in the pharmacy of Li Keyong. But Ms. Bai and Little Blue, tracing his steps, also arrive in Zhenjiang and following their smart explanation they again move in with Xu. Because Li Keyong has fallen in love with Ms. Bai's beauty, he wishes to have his way with her, so one day when they are drinking he tells a maid to take Ms. Bai to the back garden. But when Keyong is about to rape her, he suddenly sees her original shape as a huge snake, and is terrified. Xu, not knowing this, takes his leave of Keyong and opens his own pharmacy. On the seventh day of the Seventh Month, the birthday of the dragon king, Xu goes by himself to Golden Mountain Monastery for amusement. Afraid that he will suffer a disaster at the hands of the monks, Ms. Bai and Little Blue go and look for him. That very moment Fahai is preaching the Dharma in that monastery, and lifting his tin staff he scares Ms. Bai away and orders Xu to go back home.

Benefiting from an amnesty, Xu Xian returns to Hangzhou, but Ms. Bai and Little Blue have already arrived there before him. Xu insists on calling Ms. Bai a snake demon and with Li Ren he goes to the White Horse Temple, where they invite Master Dai to come and catch this snake, but Ms. Bai makes a fool of Master Dai. As a last resort, Xu goes to the Jingci Monastery to the south of the lake and asks Fahai to capture this demon. Fahai orders a divine guardian to fight Ms. Bai, and upon her defeat he captures the two demons in his begging bowl. Fahai takes Xu with him to Thunder Peak Monastery, where they bury these two demons, and place a stupa on top of them to pin them down. Xu wishes to shave his hair and leave the family, and begging for donations, he makes plans to build a seven-story pagoda to suppress these demons for all eternity. When his merit is accomplished, he is led by Weituo to the land of Ultimate Bliss.

Further Comments

The story of the White Snake originated as a folktale and was already well known during the Song dynasty. In *Poems on Miscellaneous Subjects of the Southern Song Dynasty (Nan Song zashi shi)*[5] we find a poem by Chen Zhiguang on Thunder Peak Pagoda, which states: "I've heard it said the Thunder Platform covers a monstrous snake." The commentary quotes the *Xiaochuang ziji* by Wu Congxian

---

[5] The *Nan Song zazhi shi* is an anthology of poems written in the second half of the seventeenth century on topics related to the Southern Song dynasty.

of the Ming dynasty, which states: "In Song times a master of magic stored the white snake in his bowl and buried it under the Thunder Peak Pagoda."[6] The *West Lake Rambles* (*Xihu youlan zhi*) by Tian Rucheng of the Ming dynasty, ch. 3, "The Scenes of the Southern Hills," when describing Thunder Peak Pagoda, also states: "According to popular tradition there lived two monsters in the lake, a white snake and a blue fish, which are pinned down under this pagoda." The *West Lake Rambles, A Sequel* (*Xihu youlan zhiyu*), in the chapter "Pleasures of a Prosperous Era" ("Xichao leshi") by the same author in its ch. 20, further states: "The blind men and women of Hangzhou often learn to play the lute and to sing stories and tales of past and present in order to make a living, and this is called *taozhen*. Most of the time they tell stories of the Song dynasty. It must be an old tradition from Kaifeng. ... Now stories of Red Lotus, Liu Cui, Jidian, Thunder Peak Pagoda, and the Double-Fish Fan-Pendant are all Hangzhou legends, or stories made up in imitation in recent times." Thus the story of the White Snake was already quite popular in Ming dynasty times. Chen Liulong of the Ming dynasty wrote a *chuanqi* play entitled *Thunder Peak* (*Leifeng ji*), but that has been lost. It is recorded in the *Classification of Plays from the Far Mountain Hall* (*Yuanshantang qupin*), which states: "Legend has it that the Thunder Peak Pagoda was built to pin down the demon lady Bai. It would have been doable to turn this into a short play, but now it is a full play, it lacks any coherence, so how could it capture the attention of the audience? Its language also wants to imitate splendid fullness, but there are many lapses." Ch. 28 of *Stories to Caution the World* (*Jingshi tongyan*) of Feng Menglong of the Ming dynasty consists of the vernacular story *Bai Niangzi yongzhen Leifengta*. Its incidents and characters are already relatively complete. Ch. 15 of Molangzi's *Fine Tales about West Lake* (*Xihua jiahua*), "The Miracle at Thunder Peak" ("Leifeng guaiji") is an abbreviation of this vernacular story.

This play is an adaptation of the vernacular story. The "Short Introduction" to "Actors Asked Me to Allow My Newly Composed Play, *Cloud-Dwelling Rock* (*Xiyun shi chuanqi*) to Circulate in the World" in ch. 4 of "Nanqu" in his *Complete Collection of the Pavillion for Seeing the Mountains* (*Kanshange quanji*) states: "My *Thunder Peak* is all bizarre fantasy, but I borrowed the words of earlier writers and turned it into song to amuse the eyes and please the heart with its purple flutes and red fifes in the leisure left after watching the hills and drinking wine. The incidents and characters in general follow the vernacular story with a few embellishments." According to the author's preface, the play was completed in the Eighth Month of the third year of the Qianlong reign (1738). The "Introduction" to "Watching a performance of the *chuanqi* play *Thunder Peak Pagoda*" in ch. 4 of

---

[6] This is a quotation from Wu Congxian's *Record of a Visit to West Lake* (*You Xihu ji*), in *Xiaochuang ziji* 4:49a (773).

"Nanqu" in *Kanshange quanji* states: "I wrote the *chuanqi* play *Thunder Peak Pagoda*. In total it has thirty-two scenes, from 'Compassionate Sounds' to 'Enlightenment at the Pagoda.' As soon as I had finished the draft, actors begged me for it so they could perform it." In the "Short Introduction" to "Actors asked me to allow my newly composed *Xiyun shi chuanqi* to circulate in the world" he also states: "Immediately it became quite popular and spread all over Wu and Yue." The author decribed his intention in writing the play as follows:

> The chattering birds seem to talk; the flowers seem to smile,
> Let me try to play the iron flute to come up with a new tune.
> Why should you take this tale to be true?
> So don't ask the fisherman for the ford.
>
> I love to hear the idles stories of ghosts,
> My addiction is the identical to Dongpo.[7]
> Don't say that I have made up these lies,
> It's all because of a passion too simple.
>
> (Scene I, "Compassionate Sounds," to the tune of *Pusaman*)

Once this play was performed, it was reworked by the actors. The "Introduction" to "Watching a performance of the *chuanqi* play *Thunder Peak Pagoda*" states "Thereupon there were meddlers who continued the play with the White Snake giving birth to a son who achieves the first rank. By slavishly adhering to the old conventions of the theater, they greatly pleased the eyes and ears of the audience. It became all the rage in Wu and Yue and even reached Yan and Zhao. Alas, it is the common feeling of this age that a performance can have no happy ending unless there is a top-of-the-list, and I too would not have been able to avoid this custom if I by chance would just follow the crowd. But why is it that in this play it definitely cannot be done? Lady Bai is a demon snake, and if he would enter the rank of the literati, where would that leave us? I thought that the audiences would cover their nose to avoid this dirty stench, and I could not predict that all of a sudden at wine meetings and song parties the rewards for the actors would increase. This truly is something beyond my understanding. … But in Suzhou there still are people who perform the play according to the text, without changing a single character, but alas, they do not find favor with the world, because there is no top-of-the-list happy ending."

---

[7] Dongpo is one of the sobriquets of the poet Su Shi.

Later Adaptations

In the middle of the Qianlong reign there appeared in succession the old theater manuscript *Thunder Peak Pagoda* by Chen Jiayan and his daughter, and *Thunder Peak Pagoda* by Fang Chengpei and printed by his Shuizhuju, which replaced the version by Huang and became popular in their age. As for string ballads (*tanci*) we have the *Newly Printed Eastern Tune Tale of the White Snake of Thunder Peak Pagoda*, which completely follows the vernacular story of Feng Menglong, and which is preserved in an old printed edition and in an edition printed by the Yijingtang in the Jiaqing reign (1796–1819). We also have a *tanci* entitled *The Virtuous Seductress*, which claims to be the original draft of Chen Yuqian as edited by Chen Shiqi and Yu Xiushan. It has been preserved in a printed edition of the *jisi* year of the Tongzhi reign (1869), and in general is smilar to the actors' play. Chen Shiqi was a Suzhou man of the Qianlong reign, and Yu Xiuzhan was a Suzhou man of the Jiaqing period.

In the youth books (*zidishu*) of the north we encounter "Thunder Peak Pagoda"; in Shandong in *qinshu* we find "The Tale of the White Snake"; among precious scrolls we find "The Virtuous Seductress"; and in the *muyuge* [wooden fish songs of Guangdong] we encounter "The story of the White Snake of Thunder Peak Pagoda." In recent times, Peking opera, Sichuan opera, Yunnan opera, Fujian opera, Hubei opera, Shaoxing opera, Cantonese opera, Jiangxi opera, *pingju*, Yangzhou opera, Wuxi opera, *wuju*, *tuiju*, *huangmeixi*, and shadow opera all perform "The Tale of the White Snake." In Qinjiang we have "Thunder Peak Pagoda"; in Xiangju, Hanju, Hebei bangzi, and Tongzhou bangzi we encounter "Broken Bridge." In Lüju we have "Submerging Golden Mountain in a Flood" and "Giving Birth to a Son at Broken Bridge." In the Xiangju of Hengyang we have "Submerging Golden Mountain in a Flood" and "The Meeting at Broken Bridge." In Shaoxing Gaoqiang we have "Submerging in a Flood" and "Offering at the Pagoda," and in Goajiaxi one finds "Xu Xian Offers his Apologies." All these are based on the actors' play and the *tanci*, and have no relation to the play by Huang.

2

The Actors' *Thunder Peak Pagoda*

Early References

This title is listed in *Research on Modern Plays (Jinyue kaozheng)*. It has been preserved in old manuscripts, which are found at Beijing Library and elsewhere. No author is given. According to tradition this is the version as performed in the Qianlong reign by the famous clown of the Kunqiang Old Xu Company Chen Jiayan and his daughter. When describing the actors of the Old Xu Company in his *A Record of the Painted Barges of Yangzhou (Yangzhou huafang lu)*, Li Dou writes: "Chen Jiayan was by far the best of the *sanmian* (clowns). As soon as he appeared on stage, he had people doubling over with laughter. Later he joined the Hong Company together with [Qian] Peilin." The play has thirty-eight scenes in total.

Summary

The play tells that on Mt. Emei there is a white snake, who has stolen and eaten the peaches of immortality of the Queen Mother of the West. Following self-cultivation she has become the White Cloud Immortal Maiden. Because she has not yet cut off herself from carnal longings, she descends to the mortal world. Arriving in Hangzhou, she subdues the blue snake, the leader of the water creatures, and makes her her maid.

Xu Xian, who hails from Tonglu in Yanzhou, and who has lost both his parents, is living with his brother-in-law, the Qiantang police officer Li Ren (style Junfu), and is a clerk in the pharmacy of Millionaire Wang in Iron Thread Lane. On the day of Clear and Bright, Xu goes and sweeps the graves of his parents. On his way back he runs into a shower, and stops a boat on the bank of the West Lake. The White Snake, who has changed herself into an upper-class young lady and claims to be the daughter of Prefect Bai of Hangzhou, asks to be taken on board together with Little Blue. In the boat, the two of them fall in love, and they say good-bye only after agreeing on a date for a later meeting.

The next day, when Xu Xian visits Ms. Bai, they agree to marry each other, and he returns home with the hundred tael of silver Ms. Bai has given him. Xu asks his brother-in-law to arrange the marriage, but when Li Ren sees that the silver he has brought home has been stolen, he immediately reports the case to the authorities. When the authorities search the house of Ms. Bai, they find the silver, but Ms. Bai and Little Blue all of a sudden disappear. The authorities thereupon banish Xu, and when he arrives in Suzhou he becomes a commoner.

Xu Xian stays at the inn of his friend Wang Jingxi. When Ms. Bai and Little Blue also arrive there, he tells them off, but following a reconciliation brought about by Wang and his wife, they are again reunited. Soon thereafter Xu opens his own pharmacy to make a living. When he comes one day to a temple to burn incense, the abbot, who sees him, tells him he is bewitched by a demon, and gives him an amulet. When he gets home, Ms. Bai immediately drinks the amulet, but nothing happens. She then orders Little Blue to arrest the Daoist priest, and chases him away.

On the occasion of Double Fifth, Ms. Bai, pressured to do so by Xu Xian, drinks some realgar wine, and passing out drunk on her bed, she manifests her original shape. When Xu sees this, he is scared to death. Ms. Bai ascends Mt. Song to steal the immortal herb. She defeats all immortals in battle, but is eventually captured. Ms. Bai begs for forgiveness and asks for the herb, whereupon the South Pole Old Greybeard gives it to her. When she gets home, she has Xu drink a decoction made of the herb, and so brings him back to life.

One day, when Xu Xian goes out for a walk to Tiger Hill, Ms. Bai gives him an eight-jewel, bright-pearl kerchief to wear, which is recognized by a police officer as an object stolen from the mansion of Chancellor Xiao, and he arrests Xu. When they come to arrest Ms. Bai, she has already disappeared. The official sentences Xu to be banished to Zhenjiang as a commoner.

When Xu Xian comes to Zhenjiang, he becomes a clerk in the pharmacy of He Bin (style Zhongwu). Ms. Bai and Little Blue, following him, also arrive. Xu refuses to take them in, but upon the intervention of He, the couple is reunited once again. One day, when Ms. Bai visits He Bin on the occasion of his birthday, the latter orders the maid Qiuju to take her to River-Watching Tower because he wants rape her. But Ms. Bai turns into a big-headed ghost and scares him so that he collapses from fright.

The Chan master Fahai of the Golden Mountain Monastery sets out from his temple to enlighten Xu Xian. On the road he meets with the Huaguang merchant Liu Long, who tells him in tears that his sandalwood has been stolen. Fahai tells him to return the next day to the monastery to find a solution. Then he goes to Xu, whom he asks for the donation of sandalwood for Buddha statues, and Xu secretly agrees. When Xu visits the Golden Mountain Monastery, Ms. Bai and Little Blue follow him there, and when they learn that Fahai refuses to release Xu to go home, they raise a huge punitive army and battle the gods, releasing a great flood to submerge Golden Mountain Monastery. Fahai summons the protective deities of Buddhism to give battle, and these chase the water creatures away, but because Ms. Bai is pregnant, they have to set her free. Fahai therefore orders Xu to return to Hangzhou, and to leave the family only after Ms. Bai has given birth, and he tells him to meet him in Jingci Monastery.

When Xu Xian comes to Broken Bridge on West Lake, he meets Ms. Bai. He offers his apologies, and together they go to the house of Li Ren. At this moment, Xu's sister has just given birth to a daughter, and as Ms. Bai soon will give birth, they decide to engage the unborn children. When her term is up, Ms. Bai indeed gives birth to a son. After the Full Month celebration, Xu goes to Jingci Monastery to see Fahai, and Fahai tells him he will come the next day to subdue the demon. The next day he captures Ms. Bai, while Little Blue is arrested by a protective god of Buddhism. Using the true fire of Samadhi, Fahai transforms the White Snake and buries her under Thunder Peak Pagoda, pronouncing the following gatha:

> When the Thunder Peak Pagoda collapses,
> When the water of West Lake is all dried up,
> And when the bore doesn't rise on the river,
> Only then will you be allowed to be reborn!

Xu Xian achieves enlightenment and enters the Way, and returns to the truth as a disciple of Fahai.

After sixteen years Ms. Bai's elder brother, the Black Storm Immortal, comes to Thunder Peak Pagoda and comforts her. At that time her son Xu Zilin has achieved the position of top-of-the-list, and in a memorial to the throne asks permission to tear down the pagoda and save his mother, but his request is not granted and he is ordered to offer sacrifices at the pagoda. Mother and son meet with each other, and they are filled with grief. Shilin celebrates his marriage, and the court awards noble titles to his parents. When Ms. Bai has been imprisoned under the pagoda for more than twenty years, she is eventually pardoned by the emperor of heaven, and Little Blue is also released, whereupon they are escorted to the Trayastrimsas Heaven.

Further Comments

This play is based on the *chuanqi* play *Thunder Peak Pagoda* by Huang Tubi of the Qing dynasty, and it has come about by a revision that took the popular legend into account and expanded the play by the inclusion of episodes such as the birth of a son and his success in the examinations. Scenes such as "Double Fifth," "Seeking the Herb," "Saving Xian," "Begging for Sandalwood," "The Water Battle," "Broken Bridge," "Engaging the Unborn," "Painting the Portrait," "The Spirit Meeting," "The Request to the Throne," "Sacrificing at the Pagoda," "Getting Married," and "Buddha's Completion" are all new additions but many of them have been popular on the stage. See the entry on Huang Tubi's *Thunder Peak Pagoda*.

Classified Excerpts of Qing Dynasty Anecdotes (Qingbai leichao) states: "During the Southern Tour [of the Qianlong emperor] the performance of new plays had been ordered. The salt merchants of Lianghuai thereupon invited some twenty or thirty famous types and had them compose the *chuanqi* play *Thunder Peak Pagoda*. But they also were afraid that the actors would be unable to memorize the lines, so they employed the old tunes and tempi for the ease of performance. If a singer by chance forgot his words, he could still go on singing the old tunes, and it would not conflict with the flute and the clapper. When the imperial boat took off, two boats went in front. A stage had been erected on these two boats, and they performed the play facing the imperial boat. The Qianlong emperor repeatedly watched with pleasure." The version that was performed may well have been this theater manuscript. The event took place in the thirty-fifth year of the Qianlong reign (1765). Seven years later it was once again revised by Fang Chengpei because it lacked elegance.

3

Fang Chengpei's *Thunder Peak Pagoda*

About the Author

Fang Chengpei: style Yangsong; also signs his name as Xiuyun ciyi. He hailed from Hengshan (now a part of Shexian in Anhui). In his youth he was sickly, and stayed at home to study medicine as he lacked the energy for examination study. But he was widely read in all kinds of books, and was an expert in songs and music. He collected lyrics and arias of many authors, established their prosody, and wrote *Ciju*. He traveled through Hubei and died in that area. His writings include *Tingyixuan xiaogao*, *Xiangyanju suibi*, *Feihongtang suibi*, *Diezhanglou shichao*, *Hangao xiaocao*, *Xiuyun shicao*, *Huangshan xinyong*, and *Cichen*. His *chuanqi* play *Shuangquan ji* has been lost, but his revised version of *Thunder Peak Pagoda* has been preserved.

Early References

When the *Jinyue kaozheng* lists the anonymous version, it states in a note: "There is also the revised version by Xiuyun ciyi." We have a printed edition of the *Suizhuju*, which carries a preface dated to the thirty-seventh year of the Qianlong reign (1772) of the Qing dynasty, which is found in Beijing Tushuguan and elsewhere. It is entitled *Thunder Peak Pagoda*, and the front page states "The printing blocks are kept at the Suizhuju." The first page of the main text states: "Revised by Xiuyun ciyi" and "Corrected by Haiting chaoke." This is preceded by an "Author's Preface," which is stated to have been "written by Fang Chengbei (Songyang) of Xin'an in the *xinmao* year (1771) of the Qianlong reign." It also includes "Inscriptions" by Wang Zongmin (Yin'an), Xu Deda (Youshan), and Wu Shiqi (Fengshan). At the end there is a postscript by Hong Bitai (Ruting). The play consists of thirty-four scenes in two *juan*.

Fang's Revision

This play is a revised version of the version as performed in the theater. For the transformations of the contents, see the entry on *Thunder Peak Pagoda* by Huang Tubi.

In the "Author's Preface" the playwright states: "[The *chuanqi* play *Thunder Peak Pagoda* has already a long history, and it is unknown who may have written the play. The story is found in a dispersed manner in books such as Wu Congxian's *Xiaochuang ziji* and the *West Lake Rambles* (*Xihu zhi*). An amateur collected these fragments—a rustic ignoramus not worth discussing.][8] In the year *xinmao* (1771) the Court enjoyed an inner apartment blessing (the eightieth birthday of the Qianlong emperor's mother), and the whole world shared in this joy. The Huai merchants could participate in this grand event. The Grand Secretary and Grand Coordinator Sir Gao spoke to Sir Li of the Silver Pavilion, and they ordered the merchants, apart from new plays wishing good fortune, to have this play performed for the emperor's amusement. At the house of Surveillance Commissioner Master Xu Huanku I repeatedly had the opportunity to see it, and I regretted that, while performed on the stage it well might greatly overwhelm the ears, it could not avoid raising eyebrows when perused by an expert in music. Its words were vulgar, and its tunes wrong, but I do not have the time to list all its superfluous elements. That's why I revised the play once again, spending great effort on the disposition of lyrics and the expression of ideas, to ensure that it would be of benefit to the Way of this world and align itself with the elegant and orthodox. I changed nine out of each ten of the arias in the original version and I reworked seventy percent of the prose. Scenes such as "Seeking the Herb," "Creating the Pagoda," and "Sacrificing at the Pagoda" I reworked from beginning to end, only keeping the original title. I removed eight scenes all together. "Discussion at Night" and the opening and concluding scenes, and the poems recited on leaving the stage made up of lines from Tang-dynasty poets have all been added by me. I asked for advice all the time, and I got the greatest assistance from Sir Xu Youshan (Jiangbo). ..." Following each scene there are often commentaries, and the "old version" and "original version" which are mentioned there refer to the old theater manuscript. See the entry on the anonymous *Thunder Peak Pagoda*.

The scenes that have been omitted in Fang's version are "The Theft from the Vault," "Arresting the Silver," "The Banishment," "The Theft of the Kerchief," "The Announced Visit," "The Painting of the Portrait," and "The Request to the Throne," which actually make up seven scenes. Furthermore, "The Interrogation" in the original version has been greatly abbreviated, and changed into "Sentenced and Banished." This amounts to the "eight removed scenes."

The only scene which is added in Fang's version is "Discussion at Night." It follows "Opening Shop" and describes how Xu Xian opens his pharmacy and at night goes back home where he enjoys the moon and talks love with Ms. Bai. The commentary in the upper margin states: "By adding this one scene, the whole structure becomes alive, as beginning and ending correspond to each other and opening and conclusion form one whole—it has the effects of waves on the wide sea. It also goes to show that despite all persistent delusions of

---

[8] The passage between brackets has not been provided by Guo Yingde, but has been inserted on the basis of the full text of the preface as reprinted in Cai Yi, 1989, 1821–22.

the heart the brightness of its original substance is never fully lost. So that's why there is this episode on a clear night." Fang also rewrote the scene "Water Battle" of the original version as "A Visit to the Monk" and "Water Battle."

The most important change in the plot is that in "Discovering the Crime" of the original play Li Ren makes a confession to the authorities which implied Xu Xian, but that in "Fleeing to Suzhou" in Fang's version Li first tells Xu to go to Suzhou and only then alerts the authorities. In the commentary at the end of the scene he states: "The move of allowing him to flee may be difficult to enact on the basis of reason, but cannot be missed when we consider feeling, and he lightly gets of the hook. In the old version [Li] first publicly reports [the father] to the authorities but later he also shamefacedly accepts an imperial title [because of the son]—that is truly hard to understand. It is also deplorable that the two instances of banishment are described in exactly the same manner." As for those cases where the enactment has not been changed but the arias and the prose have been fully rewritten, they occupy almost fifty percent of the play.

The playwright dates his "Author's Preface" to "the winter month of the *xinmao* year of the Qianlong reign." *Xinmao* corresponds to the thirty-sixth year of the Qianlong reign, so the play was composed in that year. The "Author's Preface" also states: "When it was completed my colleagues were so kind as to give it their approbation and wanted to have it printed. ... Sir Wu Fengshan... thereupon corrected it and had it circulated." On the basis of this, the play must have been entrusted to the printer in the same year, to be printed in the next year (the thirty-seventh year of the Qianlong reign; 1772). Haitang chaoke is Wu Shiqi (Fengshan).

Appendix IV

The Virtuous Seductress

Our earliest reference to the legend of the White Snake as an item in the repertoire of ballad singers is provided by Tian Rucheng, in his West Lake Rambles, A Sequel (Xihu youlan zhiyu), *when he writes:*

> The blind men and women of Hangzhou often learn to play the lute and sing stories and tales of past and present in order to make a living, and this is called *taozhen*. Most of the time they tell stories of the Song dynasty. ... Now stories of Red Lotus, Liu Cui, Jidian, Thunder Peak Pagoda, and the Double-Fish Fan-Pendant are all Hangzhou legends, or stories made up in imitation in recent times.[1]

The genre of taozhen, *most scholars agree, must have been a forerunner of the later* tanci, *or string ballads.*

From later centuries we have several scripts of tanci *on the theme of the White Snake legend. One version closely follows the plot as provided by the vernacular story in Feng Menglong's* Stories to Caution the World (Jingshi tongyan). *A later version, entitled* The Virtuous Seductress (Yiyao zhuan) *is said to be based on the performances of Chen Yuqian, the most famous* tanci *performer from Suzhou in the eighteenth century. It corresponds to the popular stage versions of the legend of the eighteenth century in including the White Snake's theft of the herb of immortality and the birth and subsequent successful career of her son. The* Virtuous Seductress (Yiyao zhuan) *is a typical example of the performance-related* tanci *texts of the eighteenth and nineteenth centuries. Written in an alternation of prose and verse it runs to great length, and part of the text is written in the local Wu dialect.*

The following summary is translated from pp. 44–46 in Tan Zhengbi and Tan Xun, A Descriptive Catalogue of String Ballads (Tanci xulu) *of 1981. Their summary is based on the 1867 edition of* The Illustrated Virtuous Seductress (Xiuxiang Yiyao zhuan); *also known as* West Lake Affinities (Xihu yuan).

---

[1] Tain Rucheng, *Xihu youlan zhiyu*, 368.

The Virtuous Seductress

At some date during the Yuan dynasty (1260–1368), Suzhen (Pure Chastity), a disciple of the immortal matron Ruizhi in the world above, and who is also called Liuzhi (Sixth Branch), and is a white snake who achieved her position through cultivation, is instructed by the Queen Mother to descend to earth and go to Lin'an (Hangzhou) in order to find her benefactor from an earlier life and repay his favors. When passing through Zhenjiang, she and the Pure Black Storm Great King, a blackfish (northern snakehead), become sworn brother and sister. At the mouth of the Qiantang River she also subdues a blue snake and makes her her servant. She calls her Little Blue (Xiaoqing), and they travel on together.

Xu Xian from Lin'an, whose style is Hanwen, has lost his parents at an early age, but he has been raised by his elder sister and her husband, the police officer Chen Biao, and he is now a clerk in a pharmacy. On the festival of Clear and Bright, when he is on his way back home from sweeping the graves outside the city, he runs into Suzhen and her servant girl on the banks of West Lake. Suzhen realizes that he is her benefactor from a previous life and so she works her magic to bring on a shower, and therefore she joins Xu on the boat he has hired to return together with him to the city. When they disembark upon reaching the Clear Waves Gate, she invites Xu to her house for a chat, and Xu follows her. Suzhen claims that she is Bai Xiuying, the daughter of a family of officials, and, with Little Blue acting the matchmaker, she has Xu stay to consummate the marriage that very night.

The next day Suzhen gives Xu Xian some silver and has him return home and inform his sister. But who could have known that this silver was storehouse silver, which had been stolen by the Black Storm Great King who had given it to his sworn sister. When Chen Biao recognizes it as stolen silver, he reports the case at the county office. When the county magistrate orders the arrest of lady Bai and her servant, the two of them have disappeared, but the missing storehouse silver is found in her house. Xu is sentenced to two years of banishment, and assigned to Suzhou.

When Xu Xian arrives at Suzhou he is freed from the labor camp by Wang Yongchang of the Dashengtang pharmacy, who acts as his guarantor, and he becomes a clerk in his pharmacy. When one day he enters the town, he runs into Little Blue and learns that Suzhen also has come to Suzhou and already has rented a house in which to live. Suzhen explains the earlier incident with false excuses, and husband and wife are reunited. Suzhen also provides Xu with the capital to start his own Baohetang pharmacy outside the city wall.

On the day of Double Fifth, Little Blue sneaks off to hide herself deep in the mountains, while Suzhen feigns illness and refuses to leave her room. Because Xu Xian is afraid that his wife may have caught a cold, he forces her to drink some realgar wine. Suzhen thereupon manifests her original shape of a white snake, and Xu is so frightened that he loses consciousness. When Suzhen is awakened by Little Blue, she braves all dangers to go to Mt. Kunlun and steal the herb of immortality, and then brings Xu back to life. She also makes a fake snake to dispel Xu's suspicions, and husband and wife live in harmony as before.

On the day of Mid-Autumn Festival they go to the treasure competition. Because Xu Xian does not have any treasure, people all laugh at him. Little Blue secretly borrows a treasure from the house of Mr. Gu of Kunshan, the president of the Ministry of Works, so Xu can take part in the competition. But the treasure is recognized by someone, who reports him to the authorities, whereupon Xu is arrested. Suzhen then disperses the clerks [of the pharmacy], and with Little Blue moves to Zhenjiang, where she again opens the Baohetang. Xu is found to be without any guilt, and later for some reason also goes to Zhenjiang, where he again meets with Suzhen. So he stays in Zhenjiang and does not go back.

The abbot Fahai of the Golden Mountain Monastery near Zhenjiang is ordered by the Buddha to inspect Suzhen and her servant. Under some false pretext he entices Xu Xian to come to the monastery, and there he discloses to him the background of Suzhen. A flustered and bewildered Xu wants to become a disciple of Fahai by becoming a monk, but only asks to be allowed to take his leave of his wife. By that time Suzhen, accompanied by Little Blue, has already found out his whereabouts and arrived at the monastery, where she implores Fahai to release her husband. Fahai does not give in to their requests, and intends to subdue Suzhen using his golden begging bowl. But it turns out that Suzhen is pregnant, and the child she is carrying is an incarnation of the Star of Literature, so Fahai's magical weapon is useless, and Suzhen is able to escape.

Suzhen requests the Black Wind Great King to help her and to accompany her to Golden Mountain Monastery to demand the release of her husband. Black Wind is no match for Fahai, and uses his magic to have the waters flood Golden Mountain, drowning all people throughout Zhenjiang Prefecture. Because he has committed this outrageous crime, he is killed by the dragon gods.

Suzhen and her servant return to Hangzhou following this defeat, and Xu Xian is also sent back by Fahai. They meet each other at Broken Bridge. When Xu realizes that Suzhen is pregnant, he offers an apology, but an angry Little Blue attempts to behead him, until she is finally dissuaded from doing so by Suzhen. Then they go all together to the house of his elder sister to await the date of Suzhen's delivery.

At that same moment Xu Xian's elder sister also happens to be pregnant and the two families engage the unborn children to each other. Later the two women give birth on the same day: Suzhen to a boy who is called Mengjiao, and Xu's sister to a girl who is called Bilian. When the two families celebrate the Full Month with a banquet, Fahai suddenly arrives. He subdues Suzhen under his golden bowl and makes her show her true shape. Husband and wife say a tearful good-bye. The whole family follows [Fahai] to West Lake, where Suzhen tells her whole story from the very beginning. But Little Blue sneaks away with the intent to take revenge.

Xu Xian entrusts his son to his sister and goes to the Yunxi monastery to become a monk. Later he eventually, after many travels, arrives at Golden Mountain Monastery. Mengjiao is raised by his aunt, and only learns the story of the meeting and separation of his parents when he has turned seven. At the age of nineteen he leaves for the capital to take the examinations. Visting Golden Mountain Monastery he runs into his father, and so father and son are reunited. When he gets to the capital, Mengjiao passes the examinations as top-of-the-list, and both his parents and those of his wife receive noble titles.

When Mengjiao arrives back home, he goes to Thunder Peak Pagoda in order to sacrifice to his mother. At that moment Suzhen's twenty-year ordeal has come to an end and she emerges from the pagoda, so mother and son are reunited. Suzhen thereupon returns to heaven to take up her place in the ranks of the immortals.

Mengjiao and Bilian are married, and when they leave for the capital at the end of his period of leave, they visit Golden Mountain Monastery to see his father, but it turns out that the latter has entered nirvana a few days earlier.

APPENDIX V

The Elder Brother of Zheng Defeats Duan in Yan

The title of the following story is based on a line from the opening year of the Chunqiu *(Annals of Spring and Autumn): "In the summer, in the Fourth Month, the Elder Brother of Zheng defeated Duan in Yan." The* Chunqiu *are the annals of the ancient state of Lu for the period 722–479* B.C.E., *tersely recording the most important developments at the court of Lu and in the neighboring states such as Zheng. Confucius was traditionally credited with establishing the text, and he was believed to have apportioned "praise and blame" by his subtle wording. Later commentators strove to decode the Master's intentions, and the* Chunqiu *soon attracted commentaries. One of the three ancient commentaries was the* Zuo Commentary (Zuozhuan). *The* Zuozhuan *describes roughly the same period in much greater detail. Most likely it was originally composed as an independent work, at some date between the fourth and the first century* B.C.E. *Most likely it was only later reorganized to serve as a commentary to the entries in the* Chunqiu. *In dynastic China, the* Zuozhuan *also would engender its own commentaries.*

The conflict between the Duke of Zheng and his younger brother (see p.xx of the Introduction) has traditionally been understood as history. The tale has engendered an extensive body of commentary. Most of these discussions focus on the moral character of the Duke of Zheng in his relation to his younger brother. Had he been sincere in his treatment of his younger brother and only acted against him when he had no other options? Or had he deliberately set a trap for his younger brother so he would have a pretext to go to war against him? And what about his treatment of his mother? Can a man still be called filial if he imprisons his mother, even if he later sets her free?[1] *But the persistent fascination of Chinese literati with this tale throughout the centuries is perhaps better explained if the story is understood as myth, as the earliest account of a sinning mother, and a son who frees his mother from her prison below the earth. The similarity of this story to the Mulian myth was pointed out a number of years ago by Kristofer Schipper,*[2] *but its mythical quality may well have been felt already by the*

---

[1] For a translation and extensive discussion of the various interpretations of this episode from the Zuozhuan, see Wai-yee Li, 2007, 59–84, "The Example of Duke Zhuang of Zheng."

[2] Schipper, 1989.

157

seventeenth century literary critic Jin Shengtan (1608–1661), when he commented on the line "But later he regretted this" as follows: "The preceding section is the text about hell; the following section is the text about heaven."[3]

The following translation of The Elder Brother of Zheng Defeats Duan in Yan is based on the text in A Definitive Survey of Old Prose (Guwen guanzhi), a widely used anthology of Old Prose essays of the Qing dynasty, which also includes selections from the Zuozhuan.[4]

---

[3] *Jin Shengtan pi caizi guwen*, 1986, 2. In this anthology of Old Prose essays, Jin Shengtan preceded this piece with the following introduction: "One has to understand that the first part of this long piece has its own sound and rhythm, and the second part has its own sound and rhythm. In the first half, the indictment is directed against Duke Zhuang. Wu Jiang is only a woman who is led by her nature and loves one-sidedly, and Younger Brother Duan is a pampered brat who has not been properly instructed. In the second part, the merit rests with Kaoshu of Ying, while Duke Zhuang is only an evil person whose sins have reached their full number and who eventually has remorse and corrects his mistakes."

[4] The translation is based on *Guwen guanzhi*, 1982, 1–6.

The Elder Brother of Zheng Defeats Duan in Yan

From the Zuozhuan, *"The first year of Duke Yin"* (722 B.C.E.)

Duke Wu of Zheng had married a woman of the Shen family, and she was called Wu Jiang. She gave birth to Duke Zhuang and to Younger Brother Duan of Gong. Duke Zhuang was a breech birth, and scared Wu Jiang, who therefore called him "Breech Birth." She thereupon hated him. She loved Younger Brother Duan of Gong and wanted him to be installed [as crown prince]. She repeatedly requested this from Duke Wu, but the latter did not grant her request.

When Duke Zhuang succeeded his father, she asked the city of Zhi for Duan. But the duke said: "That is a strategic city, and the Guo younger brother died there. Any other town is yours for the asking." So she asked for Jing, and the duke had Duan go and live there—Duan now was called the Great Younger Brother of the City of Jing.

Zhai Zhong said [to Duke Zhuang]: "If a large city measures more than one hundred *zhang*, it is a danger to the state. According to the statutes of the earlier kings, a big city should not exceed one-third of the capital; a middle city should not exceed one-fifth, and a small one should not exceed one-ninth. At present the size of Jing does not fit these statutes. You will not be able to suffer this." The duke replied: "This was Wu Jiang's request. How can we avoid harm?" The answer was: "When will Wu Jiang ever be satiated? The best solution is to take measures now, and not let this problem proliferate like vines, as vines are hard to deal with. If vines cannot even be removed, how much less your pampered younger brother?" The duke said: "Those who commit many acts of unrighteousness will destroy themselves. Just wait and see."

Later the Great Younger Brother ordered the western borders and the northern borders to defect to him. Prince Lü said: "A state cannot allow defection. What will you do about this? If you want to give these regions to the Great Younger Brother, allow me to serve him. But if you didn't give these regions to him, please remove him, so as to avoid unrest among the people." The duke said: "That's of no use. He will get there by himself."

The Great Younger Brother accepted the defection of other places, which he made his own, and arrived in Pinyan. Zifeng said: "This is the time for action!

With his large territory he will obtain the crowds." The duke replied: "He does not act in a righteous manner and he is not trusting. Despite his territory, he will fail."

The Great Younger Brother restored [his walls], gathered [his troops], prepared armor and weapons, and readied infantry and chariots. He was about to attack the Zheng capital, and the lady-dowager was to open the gates for him. When the duke heard that a date had been set, he said: "This is the time for action!" He ordered Zifeng to attack Jing with two hundred chariots, whereupon Jing rebelled against the Great Younger Brother Duan, who fled to Yan. The duke defeated him at Yan, and on the *xinchou* day of the Fifth Month the Great Younger Brother escaped and fled to Gong.

The duke thereupon imprisoned Wu Jiang in fortified Ying, and swore: "We will not meet again, unless at the Yellow Springs!" But later he regretted this. Kaoshu of Ying was the warden of Ying Valley. When he heard this, he offered the duke a present. The duke gifted him a meal, but at the meal he set the meat aside. When the duke questioned him about it, he replied: "My mother is still alive and she always shares my food. She has never tasted your stew, so I would like to give it to her." The duke said: "You can still bring gifts to your mother, but alas, I alone am not in that position." Kaoshu of Ying asked: "May I ask what you mean by that?" The duke told him what had happened and that he regretted his oath. He replied: "What is the problem? If you dig away the earth till you reach the sources, and then meet with her in a tunnel, who will say that you did not keep your word?"

The duke followed his advice. As he entered the tunnel he declaimed: "Inside the big tunnel/Our joy is harmonious!" When Wu Jiang came out of the tunnel she declaimed: "Outside the big tunnel/Our joy is overflowing!" Thereupon they were mother and son as before.

Bibliography

Chinese Sources and Studies

A Ying 阿英. *Leifengta chuanqi xulu.* 雷峯塔傳奇敘錄. Beijing: Zhonghua Shuju, 1960.

"*Baishezhuan*" *lunwen ji* 白蛇传 论文集 Compiled by Zhongguo minjian wenyi yanjiu hui, Zhejiang fenhui 中国民间文艺研究会浙江分会. Hangzhou: Zhejiang Guji Chubanshe, 1986.

Cai Yi 蔡毅, Comp. *Zhongguo gudian xiqu xuba huibian* 中國古典戲曲序跋匯編 4 vols. Jinan: Qi Lu Shushe, 1989.

Che Xilun 車錫倫. *Zhongguo baojuan zongmu* 中國寶卷總目. Beijing: Yanshan Chubanshe, 2000.

Chen Bojun 陈伯君. "Lun baojuan *Leifengta* de beiju sixiang," 论宝卷雷峰塔的悲剧思想 *Minjian wenyi jikan* 民间文艺集刊. No. 6 (1984), 65-80.

Dai Bufan 戴不凡. "Shilun 'Baishe zhuan' gushi" 試論白蛇傳故事. In *Baihua ji* 百花集 (pp.13-33). Beijing: Zuojia Chubanshe, 1956.

Fan Jinlan 范金蘭. *Baishe zhuan gushi xingbian yanjiu* 白蛇傳故事型變研究. Taibei: Wanjuanlou Tushu Gufen Youxian Gongsi, 2003.

Fu Xihua 傅惜華, comp. *Baishezhuan ji* 白蛇傳集. Beijing: Zhonghua Shuju, 1959.

Guo Yingde 郭英德. *Ming Qing chuanqi zonglu* 明清传奇综录. Shijiazhuang: Hebei Jiaoyu Chubanshe, 1997.

He Xuejun 贺学君. *Zhongguo si da chuanshuo* 中国四大传说. Hangzhou: Zhejiang Jiaoyu Chubanshe, (1989) 1995 (2nd printing).

Hong Bian 洪楩, comp. *Qingping shantang huaben* 清平山堂話本. Edited by Tan Zhengbi 譚正璧. Shanghai: Gudian Wenxue Chubanshe, 1957.

Hong Mai 洪邁. *Yijian zhi* 夷堅志, 4 vols. Edited by He Zhuo 何卓. Beijing: Zhonghua Shuju, 1981.

Huang Chang 黃裳, *Xixiang ji yu Baishe zhuan* 西廂記與白蛇傳. Shanghai: Pingming Chubanshe, 1953.

Leifengta mibao yu Baishe chuanqi zhan 雷峰塔秘寶與白蛇傳奇展/ *From the Legend of the White Snake: The Hidden Treasures in the Leifeng Pagoda.* Taipei: Guoli Lishi Bowuguan, 2005.

Leifengta yizhi 雷峰塔遗址/ *The Leifeng Pagoda Site.* Beijing: Wenwu Chubanshe, 2005.

Leifeng yizhen 雷锋遗珍. Beijing: Wenwu Chubanshe, 2002.

Li Fang 李昉, ed. *Taiping guangji* 太平廣記. Beijing: Zhonghua Shuju, 1961.

Liu Liemao 刘烈茂 and Guo Jingrui 郭精锐, eds. *Qing Che wang fu chaocang qubenzidishu* 清车王府钞藏曲本子弟书. Nanjing: Jiangsu Guji Chubanshe, 1993.

Luo Yonglin 罗永麟. *Lun Zhongguo si da minjian gushi* 论中国四大民间故事. Beijing: Zhongguo Minjian Wenyi Chubanshe, 1986.

Nanjō Takenori 南條竹則. *Hebi onna no densetsu: 'Hakujaden' wo otte higashi e nishi e* 蛇女の伝説:「白蛇伝」を追って東へ西へ. Tokyo: Heibonsha, 2000.

Pan Jiangdong 潘江東. *Baishe gushi yanjiu fu ziliao huibian* 白蛇故事研究附資料匯編. Taibei: Xuesheng Shuju, 1981.

Qi Biaojia 祁彪佳. *Yuanshantang Ming qupin jupin jiaolu* 遠山堂明曲品劇品校錄. Collated by Huang Shang 黃裳. Shanghai: Shanghai Chuban Gongsi, 1955.

Que Xunwu 闕勳吾, Ann. et al. *Guwen guanzhi.* 2 vols. Changsha: Hunan Renmin Chubanshe, 1982.

Shen Zu'an 沈祖安. "Zhenyuan haohao li wu qiong—Xiqu *Baishe zhuan* zongheng tan," 真圆浩浩理无穷—戏曲白蛇传纵横谈 *Yishu yanjiu ziliao* 5 (1983), 206–31.

Sun Qi 孙琦 and Chen Qinjian 陈勤建. *Bai niangzi chuanshuo* 白娘子传说. Beijing: Zhongguo Shehui Chubanshe, 2006.

Tan Zhengbi 谭正璧 and Tan Xun 谭寻, comps. *Pingtan tongkao* 评弹通考. Beijing: Zhongguo Quyi Chubanshe, 1985.

Tian Rucheng 田汝成. *Xihu youlan zhi* 西湖遊覽志. Beijing: Zhonghua Shuju, 1958.

Tian Rucheng. *Xihu youlan zhiyu* 西湖遊覽志餘. Beijing: Zhonghua shuju, 1958.

Wu Congxian 吳從先. *Xiaochuang ziji* 小窗自紀. In *Siku quanshu cunmu congshu* 四庫全書存目叢書, *Zi* 子 vol. 252. Jinan: Qi Lu Shushe, 1995.

Yu Zhuoya 虞卓婭, "*Leifeng ta* chuanqi yu *Leifeng baojuan* 雷峰塔传奇与雷锋宝卷." *Zhejiang haiyang xueyuan xuebao* 16, no. 4 (1999): 22–27.

Zhang Guoguang 張國光, ed. *Jin Shengtan pi caizi guwen* 金聖嘆批才子古文. Wuhan: Hubei Renmin Chubanshe, 1986.

Zhao Jingshen 趙景深, "Baishe zhuan" 白蛇傳, in his *Tanci kaozheng* 彈詞考證 1936; repr. Taibei: Taiwan Shangwu Yinshuguan, 1967.

Zhongguo tongsu xiaoshuo zongmu tiyao 中国通俗小说总目提要. Beijing: Zhongguo Wenlian Chubanshe, 1990.

Zhuhong 袾宏, comp. *Zimen chongxing lu* 緇門崇行錄, in *Foxue congkan* 佛學叢刊, First Series, Vol. 3. Shanghai: Shijie Shuju, 1935.

Western Languages

Translations of White Snake Stories and Plays

Anonymous. "The White Snake." Translated by Yang Hsien-yi and Gladys Yang. *Chinese Literature* (July 1959): 103–39.

Anonymous. "The White Snake." In *Chinese Village Plays from the Ting Hsien Region (Yang Ke Hsüan), A Collection of Forty-Eight Chinese Rural Plays as Staged by Villagers in Ting Hsien in Northern China*, edited by Sidney D. Gamble, 702–61. Amsterdam: Philo Press, 1970.

Chang, H. C. *Chinese Literature: Popular Fiction and Drama*. Edinburgh, UK: Edinburgh University Press, 1973.

Dars, Jacques, trans. *Contes de la Montange Sereine*. Paris: Gallimard, 1987.

Die Wundersame Geschichte der weissen Schlange (Pai she k'i chuan), Chinesischer Geisterroman. Deutche bearbeitung nach der Übersetzung van Stanislas Julien ... von Johanna Boshamer-Koob und Kurt Boshamer. Zürich: Werner Classen Verlag, 1967.

Ellis, Myra, trans. and ed. *Madam White Snake*. Singapore: Federal Publications, 1990.

Feng Menglong, comp. *Stories to Caution the World: A Ming Dynasty Collection, Volume 2*. Translated by Shuhui Yang and Yunqin Yang. Seattle: University of Washington Press, 2005.

Julien, Stanislas, trans. *Pé-ché-Tsing-ki, Blanche et Bleue, ou, Les deux Couleuvres-fées*. Paris: Charles Gosselin, 1834.

Pimpaneau, Jacques. "La légende du Serpent Blanc dans le Ts'ing P'ing Chan T'ang Houa Pen." *Journal Asiatique* 253 (1965): 251–77.

Tien Han. *The White Snake. A Peking Opera*. Translated by Yang Hsien-yi and Gladys Yang. Peking: Foreign Languages Press, 1957.

Tyan Han. "The White Snake," Translated by Donald Chang; English verse adaptation by William Packard. In *The Red Pear Garden: Three Great Dramas of Revolutionary China*, edited by John D. Mitchell, 49–120. Boston: David R. Godine, 1973.

Ueda Akinari. *Tales of Moonlight and Rain: Japanese Gothic Tales*. Translated by Kengi Hamada. New York: Columbia University Press, 1972.

Ueda Akinari. *Ugetsu monogatari. Tales of Moonlight and Rain. A Complete English Version of the Eighteenth-Century Japanese Collection of Tales of the Supernatural.* Translated by Leon M. Zolbrod. Vancouver: University of British Columbia Press, 1974.

Ueda Akinari. *Tales of Moonlight and Rain: A Study and Translation.* Translated by Anthony H. Chambers. New York: Columbia University Press, 2007.

Waley, Arthur. *The Real Tripitaka and Other Pieces*. New York: The Macmillan Company, 1952.

Woodbridge, Samuel I., trans. *The Mystery of the White Snake: A Legend of the Thunder Peak Tower*. Shanghai: North China Herald Office, 1896.

Yan Geling. "White Snake." In *White Snake, and Other Stories*, translated by Lawrence A. Walker, 1–64. San Francisco: Aunt Lute Books, 1999.

Yu, Diana, trans. "Eternal Prisoner under the Thunder Peak Pagoda." In *Traditional Chinese Stories: Themes and Variations*, edited by Y. W. Ma and Joseph S. M. Lau, 355–78. New York: Columbia University Press, 1978.

Western Language Studies

Bender, Marc, and Victor H. Mair. *Reader in Chinese Folk and Popular Literature*, forthcoming.

Chan Hing-ho, ed. *Inventaire analytique et critique du conte chinois en langue vulgaire*. Tome cinquième. Paris: Collêge de France, Institut des Hautes Études Chinoises, 2006.

Chiu, Elena Suet-Ying. "Cultural Hybridity in Manchu Bannermen Tales (Zidishu)," PhD Dissertation, University of California, Los Angeles, 2007.

Cole, Alan. *Mothers and Sons in Chinese Buddhism*. Stanford, CA: Stanford University Press, 1998.

Diamond, Catherine. "Mae Maak and Company: The Shifting Duality in Female Representation on the Contemporary Thai Stage." *Asian Theater Journal* 23 no. 1 (2006): 111–48.

Dudbridge, Glen. "The Goddes Hua-yüeh San-niang and the Cantonnese Ballad *Ch'en-hsiang T'ai-tzu*." *Hanxue yanjiu/Chinese Studies*, Vol. 8, no. 1 (1990): 627–46.

Elliott, Mark C., trans. "The 'Eating Crabs' Youth Book." In *Under Confucian Eyes: Writings on Gender in Chinese History*, edited by Susan Mann and Yu-yin Cheng, 262–81; 306-8. Stanford, CA: Stanford University Press, 2001.

Fu Hongchu. "Misogyny and Sympathy: Moral Ambivalence in Feng Menglong's Adaptation of the Tale of the White Serpent." *Tamkang Review* 29 no. 3 (1999): 47–86.

Goldman, Andrea S. "The Nun Who Wouldn't Be: Representation of Female Desire in Two Performance Genres of 'Si Fan'." *Late Imperial China* 22, no. 1 (2001): 71–138.

Hanan, Patrick. *The Chinese Short Story: Studies in Dating, Authorship, and Composition*. Cambridge, MA: Harvard University Press, 1973.

Hanan, Patrick. *The Chinese Vernacular Story*. Cambridge, MA: Harvard University Press, 1981.

Hargett, James M. *Stairway to Heaven: A Journey to the Summit of Mount Emei*. Albany: State University of New York Press, 2006.

Hsu Wen-hung. "The Evolution of the Legend of the White Serpent." *Tamkang Review* 4, no. 1 (1973): 109–27; 4, no. 2 (1973): 121–56.

Idema, Wilt L. *Personal Salvation and Filial Piety: Two Precious Scroll Narratives of Guanyin and Her Acolytes*. Honolulu: University of Hawai'i Press, 2008.

Idema, Wilt, and Haiyan Lee, *Meng Jiangnü Brings Down the Great Wall: Ten Versions of a Chinese Legend*. Seattle: University of Washington Press, 2008.

Kerr, Janet Lynn. "Pao-chüan." In *The Indiana Companion to Traditional Chinese Literature* Vol. 2, edited by William J. Nienhauser, 117–21. Bloomington: Indiana University Press, 1998.

Kuraishi Takeshiro. "On the Metamorphosis of the Story of the White Snake." *Sino-Indian Studies* 5 (1957): 138–46.

Kwok, Man Ho, and Joanne O'Brien. *The Eight Immortals of Taoism: Legends and Fables of Popular Taoism*. New York: Meridian, 1990.

Lai, Whalen. "From Folklore to Literate Theater: Unpacking *Madame White Snake*." *Asian Folklore Studies* 51 (1992): 51–66.

Lévy, André. "L'origine et le style de la Légende de la Pic du Tonnerre dans la version des *Belles histoires du Lac de l'ouest*." *Bulletin de l'École Française de l'Extrême Orient* 53, no. 2 (1967) 517–35.

Lévy, André. "Le 'Serpent blanc' en Chine et au Japon: Excursion à travers les variations d'un theme." In *Études sur le conte et le roman chinois* (pp. 97–113). Paris: École Française d'Extrême Orient, 1973.

Li, Wai-yee. *The Readability of the Past in Early Chinese Historiography*. Cambridge, MA: Harvard University Press, 2007.

Lu Hsun. *The Selected Works of Lu Hsun*, Vol. 2. Translated by Yang Hsien-yi and Gladys Yang. Peking: Foreign Language Press, 1964.

Lytle, George W. (賴傑威). "Snakes, Lovers, and Moralists: A Comparative Look at the Lamia Legends of the West, the White Snake Legends of China, and the Orthodox and Gnostic Interpretations of Genesis." *Huagang yingyu xuebao* 華岡英語學報 5 (1999): 167–79.

Mair, Victor H. *Tun-huang Popular Narratives*. Cambridge, UK: Cambridge University Press, 1983.

Mair, Victor H. *T'ang Transformation Texts*. Cambridge, MA: Harvard University Press, 1989.

Overmyer, Daniel L. *Precious Volumes: An Introduction to Chinese Sectarian Scriptures from the Sixteenth and Seventeenth Centuries*. Cambridge, MA: Harvard University Press, 1999.

Schafer, Edward H. *The Divine Woman: Dragon Ladies and Rain Maidens in T'ang Literature*. Berkeley, CA: North Point Press, 1980.

Schipper, Kristofer. "Mu-lien Plays in Taoist Liturgical Context." In *Ritual Opera, Operatic Ritual. "Mu-lien Rescues His Mother" in Chinese Popular Culture*, edited by David Johnson, 126–54. Berkeley, CA: IEAS Publications, 1989.

Scott, Mary, trans. "Three *Zidishu* on *Jin Ping Mei*, by Han Xiaochuang" *Renditions* 44 (1995): 33–65.

Seaman, Gary. "Mu-lien Dramas in Puli, Taiwan." In *Ritual Opera, Operatic Ritual. "Mu-lien Rescues His Mother" in Chinese Popular Culture*, edited by David Johnson, 155–90. Berkeley, CA: IEAS Publications, 1989.

Teiser, Stephen F. *The Ghost Festival in Medieval China*. Princeton, NJ: Princeton University Press, 1988.

Ting, Nai-tung. "The Holy and the Snake Woman: A Study of the Lamia Story in Asian and European Literature." *Fabula* 8 (1966): 145–91.

Ting, Nai-tung. *A Type Index of Chinese Folktales in the Oral Tradition and Major Works of Non-Religious Classical Literature*. Helsinki: Suomlainen Tiedeakatemia, 1978.

Wadley, Stephen A. "The Mixed-Language Verses from the Manchu Dynasty in China." *Papers on Inner Asia* 16 (1991).

Waley, Arthur. *Ballads and Stories from Tun-huang: An Anthology*. London: George Allen and Unwin, 1960.

Wang, Eugene Y. "Tope and Topos: The Leifeng Pagoda and the Discourse of the Demonic." In *Writing and Materiality in China: Essays in Honor of Patrick Hanan*, edited by Judith T. Zeitlin and Lydia H. Liu, 488–552. Cambridge, MA: Harvard University Asia Center, 2003a.

Wang, Eugene Y. "The Rhetoric of Book Illustrations." In *Treasures of the Yenching: Seventy-Fifth Anniversary of the Harvard-Yenching Library Exhibition Catalogue*, edited by Patrick Hanan, 181–217. Cambridge, MA: Harvard-Yenching Library, 2003b.

Wu Pei-yi. "The White Snake: The Evolution of a Myth in China." Dissertation, Columbia University, 1969.

Wu Yuantai. *Pérégrination vers l'est*. Translated by Nadine Perront. Paris: Gallimard, 1993.

Yan Yuan-shu, "Biography of the White Serpent: A Keatsian Interpretation." *Tamkang Review* I, no. 2 (1970): 227–43.

Yang Erzeng. *The Story of Han Xiangzi: The Alchemical Adventures of a Daoist Immortal*. Translated by Philip Clart. Seattle: University of Washington Press, 2007.

Yen, Alsace. "The Parry-Lord Hypothesis Applied to Vernacular Chinese Stories." *Journal of the American Oriental Society* 95, no. 3 (1975a): 403–16.

Yen, Alsace. "*Shang-ssu* Festival and Its Myths in China and Japan." *Asian Folklore Studies* 34, no. 2 (1975b): 45–85.

Yü Chün-fang. *Kuan-yin: The Chinese Transformation of Avalokitesvara*. New York: Columbia University Press, 2001.

Glossary of Chinese Terms

Bai 白
bai 白
Bai Juyi 白居易
Bai Suzhen 白素貞
Bai niangzi yongzhen Leifengta
白孃子永鎮雷峰塔
Baishe zhuan 白蛇傳
Baishi baojuan 白氏寶卷
baojuan 寶卷
bianwen 變文
Bilian 碧蓮
Boyi ji 博異集

chan 禪
Chang'e 嫦娥
Chen Jiayan 陳嘉言
Chen Liulong 塵六龍
Chen Tuan 陳摶
Chen Yuqian 陳遇乾
Chen Zhiguang 陳芝光
Chenxiang 沉香
chuanqi 傳奇
Chunqiu 春秋
Chuta 出塔

Dong Yong 董永
Dongbo 東坡
Dongfang Shuo 東方朔
Dongyou ji 東遊記
Du Fu 杜甫
Duanjia qiao 段家橋
Duanqiao 斷橋

Fahai 法海
Fang Chengpei 方程培
feng 鳳
Feng Menglong 馮夢龍

Gu 顧
Guan Suo 關索
Guan Yu 關羽
Guanshiyin 觀世音
Guanyin 觀音
guci 鼓詞
Gushenzi 谷神子
Guwen guanzhi 古文觀止

Han Xiangzi 韓湘子
Han Xiangzi quanzhuan
韓湘子全傳
Han Yu 韓愈
Hanwen 漢文
Hebo 合鉢
Hong Bian 洪楩
Hong Mai 洪邁
Hu Die 胡蝶
Huaguang 華光
Huang Tubi 黃圖珌

Jiangnan 江南
Jin Shengtan 金聖嘆
Jingshi tongyan 警視通言
Jinshansi 金山寺
jiedishen 揭諦神
Jita 祭塔
juan 卷

kaipian 開篇
Kuta 哭塔

Leifeng ta 雷峰塔
Leifengta qizhuan 雷峰塔奇傳
li 里
Lao Laizi 老萊子
Leifeng baojuan 雷峰寶卷
Leifeng ji 雷峰記
Leifeng ta 雷峰塔
Li Bihua 李碧華
Li Dou 李斗
Li Huang 李黃
Li Jing 李靖
Li Junfu 李君甫
Li Keyong 李可用
Li Rui 李銳
lian (lotus) 蓮
lian (love) 憐
Liezi 列子
Lin Bu (Hejing) 林逋和靖
Lishan laomu 驪山老姆
Liu Bei 劉備
Liushijia xiaoshuo 六十家小說
Longhushan 龍虎山
Lu Xun 魯迅
Lü Chunyang 呂純陽
Lü Dongbin 呂洞賓
luan 鸞

Ma Chao 馬超
Ma Rufei 馬如飛
Ma Rufei xiansheng nanci xiaoyin chuji
馬如飛先生南詞小引初集
Mao 茅
Meng Jiangnü 孟姜女
Mengjiao 孟蛟
Molangzi 墨浪子
mu 畝
Mulian 目連

Nan Song zashi shi 南宋雜事詩
Nanyou ji 南遊記
nianhua 年畫

Penglai 蓬萊

Qi Biaojia 祁彪佳
qing (6.66 hectare) 頃
qing (dark, blue, or green) 青
Qingbai leichao 清稗類鈔
Qing'er 青兒
Qingping shantang huaben
清平山堂話本
Qiongying 瓊英

Renshi zhuan 任氏傳

Shangqing 上清
Shen Jiji 沈既濟
si (longing) 思
si (thread) 絲
Su Shi 蘇軾
Sunü 素女

Taiping guangji 太平廣記
Tanta 嘆塔
tanci 彈詞
taozhen 陶真
Tian Han 田漢
Tian Rucheng 田汝成
Tianzhu 天竺

Weituo 韋陀
Wulin 武林

Xi Shi 西施
Xi Xuanzan 奚宣贊
Xiangshan baojuan 香山寶卷
Xiaoqing 小青
xiaoxin 小心
Xihu jiahua 西湖佳話
Xihu santa ji 西湖三塔記
Xihu shiyi 西湖拾遺
Xihu youlan zhi 西湖遊覽志

Xihu youlan zhiyu 西湖遊覽志餘
Xihu yuan 西湖緣
Xiuxiang Yiyao zhuan 秀像義妖傳
Xixiang ji 西廂記
Xiyou ji 西遊記
Xu Xian 許仙
Xu Xuan 許宣
xuanzan 宣贊

Yan Geling 嚴歌苓
Yangzhou huafang lu 楊州畫舫錄
Yijian zhi 夷堅志
Yingzhou 瀛洲
Yiyao zhuan 義妖傳

Yuan 袁
yuan 園
Yuanshantang jupin 遠山堂劇品
Yue 越
Yue Fei 岳飛

Zhang 張
zhang 丈
Zhengbo ke Duan yu Yan 鄭伯克段於鄢
Zhengyi 正一
zhuangyuan 狀元
zidi 子弟
zidishu 子弟書
Zuozhuan 左傳